TRAITOR'S CODEX

TRAITOR'S CODEX

A Crispin Guest Medieval Noir

Jeri Westerson

This first world edition published 2019
in Great Britain and the USA by
SEVERN HOUSE PUBLISHERS LTD of
Eardley House, 4 Uxbridge Street, London W8 7SY.
Trade paperback edition first published
in Great Britain and the USA 2019 by
SEVERN HOUSE PUBLISHERS LTD.

British Library Cataloguing in Publication Data
A CIP catalogue record for this title is available from the British Library.

ISBN-13: 978-0-7278-8875-4 (cased)
ISBN-13: 978-1-84751-987-0 (trade paper)
ISBN-13: 978-1-4483-0213-0 (e-book)

All Severn House titles are printed on acid-free paper.

Severn House Publishers support the Forest Stewardship Council™ [FSC™],
the leading international forest certification organisation.
All our titles that are printed on FSC certified paper carry the FSC logo.

Typeset by Palimpsest Book Production Ltd.,
Falkirk, Stirlingshire, Scotland.
Printed and bound in Great Britain by
TJ International, Padstow, Cornwall.

To Craig, the only man more loyal than Crispin

AUTHOR'S NOTE

Many events and characters from previous volumes will be mentioned here. You may wish to refresh and enhance your memory by revisiting *Veil of Lies*, *The Demon's Parchment*, and *The Silence of Stones*.

GLOSSARY

Anchorite, Anchoress – a religious recluse anchored to a church by a specially built cell or **Anchorhold** – usually attached to the side of the church itself.

Breviary – A small prayer book.

Cod – Middle English word for scrotum.

Domus Conversorum – Residence for converted Jews during the reign of King Edward III in 1232. It was granted to the Keeper of the Rolls of Chancery in 1377 to house the close roll records – records of activities, grants, and other official documents. These were written on parchment and sewn together by year into the close rolls.

Lollard, Lollardy – Reformist movement of John Wycliffe who, among many differing beliefs, felt the Bible was the supreme authority, and that baptism and confession were not necessary to salvation.

Mummer – An actor. There were few plays as such. But a **Mummery** or performance of a satirical or religious nature was more common, particularly on certain feast days.

Rood Screen – A decorative wooden, sometimes stone, screen spread across the nave of a church, blocking the assembly from the altar. Above it was generally a crucifix, or 'rood'.

Watching Loft – A second story in a church or hall as big as a gallery or as small as a narrow passage, where watchers could look down on to a shrine or other important area below.

ONE

London, 1394

C rispin Guest eyed the room. His favorite tavern, the Boar's Tusk, was raucous with the noise of men talking and laughing, a man playing a pipe, cups clinking, and a hearth crackling. A permanent lingering haze of smoke hung in the air just at eye level. He'd spent many a day here in an earnest attempt to get himself good and drunk on the wine he barely had coin to pay for, wallowing in the misery that had characterized his life since being banished from court and losing his lands, his wealth, and his sense of himself.

But that had been some years ago.

Today, drinking ale in a horn beaker, he relaxed somewhat in his usual place against the wall with a view of the door (some habits were hard to break), and amusing himself – sober these days – on the goings-on around him.

There were fewer men in the tavern than usual. The plague always struck in late spring and summer, when the weather warmed. He used to leave with the rest of court and summer in Sheen on his estates or at Lancaster's. Now, of course, he stayed in London, doing his best to avoid certain streets, keeping an eye out for the telltale signs. Perhaps it should have made him more cautious in London this time of year, but he didn't see the point. Either God would protect him or He wouldn't. There was no use bargaining for it.

A shadow of a large man fell over him; and then the man sat on a stool opposite. Crispin raised a smile to Gilbert Langton, the tavern keeper.

'Well, look at you,' said Gilbert in a smoke-roughened voice. 'I never thought I'd be serving you ale, Crispin Guest, when you always groused for your wine.'

Crispin glanced at his cup and tipped it to his lips. 'Well, I have a whole houseful of Tuckers these days, and I must save money where I can.'

Gilbert laughed, a hearty sound. 'You'd think they were *your* family, the way you carry on.'

He didn't take offense. Once, in an earlier day, and a jug full of wine in him, he would have scowled and railed that a servant meant nothing to him. But today, he merely offered a crooked smile. 'I do indulge them. It is still strange to me how my own servant can take over my life.'

'Because Jack is more than a servant to you. He's a friend, a companion.'

'That is the truth of it.' Who would have thought it? Certainly not him. Not in the days when he was Baron of Sheen, with his manor house, his knighthood, his place at court, where servants were invisible to him. It was different now in his life on the Shambles, the stinking butcher's district of London. Living in a poulterer's shop because it was all he could afford, Crispin had made a life for himself with his apprentice Jack Tucker. And then his servant brought a wife and child. And then it was two children, and the girl was pregnant again. Jack was as studious a husband as he ever was as an apprentice.

'It's good to see you happy, Crispin. I know that has not always been the case.'

'You've always told me how I should reconcile myself to my lot, Gilbert, and I have been . . . reluctant.'

Gilbert laughed again, harder this time. 'Reluctant? There's a word.'

'Very well. Decidedly unpleasant about it.'

'And it only took Jack Tucker taking my niece to wife to mellow you, eh?'

'Perhaps. But it is in days like today that I find my escape to the Boar's Tusk most necessary.'

'Oh?'

'I have never lived in such close quarters with squalling infants, Gilbert. The boy has his moments, and the babe is a colicky child.'

'And so now you understand why many a man spends his time and his coin here.' He swept the room with a brawny arm.

'I do indeed. But . . . tell me.' He sipped again, and just over the rim of his cup, he said, 'I have noticed yon man with the blue houppelande, staring at me for some time. Do you know him?'

Gilbert made a sly turn of his head, taking the man in before turning back to Crispin. 'Can't say that I have. Shall I have him tossed out?'

'No, no. I would see what transpires.'

'On the scent again, are you? Then I'll leave you to it. Give my best to my niece.'

'I shall.'

Gilbert rose, straightened his stained apron, and rumbled his way through the crowded room. Crispin poured more ale into his cup from the clay jug in front of him. He sat alone, as he was wont to do. And because most of the patrons knew who he was – and who he used to be – they allowed him his privacy.

Drinking, Crispin watched the man who still seemed to be staring at him, watched as he rose from his table, and pushed his way in a slow stride toward Crispin. When he stood over the table, Crispin merely gazed up at him.

The man hid his face in the shadow of his hood, but there was a trace of blond beard and hair. His eyes were brown but little could be read there. His clothes were that of any man on the streets of London, nicely made, even a bit of fur, legs encased in dark stockings.

'Are you Crispin Guest, the Tracker?'

'Who's asking?'

The man reached into his scrip, pulled out a wrapped bundle tied with twine, and dropped it in front of Crispin, nearly knocking over the jug.

'Don't open it here. Best to keep it off the table. You'll know what to do.'

And then he walked away. His quickened steps took him to the door.

'Wait!' said Crispin, rising. 'What am I supposed to—'

But before he could even hope to get to the man without making a spectacle of himself by leaping up on tables and throwing men aside, the stranger was gone.

He stared at the package. It was covered in soft leather wrappings and tied tightly. He could not tell from its rectangular shape what it might be and, without knowing the man who left it, it was a mystery burning him with curiosity.

Casting a glance about, no one appeared to be looking his

way. He scooped the package off the table and dropped it into his scrip. Nothing for it but to take it home.

He walked down Gutter Lane to West Cheap. On the corner a few people had gathered, listening to a man preaching.

Crispin only heard a little of what the man said, but it soon became clear that the preacher was a follower of Wycliffe, a Lollard, a religious reformer. He spoke loudly how the Bible was supreme even over that of the words of priests and bishops, and how those clergymen should not hold property but be as poor as Christ. The man was holding a book that he waved around. No doubt a Bible written in English. Was the man tempting the authorities to seize him?

Though the crowd mostly booed him and hurled insults, some seemed intrigued. With friends like the Duke of Lancaster, many emboldened Lollards seemed to go about these days preaching their beliefs. Crispin was of the opinion that a man's beliefs should be left alone; though he agreed with some aspects of Lollardy, he did not like their doctrine that baptism and confession were not necessary for salvation.

He slowed and listened for a few moments before he turned away and took Cheap till it became the Shambles, leaving the ranting preacher behind. Stalls of butchers selling meat filled the air with a special kind of lingering smell that never seemed to leave his clothes. A boy with doves kept in small baskets hanging from a yoke over his shoulders moved carefully down the lane, where he headed toward a shop that specialized in game birds. Crispin sidestepped a plump woman moving geese down the trodden mud, gently urging them on with a stick.

Hands suddenly clamped to his arm and he swung away, ready to pull his dagger.

A man in ragged clothes and a dirty face smiled a crenellation of missing teeth. 'The dead are all around us. Do you hear them speak?'

'Sometimes too often. Away with you, beggar.'

'I'm not no beggar. I just tell what I hear. And the dead speak to me. But they mostly speak to you.'

A shiver ran up his neck. He shook the man loose from him and reached into his money pouch. 'Maybe this will quiet them,' and he handed the man a farthing.

The man took it, looked at it as if it were a foreign thing. 'When the dead speak again, you *will* listen . . . Crispin Guest.'

The beggar clutched the farthing in his dirty fist and shambled away, seeming in his manner that he had forgotten he had ever stopped Crispin.

Crispin let out a long breath. 'London,' he muttered.

Once the prophesying beggar disappeared into the crowd, Crispin finally turned toward the old poulterer's, a rickety structure with two bedchambers above and a shop below. All the shutters were open, letting in the breezes of June, and he hopped up on to the granite step and let himself in.

A small boy, barely two years old, ran headlong into him before he could speak a word.

'Crispin! Get your arse over here!'

Crispin startled, as he always seemed to these days when his servant Isabel Tucker yelled at their oldest child. They had named the little boy 'Crispin' to honor their master, but he was beginning to think it wasn't so much of an honor after all.

Crispin bent to grab the boy and hoist him in his arms. The pale skin and bright red hair was definitely the face of his apprentice Jack Tucker. 'My lad,' he said sternly, 'what have you got up to that makes your mother so cross?'

Isabel burst through the back door and put her hands to her ample hips. Pregnant again with her third, she had a scolding look to her face. 'Now, Master Crispin, you must not indulge him.'

'Indulge him? I was saving his life from a terrible dragon, wasn't I, boy?'

Little Crispin giggled and chortled and muttered nonsense words that only his mother seemed able to decipher. He reached for her arms and she took him. 'He was pulling poor Gyb's tail and chasing the chickens.'

'He was merely being a boy. I'm certain I did my share of pulling cats' tails and chasing chickens.'

She laughed and brushed a lock of hair from her face. 'I cannot imagine it.'

'Madam, do you think I arose from my mother's head fully formed as you see me now?'

'I wonder.'

He snorted at her back as she turned away toward the hearth, the boy clinging to her like a vine, she stirring the pot on the trivet. The babe, Helen, lay in her cradle, sleeping between the hearth and window, amazingly quiet even with the loud conversation.

Gyb jumped up into the window then, flicking his aforementioned pulled-tail and eyeing Little Crispin judiciously. Little Crispin nearly leapt out of Isabel's arms and cried, 'Gyb!', one of the few words Crispin could interpret.

But the black-and-white cat was having none of it. He dropped down on the other side of the sill to the street and was, no doubt, going to his other favorite occupation of watching the chickens Isabel had acquired. In all his years on the Shambles, Crispin had never kept chickens. When would he have had the time or fortitude – or indeed, the knowledge – to tend to them? But Isabel was a good wife and servant and managed it all.

The front door opened and Jack strode into the hall and smiled at his wife and child. 'There they are.' He gathered them both in his arms, much to the squeals of wife and son.

Jack was now twenty-two, and there was never a more formidable man. Tall, broad-shouldered, with flaming red hair and beard, he was like a fearsome giant from tales of old. Yet Jack was neither fierce nor much of a giant, all told.

'Master, where'd you go off to this morning?'

'Getting away from . . . er, from my . . .' He shut his mouth. He would not hurt the feelings of his apprentice for anything in the world. And then he admonished himself for being so soft on a servant.

'Looking for a bit of peace and quiet?' Jack smiled and winked.

'As it turns out,' said Crispin, taking the parcel from his scrip and placing it on the table in the middle of the room, 'it was a good thing I did. I think.'

'What's that?' said Jack, looking the package over before pulling up a chair to the table.

Isabel, still clutching Little Crispin and letting him hold the stirring spoon, got closer and peered over Jack's shoulder.

'It is a mystery,' said Crispin with a twinkle in his eye. 'I was minding my own business at the Boar's Tusk when a man I did not recognize left it with me. All he would say was not to open it in public and I would "know what to do".'

'Oh dear,' Jack muttered.

With his fingernail picking at the knot of twine, Crispin pried the strings loose and folded back the wrappings.

'It's a book,' said Jack.

Leather-bound and thick, Crispin made a sound of assent. He opened the cover and looked at the pages. Written in a language completely unfamiliar, he nevertheless tried to make sense of the carefully penned writing. 'Greek. Ἰησοὺς . . . No. Only a few words in Greek here and there. Yet . . . not quite right.' When he turned a page, he ran the edge through his fingertips, running his hand down its strangeness, its almost basket-weave surface.

'This is strange,' he said quietly. 'It isn't like any parchment I have ever seen before.'

Jack leaned closer. 'What is this writing, Master Crispin? It's not Latin. Or Greek exactly.'

Crispin turned another page. 'I don't know.' He closed the cover and picked it up, turning it, examining the edges, the binding. 'Why would that man leave this with me?'

'Because it's dangerous.' Jack unconsciously put his hand to his dagger hilt hanging from his belt. 'Why else would they burden *you* with such?'

'He did ask if I was the Tracker.'

'Then he left it with you for safekeeping.'

'That would appear to be true. On the surface.'

'Meaning?'

'Meaning that he might also wish to rid himself of it. But a book is a valuable commodity.'

'Is it a Bible, sir?'

'No, I don't think so. Perhaps a *Liber Usualis*, a book of chants. Though . . . I see no musical notation.'

Jack shook his head. 'But a book is a rare thing. You've got that book of Aristotle.'

'And it was hard to find for the price. But there are books of all sorts, Jack. Books of science. Books of histories. I used to have my share of them. And Abbot William de Colchester of Westminster Abbey has a mere few.'

'Our landlord, Nigellus Cobmartin. He has law books. Being a lawyer, he'd need them.'

'Indeed. He came from wealth, though little of it does he have now.'

'A man foisting a book on you, sir. That's leaving money on the table is what that is.'

'Yes, it is.' Crispin had not stopped touching it, fingertips riding over the cover, the edges of the strange material that made up its pages.

'Then the first thing to do is find out *what* it is, eh?' said Jack.

'That would seem the logical choice.'

'A book dealer.'

Both Crispin and Jack looked up at Isabel.

'A book dealer,' she said again, running her hand gently over the crimson hair of her son. 'Didn't you mention him once? On Chauncelor Lane?' She shrugged. 'Or a monastery. They would know about books.'

'An excellent suggestion. Chauncelor Lane. Let us proceed there.' Jack kissed his wife, ruffled the hair on the little boy's head. 'Now you mind your mother, Little Crispin.' Then Jack grabbed his master's sword hanging in its scabbard by the door.

Crispin quirked a brow at Jack, but his apprentice merely turned him and strapped the scabbard around his master's waist. 'It doesn't hurt to be too careful,' Jack said.

Crispin smiled and preceded his apprentice out the door, book dropped into his scrip once again. 'I am regretting allowing you to name that boy after me.'

'Why, sir?'

'Because whenever she scolds *Crispin* and cries out his name with a harsh tone, I feel *I* am caught at something.'

Jack laughed. 'It's guilt you feel. You feel she is scolding you for something you got away with. She's God's messenger.'

Crispin snorted, adjusting his scabbard. 'Wretched man,' he muttered.

They proceeded up Newgate, ventured out past the arch and iron-bound wooden gates, and continued out of London proper to Holborn. From there it was a good stretch of the legs to Chauncelor Lane. There on the left was the squarish building that used to be the Domus Conversorum, the residence of converted Jews, but its last resident had long since moved away and the building was dedicated to the Keeper of the Rolls of

Chancery. Years ago, Crispin had dealt with converted Jews, and with those who had not converted but secretly lived in London well after King Edward I had turned them out of England. The street reminded him of that long-ago day of his investigation, and the treachery that followed. Glancing at his tall, young apprentice, the feeling of unease quickly dissipated, knowing that Jack had escaped the worst of what they had encountered.

'I have never heard of a dealer in books, sir,' said Jack, striding up the lane without seeming to share his master's frightening memories. 'Leave it to me wife to know better than me. They come dear, don't they, them books?'

'Indeed, they do. But the man we are about to meet travels far and wide, picking up small books of philosophy, law, and other such tomes. Books are so dear that they are left to children in dead men's wills. Yet some of the children don't appreciate them as you or I do. They sell them. And he buys them.'

'Is that where you got your Aristotle book, master?'

'Yes. I have since gone back many a time, but alas. I'd much prefer to keep you all fed than to spend our few coins on another book.'

'Well, thanks be to God for that.'

It was a thin little shop, as if its taller neighbors were trying to crush it between them. There was no display stand, as had many other vendors along the lane, for the shop's precious inventory could not be allowed to be ruined by a sudden rainstorm or snatched away from an inattentive shopkeeper. Instead, there was a wooden sign painted with the image of an open book. The door was shut, but the shutters were open.

Crispin got to the window and leaned in. He couldn't keep himself from smiling as he ran his gaze over the many books and scrolls. He sighed a breath full of regret, of a past that was never to return.

The shopkeeper, a man in his middle years with brown hair streaked with gray under a black felt cap, wore a long, dark gown like a priest's. 'May I help you, sir?' he said to Crispin, a hand at his heart, and a slight bow to his head.

'Indeed you can. May I come in?'

'Of course. Say! Are you not the man who bought my book of Aristotle?'

Crispin opened the door and walked in. 'Yes. But that was many years ago.'

'I always remember the books. Each one.' He looked over his own shop with a gleam of pride in his eyes. 'Some of them have traveled great distances. I obtained these law books from Rome,' he said, pointing to several books stacked upright. 'Would you like to know which one has been the farthest?'

Without waiting for Crispin or Jack to answer as he ushered them in, the man shuffled to a shelf at the back of the shop. It was a small breviary, or looked to be. Its leather cover was ornate with gold-leafed scrollwork. 'This tale of Launcelot was penned in London over fifty years ago, but you'll never guess where I found it?'

'Where?' said Jack, caught up in the man's excitement. Crispin couldn't blame the boy. The bookseller was as much a storyteller as were his wares.

'I found it in the Holy Land, young man. Bought it off a knight making a pilgrimage.' He turned the finely wrought cover in his hands tenderly. 'He felt it was a sin owning such a foolish book, as he called it. Took my money just the same.' He chuckled. With a sigh of contentment, he returned it to its spot. 'But you, sir, are a man of distinct qualities. I have a Socrates I have newly acquired.'

Crispin closed his eyes and waved his hand. 'Don't tempt me, sir. I came not to buy – though I wish with all my heart that I could – but to ask your advice.'

'Oh? Well then?'

Crispin reached into his scrip and pulled out the book. He laid it on a table in the middle of the narrow shop. The man approached it as if it were a wild bird and liable to take flight. When he first touched it, his fingertips ran up the surface, examining the leather. He examined the spine, nodding and muttering. And, finally, he gripped the edge and carefully opened the cover. He blinked down at the careful script, gray eyes tracking over each line.

'Intriguing.'

'Indeed. Can you tell me what it is, what it says?'

'Dear me, I was hoping you could enlighten *me*. It is very old, that much I can tell you.'

'Is it?'

'Well, the binding, the cover is new. Fairly new. But the pages inside. The ink is faded. And it was not originally bound as a book.' He ran his hand down the center where the stitches could be seen. 'It was likely several scrolls. But the most interesting thing is this. Look here.' He lifted a page and rubbed his fingers very gently on either side of the corner of the page. 'Here. Touch it, good master.'

Crispin ran his fingers over the strange texture. 'It isn't like any parchment I have ever seen. It's thin . . . with this pattern.'

'That's because it isn't parchment. It's papyrus. It's made of reeds. Isn't that ingenious? Reeds that grow in only one place. In Egypt, where Moses was born.'

Crispin looked at it anew. He couldn't help reaching out with his fingers again to touch the intriguing page. 'Can you read this language?'

'Alas . . . no.' He looked the text over again and shook his head. 'I am versed in French, Latin, Greek, even a little Italian, and I can recognize a few other languages by sight.' He squinted over the page once more. 'Yes. I believe *this* is Coptic.'

'And what is Coptic?' asked Crispin.

'A very old language, my good sir. Spoken in Egypt and Palestine by our early Christian fathers.'

A chill rippled over Crispin's shoulders. Something old. Something from the Holy Land. If not a relic then surely related to one.

'Master,' said Jack quietly. Yes, he'd worked it out, too.

'Not now, Jack. Good sir, do you know of anyone who can translate such a book?'

'Well. That *is* specialized. I don't know that there is anyone in London . . .'

'Do you have any idea who would want such a book?'

'Anyone would want this book,' he said, seeming perplexed at the question. 'A scholar of Christian texts, certainly. A monk, a priest, a bishop. But alas, few could actually read it.' He turned a few more pages. 'Could you tell me, good sir, where you acquired such an unusual codex?'

'It . . . dropped into my possession quite by accident.'

'If you should like to sell it . . .'

'I fear it is not mine to sell. If you should recall anyone who might be able to read it, please contact me at your earliest convenience. I am Crispin Guest, Tracker of London, and I can be found on—'

'Blessed saints! *You* are Crispin Guest! Why didn't you say so? I have been a great admirer of yours, sir. Why, just the other day, you saved a woman in great peril not more than a street away. Solved the murder of her betrothed. A stunning tale of valor.'

'Did I?' He looked back at Jack, who frowned. 'Er . . . solved a murder?'

'Yes, indeed! We've all been talking about it. It is a very great honor your being in my humble shop, sir.' He grabbed Crispin's hand and pumped it with both of his.

Crispin politely extricated himself. 'I thank you, but . . . I have done no such valorous deed of late. Could you be mistaking me for someone else?'

'I hardly think so. There was much celebration. I've met the woman. You are too humble, Master Guest. If I find anything about this book, I will send a message to you on Bread Street.'

'Bread Street? I live on the Shambles.'

'Surely not. For during the celebrations, all said that the Tracker resided on Bread Street.'

'I can hardly be mistaken where I have lived these last seventeen years. It is still the Shambles, though now in a poulterer's old shop.'

The man put a hand to his mouth. 'I wonder that I had misheard. Well, it matters not. I will send for you, wherever you are.'

'Good then. I thank you.' He bowed, took the book back into the scrip, and signaled Jack to depart. Once on the street, his hand rested thoughtfully on the book inside its pouch.

'I don't recall you solving no murders of late, master.'

'I'm sure it's an honest mistake.' He looked down the lane, remembering the case of that long-ago day that dealt with secret parchments, with even more secret Jews, and with a monster that may or may not have been. 'I think I have an idea. We'll need to head to Westminster . . . to a goldsmith's shop.'

TWO

He wondered if Jack remembered when he was in the clutches of a man who murdered and abused young boys. Crispin said nothing as they headed up the Strand to Westminster proper and dove into the streets nearest the Thames. It had been a long time but Crispin recalled the way. Yet it wasn't until they'd reached the goldsmith's shop that Jack suddenly stumbled to a stop.

'So you remembered,' said Crispin carefully.

His apprentice was stiff and stone-faced. 'Aye, sir. Why are we here?'

'It was a long time ago. When you were only a boy.'

'Like yesterday,' said Jack in a less than steady voice.

Crispin rested his hand on the man's shoulder. 'I'm sorry. I did not mean to awaken such memories. That man is long dead and cannot harm you now.'

Jack swallowed hard and passed a hand over his brow. 'This is foolish. I'm a man now. I've been back to Westminster so many times since . . .'

'But you were such a vulnerable child then. And I have never forgiven myself for putting you in such danger.'

'Now I do feel foolish, sir. It makes no matter. I am not that child no more.'

Crispin stepped back and looked him over. That gray look to him had gone. His face was flushed and pink, and the freckles were still in evidence, as was the proud upward tilt to his nose and the determination in his amber eyes.

'Very well. Let us proceed.' Crispin led the way to the goldsmith's door and smartly rapped upon it.

Soon the door was unlocked and answered by a man, somewhat grayer and more stooped than when Crispin had met him twelve years ago. His beard was longer, his clothes hung on a thinner frame. Crispin didn't have any reason to believe this man had not left with his compatriots when a sweep had occurred in

London looking for stray Jews who had avoided King Edward's expulsion. He had sent word to the man, in fact, warning him, and many of his friends had left London. Yet this man had remained, untouched, unknown to those who would see his kind all expunged from the land.

The man well remembered Crispin, too, for his eyes rounded and he tried, as he had twelve years ago, to shut the door on Crispin.

'Have no fear of me, Master Middleton. It *is* Master Middleton, is it not?'

The man stopped and wearily let go of the door. 'And you are Crispin Guest. I remember you.' He gestured them through and looked both ways down the lane before closing the door after them. A goldsmith couldn't be too careful.

'It was a long time ago.'

'Yes,' said Middleton. He looked Jack over. 'If this is your same apprentice, it has been a *very* long time indeed.'

Jack bowed.

'The last time we talked was because of dangerous parchments. This time, it is because of a book.' Crispin took it from his scrip, opened it, and showed Middleton the pages.

'Why have you come to me with this, sir? I am but a goldsmith.'

'I thought, perhaps, you might be versed in languages. Have you seen this script before?'

The man looked the page over. 'I am not. Hebrew is the only other language I can read.'

'And this is not Hebrew.'

'I think you know that is true, Master Guest. But . . .' He touched the page. 'Unusual.'

'I am told it is papyrus, made in the Holy Land.'

Middleton drew back. 'I have never been there.'

'No?'

He smiled. 'I was born in Westminster, Master Guest, and have never left it. Do you presume to think that all Jews have come directly from the Holy Land? A pilgrimage is for wealthy wayfarers, knights and lords and their ladies, not humble tradesmen. And, of course, they are going *to* Palestine, not *from*.'

'I see.' Crispin instantly felt foolish. He had assumed that very thing, erroneously, it seemed. 'You are quite right, Master Middleton. Forgive me. I have also been told that the language in which it is written is something called Coptic, from Egypt.'

'Hmm,' he said, stroking his beard. 'I know of a scholar on Wood Street in London . . . a Jewish scholar,' he said quietly. 'He knows many languages. He is . . . he is, in fact, a rabbi and well-respected, who also lives in secret. He knows of you and will, I think, help you if he can. Our community is grateful to you for your discretion.'

Crispin made an exasperated sound. 'I thought all of your race left London when I warned you to flee. Why did you stay?'

'Some of us did indeed depart, fearing to be arrested. But many of us, like myself, are old and wish to live out the rest of our days in the country we have always called home.'

Crispin sighed. How could he argue with that? He would have been satisfied to die at Sheen where his lands and manor house had been. Alas, they had burned to the ground. He had no country but London, it seemed.

'I understand, Master Middleton. What is this man's name?'

'Peter Pardeu. He is a barber surgeon.'

'Then it's back to London for us.' He bowed to Middleton, who looked happy to see the back of him, and proceeded with Jack.

'Sir,' said his companion after a mile or so. 'I'm worried about this book.'

'It is a strange thing.'

'What if we can't find out what it is and who it belongs to?'

'Then we will add another book to our . . . one.'

'But master, it's old. It's . . . almost biblical itself. Is it another one of them relics . . . or something else?'

'I haven't the faintest idea, Jack. That is why one investigates. To collect the facts and cull the rest.'

'I'm just waiting for the dead body to fall into our laps.'

'That's a horrible thing to say.'

Jack crossed himself. 'I know, sir, but I also know how these things turn out for the two of us.'

'You'd better pray for a worthier outcome.'

'I do, sir. All the time.'

'Tucker, you'll be gray before you're twenty-five if you keep up that sort of worrying.'

'If I'm a cynic it's because I got it from you.'

Crispin said nothing. The man was probably right.

They reached Newgate and headed up Wood Street from West Cheap. They passed several shops and houses. Crispin noticed that beggar again, leaning against a wall and gazing casually at him. He thought of sending Jack to shoo him away but he felt foolish suddenly at the notion. He turned away from him and spied the barber pole, dirty and grayed from soot. He and Jack turned at the same time and went in.

A man was sitting backward in a chair. His coat lay aside, and his chemise rucked up over his shoulders, exposing his back. And on his back, a series of ceramic cups were stuck like barnacles, puckering the flesh around them. An old man who looked more like an alchemist than a barber, with a black merino cap and long robes, bent over him, examining the cups to make certain they stayed in place. He took one more from the hearth where it was warming and, holding it with a cloth, quickly applied its open end to the man's back. The client hissed and writhed in pain but soon settled down as the old man soothed with calming words and a steady hand to the back of his neck.

'There now, Master Field. You sit there and relax. The pain will soon recede.'

'Thank you, Master Pardeu,' he gritted out.

It was then that the old man turned and spied Crispin. 'Masters,' he said with a bow, stroking his long beard. 'I shall be with you shortly. This man requires only a few moments more for his cure.'

'We will wait,' said Crispin, both hands on the scrip he held before him.

The barber offered the man a small cup of what looked like wine. He took it and drank. The barber set about putting his tools away, sweeping the ashes back into the hearth, and then looked back at his client. 'Well now. Let's take a look, shall we, Master Field?' He carefully pried off one cup and touched the reddened ring left behind. 'Excellent. Those foul humors were adequately removed.' He took off each cup carefully in turn and laid them in a row on the hearth. Examining the man's back, he nodded his satisfaction. 'Master Field, you should feel the easing of your pain in a day or so. Remain as warm as you can tonight and take wine if possible. Two pence, if you will, master.'

The man pulled his shirt down carefully over the red rings on his flesh, and grabbed his cote-hardie, shrugging into it. He buckled his belt loosely around his waist and dug into a pouch hanging from it. 'Here you are, barber. And for this, much thanks.'

He nodded to Crispin, buttoned up his cote-hardie, and left the shop.

'Now, my good master,' said the old man, facing Crispin. 'What can I do for you? Or is it the young man who ails? For with such a proud red beard I can see he has no need of a shave.'

Jack reddened and brought a hand self-consciously to his trimmed beard.

'Nothing of the kind, Master Pardeu,' said Crispin with a chuckle. 'We have come from a certain goldsmith in Westminster who recommended we go to you.'

'Oh? Well, it is good when clients make recommendations.'

Crispin stepped closer and glanced at Jack over his shoulder. Jack went to the door, and positioned the bar over it, locking them in. He strode to the window and closed the shutters.

'What is this?' cried the old man. 'If you've come to rob me, I warn you. I am paid very little.'

'Be at peace, Master Pardeu. Or should I say . . . *Rabbi*?'

The barber stilled. His blue eyes searched Crispin's face, then Jack's, and then toward the window. 'What nonsense,' he said tentatively.

'Perhaps I should have first introduced myself. I am Crispin Guest. I am known in London as the Tracker. And this is my apprentice, Jack Tucker.'

The man's face changed from stark fear to careful hopefulness. 'You are the Tracker. I have heard of you. Almost . . . legendary.'

'Yes. Master Middleton would not have told us to come if he did not trust me. You recall twelve years ago . . .'

'Yes, indeed, Master Guest,' he said quietly, softly. 'There is not a Jewish household within my care who does not praise and pray for Crispin Guest.'

Crispin scuffed the stone-laid floor with his boot. He grunted his reply. 'Then . . . you realize that it is no mere fancy my being here.'

'No, of course not. What is it I can do for you, sirs?'

'I have this book. I hoped that you could translate it for me.'

'Translate? Is it . . . is it in Hebrew?'

'No. It is in a language called Coptic.'

The old man's eyes lit with a sense of excitement. 'Is that so?' He gestured Crispin forward toward a table. Following, Crispin removed the book and laid it down on the surface. Pardeu touched it reverently, running his fingers over the leather cover. 'The cover seems new,' he said, 'though well-traveled.' He opened the cover and touched the paper. 'By my life,' he muttered. 'Papyrus.'

Crispin edged forward and peered over the man's shoulder. 'Can you read it, sir?'

The man's hands trembled slightly as they glided over the page. 'Where did you say you obtained this, Master Guest?'

'I didn't. It came to me anonymously.'

'I see.' He took a quick glance toward the shuttered window, as if checking to make certain it was still shut. He pulled the candle closer and seemed to be looking over the script, line by line.

'What is it, Master Pardeu? Can you read it?'

He slowly turned toward Crispin. His eyes, a little yellowed with age, gazed at him with some concern. Softly, he said, 'Perhaps it is best you take it away and burn it.'

'What? Why?' His patience tightened. 'What the devil does it say, man?'

His gray brows winged upward, cradling the steps of his forehead. 'Very well. But I did warn you. I shall translate.' He put his finger to the top line, licked his lips, and read: '*The secret revelation by which Jesus spoke in conversation with Judas Iscariot, during eight days, three days before he celebrated Passover.*'

THREE

Frowning, Crispin leaned over the table, staring at the words that were frustratingly beyond his deciphering. 'Our Lord . . . in *conversation* with Judas?'

Pardeu rubbed his hands nervously. 'It might be rightly interpreted as a . . . erm . . . a *gospel*. Of Judas.'

Crispin glared. Until he remembered Pardeu was a Jew. He stood up and stared down his nose at him, unsheathing his dagger. 'Do you toy with me? What does it truly say?'

'I swear to you, Master Guest, that I am not lying. My eyes are old. Perhaps I mistook the words—'

'Perhaps you are making it up out of whole cloth!'

Pardeu raised his hands as if to fend off a blow. 'I am not. You said you trusted me, trusted Master Middleton. Then why can you not trust the words written herein? I have never seen the like before.'

'You said the cover was not old.'

'But the pages within are. They are faded, torn, some even lost. I fear it is very old. And made of papyrus and written in Coptic . . . this is evidence that it came from far away, in the only place such things can be acquired: the Holy Land.'

'Master.' Jack's anxious voice came from behind him. 'Why would Master Pardeu have cause to lie to you, sir? Did not the bookseller say as much? Put your weapon away and let us hear what he has to say. No matter how blasphemous.'

Crispin was not as godly a man as Jack was, but he had prayed, felt he'd done his best under the eyes of God, and even got the blessings of two abbots of Westminster Abbey. Surely that meant he could tell truth from a lie.

Would this man, given what he said about Crispin, lie to him now?

He slowly lowered the dagger and sheathed it smartly with a snap. He grabbed a chair and pulled it out, stepped over the seat, and sat hard. 'Read it, then.'

Pardeu glanced toward Jack. The boy gave him a weak smile and an encouraging nod. Pardeu warily seated himself and pulled the book toward him.

Crispin stood at the barber's hearth and stared into it. He and Jack had remained quiet during the brief reading. Peter Pardeu's voice was soft and gentle as he had read, saying aloud the outlandish words. It was such a strange tale. And yes, it sounded very much like a gospel. The man had called it a secret text, much in the realm of heretical sects that claimed to have special and enlightened knowledge beyond what the Church taught. Like these damned Lollards.

Crispin knew his Scripture. And what was in this Judas 'gospel' was nothing like he'd ever heard before.

'If I understand this book aright, Master Pardeu,' said Crispin, never taking his eyes off the fire, 'then our Lord is not Savior because of his sacrifice, but because of this . . . "special knowledge" he imparts to . . .' He paused to shake his head. 'To Judas, of all people. The one man this text seems to say was the most enlightened of all his Apostles?'

'It seems fantastic,' said Pardeu, 'but that is what it says.'

'And so Judas is not the villain, deviously living side by side with our Lord and his saintly Apostles and plotting his demise, but as a *friend* to Jesus, doing his bidding – even unto turning Him in to the authorities – and understanding his secrets better than the others.'

Pardeu fingered the book's edges. 'That is what it seems to be saying, Master Guest.'

'But how can this be? This is not anything like what has been preached to Christians throughout the ages. It is not what crusades were fought for.'

The man gently pushed the book aside and folded his hands together on the table. 'Master Guest, I wonder if you are knowledgeable of the Council of Nicaea, the first important Christian council convened by Emperor Constantine over one thousand years ago.'

'Of course. We profess the creed that came out of that council.'

'But are you aware of its significance?'

'I suppose you're going to tell me. How is it that a Jew knows about Christian councils and their significance?'

'Be at peace, Master Guest. I may be a humble barber to all of London, but in secret, I am a rabbi, a man of learning. A scholar of the religion of my race, but also that of the Christian faith. Who would not study such a thing that can express its might in so many harmful ways to my own people?'

Crispin's smirk was black. 'Lancaster often told me to know my enemy.'

Pardeu made a noncommittal tilt to his head. 'It has been important to know and to impart this information to my fellow Jews who live in secret but outwardly as Christians.'

Such was distasteful to Crispin, and he couldn't help scowling. But his experience on the matter also made him empathize. He had seen these English Jewish children cower in fear, the mothers encircling their charges within the safety of their arms, a safety that could have been easily snatched from them had Crispin reported them to the sheriffs. He could have turned on them, especially when the maiden – the *Jewish* maiden – he had been falling for, proved herself false and soured him even more on her race. But that had not been the fault of these Jews. They had been living peacefully, even industriously, in London and Westminster for a hundred years. Their fate had been in his hands. They had everything to lose if they revealed themselves, and much to gain by playing at Christian.

Still, it left a bad taste in his mouth.

'I concede it, Master Pardeu,' he said after a long moment. 'Then what was the significance of the Council of Nicaea?'

'As you said, sir, the creed which you profess. But that creed was born of that council of bishops to truly decide on what it was that all Christians *must* believe. In those early years after Christ's death . . .' he paused and added, 'and resurrection . . . it was debated between the many sects of Christianity that were spreading throughout the Holy Land and beyond, who Jesus actually was.'

Jack stepped forward, his face full of concern. 'But we know who he was, Master Pardeu,' he said in a stern but gentle tone. 'He is our Savior and our Lord. He is the Son of God.'

'Yes, this is what you know now, and it came from this council.

You see, much to the contrary of what you may have been taught, in the many places that Christianity had spread in those early days, there was no one unifying belief. The divine nature of Jesus the Son in relation to the Father was hotly debated among the bishops and scholars of the time. They feared a schism. Was the Son as great as the Father? In the Church in Alexandria they believed that the Father was supreme and a Son could not be equal. In other words, the Son was not God but created by Him and had not the eternity or the power of the Creator. Or was it – as the Roman Church believed, as you understand now – that the Son is the true God, coeternal and equal with the Father, *begotten* – as you say in your creed – not *made*, proclaiming that he was not a mere creature brought into being out of nothing, but the true Son of God, brought into being from the very *substance* of the Father.'

Crispin nodded, watching the now-scholarly face of the man before him, all trappings of a barber washed away, replaced by that of the teacher.

'Now the former was heretical and dangerous to the very notion of the salvation of one's soul,' Pardeu went on. 'This difference in thought was causing errors and heresies. And so, Emperor Constantine wished to settle the matter and unite his entire empire under this one creed.'

Jack looked questioningly toward Crispin. 'Is that true, master? Did those in the Church ever believe different?'

'It is true. I have heard of this before.'

'How can that be?' said Jack. 'They were living in the time of Jesus. How could they not be touched by God to spread the one true gospel?'

'But Master Tucker,' said Pardeu, 'this was many years *after* Jesus walked the earth, and the message had spread far and wide. Some regions of the far east had to interpret what they were told. There was need to strictly define this revealed doctrine. You must remember, in the very early days of the Church, it was forbidden to be Christian and they held their faith in secret, much as my people must do now in England.'

Jack shuffled uncomfortably.

'And there was yet to be a written gospel,' Pardeu added.

Jack shook his head. 'No gospel? But didn't His Apostles write it all down?'

'Not immediately. And some of the gospels were written later by others. The bishops were only beginning to decide which of the many gospels should be included in what you call the New Testament. Though much of this had been decided well before the Council of Nicaea, of course, but they were still not entirely settled.'

Jack frowned and stroked his beard.

'Tell us more of this council,' said Crispin.

'Well, the bishops met, discussed, and debated – much as the early rabbis discussed and debated our Hebrew Scriptures, what you call the Old Testament. We, too, needed to know what the true message of God was for us. And so Constantine invoked a council wherein your bishops met to decide the very basic tenets of Christianity itself and a worldwide profession of belief, silencing the heresies.'

'And did it silence the heresies?' asked Jack.

'Recall the Lollards, Jack,' said Crispin, 'who have their heretical beliefs about the sacraments and other tenets of the faith. It goes on even today.'

'As your master says. There were those whose steadfast beliefs were hard to break. As I said, the gospels were joined before the Council of Nicaea, but it might interest you to know that there were many more gospels than the four you know today.'

'Like this one,' said Crispin, gesturing toward the book.

'Yes. Just like this one.' Pardeu stretched his hand over the papyrus page. 'Many more synods were called to question these new gospels that appeared. These synods decided which gospels most conformed to what they called the true word.'

'They *decided*,' said Crispin. He did not like the sound of that.

'Moved by God to do His will, of course.'

'I have seen how bishops do the will of God,' he muttered.

'The orthodoxy of your canon is held very dear. And, as you say, there are heretics in every age. They cause havoc, disruption . . . even wars. Your Church holds tight to its doctrine, and any that defy it are put to the torch. Do you now understand, Master Guest, the danger of this book?'

'I'm beginning to.'

'What?' said Jack, stepping forward. Crispin had noted that Jack was particularly quiet during the reading of the book itself

– as much of it as Pardeu was able to read with its many torn and faded pages. 'What does it mean, sir? Why should our Lord be so close and friends with the one who betrayed Him?'

Crispin ran his hand down his face before fitting his thumbs in his belt. He swiveled toward Jack. 'It means, Jack, that in *this* gospel, Judas did not betray Him, but did His bidding. A plan, as it were. And it is this *knowledge* that Jesus imparts to Judas that saves us from the pits of Hell – this sanctifying of self – not of Jesus' sacrifice on the cross.'

'But . . . that can't be right, sir. Can it?'

'Not according to all the Scripture *we* know.'

Jack stared at the book a long time. 'Is this Scripture we *don't* know?'

'Don't be absurd!' Crispin walked to the table and slammed the cover shut. But much like Pandora and her mythical box, the Creatures of Ideas had already escaped, casting doubt by their mere mention. He stared at the book and brooded. 'If He did not sacrifice, then He did not need to rise from the dead. And if none of this is true, then where can we go to shed our sin and reach Heaven? Our sin is still with us if it is not expunged by Jesus on the cross. All of what we recite in our creed is then wrong.'

Jack's eyes widened. 'Then it's blasphemy.'

'Very old blasphemy.' He could not help himself, and lifted the cover again to stare at the ancient pages.

And yet . . .

This was why the old Jew told him the tale of the Council of Nicaea. That there *were* differing views when the Church was new. There were doubts. But the true way had only to be revealed to the bishops at the council, just as the true word was revealed when they met to find the true gospels.

But as Pilate himself had said, *Quid est veritas?* What is truth?

And yet Lancaster was a Lollard, as were many knights of King Richard's court. Wycliffe might have been suppressed in death, but there were wealthy men who ascribed to his doctrine, even today. And, though Crispin couldn't agree with all of it, he had to admit quietly to himself that some of it made sense to a thinking man.

'There are those who would kill to suppress this,' said Pardeu quietly, glancing once more at his shuttered window.

Crispin had come to the same conclusion. 'Then who was it that gave it to me? And why?'

'This person knew you would do the right thing?'

'And what is that right thing, for God's sake?'

'Only you will know that, Master Guest.'

You must forget what you think you know . . . Beware of what you find . . . The dying words of Abbot Nicholas de Litlyngton of Westminster Abbey. It was damnable. This was worse than any relic. Far, far worse.

His head ached. 'Where . . . where should I take it now, Master Pardeu?'

'Ah, well. If it were me, Master Guest – and you must be aware that a Jew prizes Scripture above all other books, but prizes all books greatly – I think that, given the words in this codex, even *I* should burn it.'

'If that were true, then why did not the man who gave it to me burn it himself?'

'I do not know, Master Guest.' Pardeu rubbed his hands together and anxiously eyed Crispin. 'Master . . . I must reopen my shop. I fear that barring my door has sent clients away. A man must make a living.'

'I'm sorry. Yes. Yes, of course.'

'And Master Guest,' he said, watching Crispin retrieve the book and stuff it once more into his scrip, 'I hope you tell no one that you brought that codex here.'

'I see. No. I would not bring danger to your threshold.' He nodded to Jack, who threw back the bar and opened the door. Crispin had almost forgotten that it was daytime and nearly summer, full of birdsong and the sound of humanity going about their business.

He dug into his money pouch before he turned to go and left two small silver coins on the table. 'For your trouble, sir, and your time.'

Jack went ahead of him out the door and they both stood in the sunshine. The sun warmed their shoulders and he raised his face to it, smelling the wet grass of the meadows beyond, and even the dank scent of the Thames as it wended its way just beyond the streets and fields.

Was it possible, all the things that were in this book, this Judas codex? Could they be true? Was his faith far more complicated than the words of Scripture he had learned all his life? Were there nuances? Was there more?

Or . . . was it wrong?

He sniffed the June air again – less full of smoke and stench away from London's walls – and rubbed his chin in thought, hiding his face under the fall of his hair.

'Master, maybe it's best that we go to Abbot William.'

When he raised his head, Jack was looking at his scrip as if it held a demon. And that wasn't that far from the truth. What *would* the abbot say? He might burn it on the spot. He might—

A commotion behind him on the next street over. He could hear the shouting over the rooftops from where he stood. He flicked a glance at Jack before he took off in a trot, curious at what he might find.

FOUR

They hurried up to Holburn Street and there Crispin spied the commotion of milling people, their voices raised into a chatter. Crispin didn't burst through as he was wont to do when he was a lord. Instead, he stood at the back, observing, listening to the snippets of what people were saying. But it wasn't enough. He tapped a man on the shoulder.

The man turned a face of unkempt scruff and eyed Crispin under thick brows.

'What's happened?'

'A man was struck and robbed, but the Tracker saved him *and* recovered the man's goods.'

Crispin looked at Jack.

'The Tracker, you say?'

'Aye. Crispin Guest. Haven't you ever heard of him?'

'I have,' Crispin admitted. He turned to his apprentice and asked quietly, 'What curiosity is here? Jack, wriggle your way into this crowd to see what the devil is going on.'

'Right, sir!' In he went, as slick as an eel. All was forgotten in that moment, and anything about mysterious books that could bring down the very soul of the Church languished behind this new mystery.

He watched Jack move through the throng and then lost him. Crispin walked slowly around the circle of people, watching as they excitedly talked. Strange to watch people talk about him in this way, almost as if he were a ghost.

It wasn't long till Jack made his way toward Crispin, dragging a man behind him.

Jack let the man go and nodded toward him. 'Go on. Tell my master what you told me.'

The man – in his thirties, a tradesman of some kind, decent clothes, trimmed beard – looked Crispin over suspiciously. 'As I was telling this young man here, I was robbed. I'm a cordwainer, and I was delivering my goods to my client. Two pairs of fine shoes I had just completed. A finer set of shoes you've never seen, good master.'

'Yes, of course,' said Crispin impatiently. 'And what happened?'

'A man ran up behind me, slammed me at the back of my head, snatched my parcel, and started running. I yelled at the top of my lungs and gave chase. So did others on the street. He was bold as brass, was this thief. Then, out of nowhere, a man emerged from an alley. Drew his sword on the knave. The man dropped the parcel and ran off. The man with the sword sheathed it, picked up the parcel, and returned it to me. Oh, he had nice manners, like a lord. I thanked him, offered to pay him. He wouldn't hear of it. Then he told me his name was Crispin Guest. You must know of that fellow. They call him the Tracker. He solves crimes.'

'He does indeed,' said Crispin with a scowl. 'What did this man look like?'

'Well, he was a man in middle years, black hair, gray eyes. Wearing a red cote-hardie and blue . . . stockings . . . say. He looks a lot like you, sir.'

'Does he now?'

'Funny that. You could be his brother. Well, I finally convinced him to take some coins for his deed. He saluted me and strode off. He finds things, doesn't he? Lost things, so they say. He also confounds the sheriffs, beats them at their own game, finding murderers and such. Oh, I've heard all the tales but I never expected to meet him myself. I feel quite honored. They say he lives on Bread Street.'

'That's very interesting. Thank you.'

'I don't mind saying, I feel better on the streets of London knowing Crispin Guest is there.'

'So do I,' said Crispin with a sneer.

Jack stood beside him and watched the man depart. 'What by God's blood was all that?' asked Jack. 'You were with me the whole time.'

Crispin felt an uncomfortable war of feelings. Pride that the citizens of London were aware of his deeds, but strangely insulted that there was another taking credit for his work. Or were they? 'It seems I have a double.'

'Pardon my saying, sir, but . . . why? It isn't as if . . . well . . .'

'It isn't worth impersonating me, as poor as I am, is what you meant. I well know it, Jack. But I am curious. Who is this miscreant who uses my name, and what could he be after?'

Jack screwed up his mouth and stood straighter. It seemed his indignity for his master was coming to the fore. 'To Bread Street, sir?'

'Most assuredly.'

Bread Street was full of bakers and the aromas were as sweet as the Shambles' were sour. But since they didn't know where this man's lodgings were, they'd have to ask. Crispin pulled his hood up over his head. Even though it was warm, he thought it best to hide his face. 'Jack, you should probably do the asking.'

Jack nodded. 'Aye. That's best.' They approached a woman putting out round loaves of bread on her shop stall table. 'I beg your mercy,' said Jack with a fluid bow, 'but I've heard that the Tracker Crispin Guest resides on this street.'

Her face burst into a smile. 'You are correct, sir. I'd always heard he lived on the Shambles, but we are fortunate indeed to consider the Tracker in our own parish.'

'We are in need of him, madam. Can you point out the house to me?'

'Dear me,' she said, a hand to her chest. 'It is just past an alehouse, the Fox Tail. See the stake just down the lane?'

'I do. Thank you, fair mistress.' He bowed again, and she giggled at his courtly manner.

'You do that very well,' Crispin commented as they walked together up the street.

Jack blushed. 'Oh, that. I've learned a thing or two as the Tracker's apprentice.'

'I wonder if you will meet your double as well?'

'Eh?' Jack's cheer suddenly fell flat. 'There had better not be!'

Crispin chuckled and proceeded up the street. They passed the ale stake and found a modest structure beside it, sharing a wall on one side, and an alley on the other. Crispin nodded for Jack to proceed and his apprentice knocked smartly on the door.

No one answered.

'Must not be home yet,' said Jack, gazing up and down the building. 'What do you suppose he's up to, master?'

'I haven't the faintest idea. I am the last person anyone would
wish to impersonate.'

'What are we to do now?'

Crispin looked one way down the lane, and up the other. 'Why
. . . see inside.' He rattled the door but it did not open. 'Jack,
do me the kindness of blocking me from the street.'

Jack moved to stand in front of Crispin, his hands at his hips
so that his mantle was spread wide. Crispin knelt, got out his
lock picks from his pouch, and worked on the lock. It was easily
done and he stood, tapping Jack's shoulder. In they both went
into the darkened interior.

It was a simple one-room lodgings, much like his old place
over the tinker shop, only a bit wider. One bed, a coffer, a table
with four chairs, a stool by the hearth, and a few items on a
pantry shelf.

Crispin looked over the razor and strop, picking them up.
There was a comb and there were, indeed, black hairs still clinging
to it.

He went over to the modest bed and sat on it. The crunch of
straw under him made him feel somewhat better, since his mattress
was stuffed with horsehair. He went to the coffer and lifted the
lid. Extra chemise and braies, stockings. Nothing else of any
consequence, but he took the items out and carefully laid them
aside, first holding up the patched chemise to his own frame. He
showed Jack who nodded in approval. The man was obviously
Crispin's match in height.

He next ran his hands on the inside walls of the emptied coffer,
knocking on them, when something made a soft click and a secret
door opened.

'Oh ho,' he murmured and looked in it. Coin and other gold
baubles, brooches, necklaces. He wondered if this 'Tracker' came
by them from fees or by some other means.

Jack whistled. 'Look at that, master. You never got no fees
like that.'

'I'm beginning to think I'm underpaid.' He shoved it all back
in and clicked closed the door. He replaced the clothing items
inside and shut the coffer's lid. When he stood, he looked around
the room, scratching his head,

'I don't know what's going on here, Jack, but I will find out.'

'Are we going to stay to wait for him?'

'No. We have other business at Westminster.'

Jack looked around one more time. 'At least there appears to be no other Jack Tucker.'

'No, Jack. You are one of a kind indeed.'

Even so, Crispin hovered in the area, standing under the shadow of an eave and watching the place. No one came near it.

'I can't help wondering,' said Jack, after they had started walking, 'why a man would impersonate you. They say he solved crimes.'

'I can't begrudge him if he is doing good. But I cannot have a man steal my name. It's all I've got left.'

'You've got me, sir. And Isabel. And the children.'

'I didn't mean that. Of course I consider myself fortunate to have you and your family in my household. But . . . a man is only as good as his name. I haven't anything else of value. Oh, I have my family ring and my sword, but nothing else. If a man goes about and uses my name, there's no end of mischief that can be done. And, believe me, I've done enough harm to that name.'

'The people love you now, sir. They've forgotten the . . . other.'

'They've laid it aside, perhaps, but they have never forgotten that I committed treason all those years ago. And they never will.'

Jack was silent for a moment. Until . . . 'It don't matter to me.'

Crispin turned to watch the profile of his apprentice but said nothing. Something heavy, something deep inside his heart lifted. It was revelatory that each time Jack expressed such an opinion it should carry so much weight.

But well before they reached Charing Cross or the towers of Westminster Abbey came into view, Crispin stopped. Jack stumbled as he looked behind him at his master. 'What's amiss, sir?'

'Jack, the more I think on it, the more I believe it *not* a good idea to talk with Abbot William about this.'

'Eh? Why not?'

'Because the abbot would be obliged to destroy such a book.'

'He wouldn't be far wrong, if you ask me.'

'But you see, Jack. Someone has gone to the trouble to deliver this to me. To *me*. He could have very well destroyed the book himself. But he didn't. He came to me and told me I'd know what to do.'

Jack set his fists to his hips. 'And do you?'

Crispin huffed a bitter laugh. 'No, by God. But I cannot hand it over to be destroyed. Not yet. Not until I find out why this has been given to me. I'll tell you what you should do.' He pulled the scrip's strap over his head and proffered the bundle. 'You take this back home and secure it. I have some thinking to do.'

'You aren't coming home?'

'In a while. I must think first.'

Jack pulled the strap reluctantly over his shoulder, letting it land diagonally across his chest. 'Well, I'll be waiting, master.' He strode back the way they had come, glancing back over his shoulder with a frown.

Crispin threw back his hood and ran his hand through his hair. Think, yes, but what to think? He'd never find that man again, the man who gave him the parcel. How could he ever discover his purpose?

With careful strides, he, too, started back toward London, staring down at the stony road ahead of him.

So deep was he in contemplation – of this hand and that hand and choices back and forth – that, when he looked up, he was surprised to find he had walked past the Shambles and on to Mercery Lane. And with a 'God's blood' on his lips, he further realized he was standing in front of the Walcote residence.

'Damn,' he muttered. And the front door to it was opening. Like any thief – or fool, he chided himself – he ran for the nearest corner and hid in the shadows. But instead of going onward as he should have done, he clung to that corner and watched, hoping – dreading – for a glimpse of her.

And there she was. Philippa Walcote, married to surely the richest cloth merchant in London. She had been a scullion in that household and had risen far above her station when she married Nicholas Walcote. But he had turned out not to be who he had said he was. And murdered, to boot. Murdered because he masqueraded as Nicholas but was an imposter. In the end, she had married the real Nicholas's brother, Clarence, and had kept her place after all.

Yet during that time when Crispin himself investigated the

murder and theft of a relic, he had fallen in love with the brash
Philippa, and she with him. But in those long-ago days, he had
been too proud to bring a scullion to wife.

She was still beautiful, still rosy-cheeked, her hair bright like
brass, caught up in a fashionable horned headdress and covered
with a gold netting veil. She was holding the hand of her young
son, now ten years old. Crispin's breath caught. He had not seen
the boy for some years, and now, more than ever before, he was
struck at how much the boy looked like him . . . for it *was* his
son. Christopher.

He thanked God Clarence Walcote didn't have a clue.

Watching them avidly, he memorized their features, hungry to
talk to them but knowing well he was best out of their lives.

And then the boy spotted him.

Crispin jerked and tried to vanish around the corner.

'Master Crispin! Is that you, sir?' the boy called out. A male
servant with them tried to hush the boy.

Caught. It was useless to run, to ignore the summons. But
worse. He didn't want to.

Slowly, he revealed himself and stood firmly on the lane. He
bowed stiffly. 'Master Walcote. It has been many a day.' He flicked
a glance at Philippa, who was gazing at Crispin with a tender
expression.

The boy's face screwed up with anger. 'Master Guest, you
told me a fib. You said you would return to teach me arms.' The
boy was all seriousness and carried himself much like a lord.
Crispin swore at himself for allowing this. He hadn't been careful
and he well knew he'd done it on purpose.

'It made me sad, sir, that you would abandon me so. And we'd
become such friends. Or so I thought.' His face drooped to
melancholy and the sight of it made Crispin's heart lurch.

The boy had grown since last he'd seen him two years ago.
He was taller, more graceful. His black hair shone blue in the
sunshine, and his gray eyes scrutinized Crispin judiciously.

Crispin bowed again. 'My heartfelt apologies, Master
Christopher. But I had much work to attend to. And I feared to
interrupt your studies. You should know, however,' he said, taking
a step closer, 'that you could never lose me as a friend.'

The child's face cheered. 'I'm heartily glad to hear it. And as

far as interrupting my studies, bah! I could always have found
time. Couldn't I, Mother?'

She patted his hand and released him. 'You well know Master
Guest is a busy and important man.' Her accent was still that of
the scullery, though she worked hard to pronounce each word
and lessen the harshness of it.

'I know, Mother. I listen to tales of Master Guest all the time,'
he said eagerly. 'Mother and I are shopping today, but you must
come back and do as you promised, Master Crispin.'

Crispin hesitated. He didn't want to lie to the child, but he
didn't see how he could be seen at the house. It wouldn't be long
till a servant speculated as to why the child looked more like
him than his own father.

Philippa rescued them both. 'You mustn't delay Master Guest.
Can't you see he's on his way somewhere? Now run along ahead
with John, Christopher.' She nodded to their servant. 'I will talk
to Master Guest.'

'Very well,' he said reluctantly. 'You promise? I will see you
again?'

'Go on now,' said Philippa, shooing him on.

Their retainer followed the boy. Christopher skipped onward,
turning to wave. 'God keep you, Master Crispin!'

Once he and his servant disappeared around the bend in the
road, Crispin hastily turned to her. 'I apologize for presenting
myself. I never meant for you to see me.'

She smiled. A dimple in her cheek had always meant mischief.
'And yet we did. In fact . . .' Her heavy-lidded eyes looked away,
surreptitiously scanning the street. 'I've seen you many a time
outside our house, hiding in the shadows. Not so stealthy, are
you, Master Tracker.'

His face burned with embarrassment. 'Perhaps I wasn't trying
as hard as I could have done.' He winced at his blatant foolishness and dared raise his eyes to her face. How he wanted to kiss
her! But out in the street as they were, it was impossible. And
anyway, he wouldn't – couldn't – cuckold Clarence Walcote,
who had been kind to him.

'How are you?' he asked softly.

'I am well.'

'And . . . Christopher?'

Surprised and suddenly stiff that she should slip her arm in his, he did his best to comport himself with dignity as they walked slowly down the lane. 'He was in a state after . . . after what happened. His best friend, after all. He was devastated that you left and never returned, never fully explaining to him what had transpired. He thought it was his fault that he had somehow lost your friendship.'

'Damn. I never meant for that to happen. Did you tell him? Explain to him why I couldn't—'

'I did my best to explain that you were still his friend, even though he had lost the other who was dear to him. That . . . you might return to him some day.'

'But you must surely see why I can't.'

'Oh yes. He is the very image of you. And even Clarence might come to notice . . .'

'Yes. I mustn't return.'

'But perhaps . . . he can come to you.'

A flame of hope burned in his chest. He had wanted to get to know his son. To simply know that he was out there in London kept his heart lighter than it had ever been. But he hadn't dared dream it possible to know the boy and the boy to know him.

'That *might* work . . .'

'There are things he should learn. Things that only you can teach him.'

He reined in his excitement. 'He already asked once why we looked so much alike.'

'Hmm. He is a clever boy.' She squinted into the sunshine before gazing at Crispin with those sultry eyes he could not make himself forget. 'Perhaps some day when he's old enough to understand . . .'

'We'll see.' But secretly, Crispin hoped.

'And how is Master Tucker? He was quite the young man when last I saw him.'

'Well and truly married, with two children and another on the way. The oldest . . . they named him after me.'

She stopped. 'Oh Crispin! What a fine testament to you.'

His cheeks burned again. He couldn't deny he was proud that they'd done it. 'Yes. Well . . .'

'That must be a full household. Are you pleased?'

He shook his head in disbelief. 'I am unaccountably pleased at it. I've . . . changed, Philippa.'

'Indeed, you must have. Is this the same man who refused to wed a scullion?'

'You don't know for how many years I have regretted that decision.'

'Well! You *have* changed.'

'Too late, I'm afraid. Too late for us.'

She laid a hand to his arm. He felt it burn him. 'But not too late for another. Crispin, you need not be alone.'

'I am not alone. I have a herd of Tuckers under my feet.' The truth of it eased the hurt a little.

'So you do.' She appraised him boldly before dropping her eyes and her hand from his arm. 'Much time has passed. We are all different these days.'

'Nothing is amiss at home, is there? Clarence is good to you, isn't he?'

'Oh, aye. He is ever kind. A good husband and father.'

Crispin tried to keep his face neutral.

'You're thinking very loudly, Master Guest,' she said with a laugh.

He scowled. 'Madam, do you presume to know what I am thinking?'

'I know exactly what you're thinking.' She reached up and kissed his cheek lightly. It flushed his face with heat. 'And I love you all the more for it.'

'Philippa!' he rasped, looking up and down the lane.

'It is true. I will not deny it.'

He pressed his arms to his sides, fisting his hands. It was the only way he could keep from embracing her. 'And I love you still,' he said quietly. 'I prayed for relief, but God will not grant it to me. Perhaps I am too much of a sinner.'

'Nonsense. You are a kind and honorable man. The Almighty knows it, surely.'

They gazed at each other. He sopped up her features like bread in a bowl, trying to hold them dear, when he realized she was doing the same thing.

Reluctantly, he bowed. 'It was a pleasure seeing you again, madam.'

She clasped her hands together, perhaps for the same reason Crispin clenched his fists. 'For me as well. Be looking for a message from me. I'm sure Christopher will be pleased to meet with you.'

'Philippa . . . do you truly think that this is a good idea?'

'Having a child has taught me much, Crispin. It has taught me that there is a great deal I would sacrifice for his sake. And I would even risk losing him if in knowing himself better – knowing you and who you are – he would come to hate me for it.'

'Never that. He'd be a fool.'

'When he knows the truth some day, he might.'

He expected tears in her eyes, and perhaps if she were any other woman there might have been. But in her eyes, he saw only determination.

He bowed again. 'As you wish. I fear I cannot deny you anything you ask of me.'

'Anything?' There was a sparkle in her eye. 'We shall have to see about that.' Before he could admonish her, she turned away, leaving him a view of sparkling netting and a long trailing skirt.

He took a deep breath and let it out slowly. Damn the woman. But it was good to see her, to talk with her. The smile on his face didn't surprise him.

He turned and made his way between the houses and abruptly stopped short. That beggar was there again, eyeing him warily. He didn't want to draw his sword, but he kept it in mind.

'Are you following me, knave?'

The beggar sat with his knees drawn up. His stockings were more holes than material. His cote-hardie was in tatters, but his leather hood – which had seen better days – was still useful to cover his head. His unfocused eyes turned toward Crispin. 'Ah, it's the man who listens to the dead. The other man, that is.'

'I *don't* listen to the dead. Why would you say such a thing?'

'Oh, but you do, master. Just as I do. They speak to me, especially the newly dead. Or the soon to be. It's the murdered that talk to you and you listen, don't you? You hear them as clear as I am speaking to you.' He rose unsteadily, using the wall to brace himself. Stalking toward Crispin, he got in close. 'I hear them too!' he whispered.

'Away with you. I don't know what you're talking about.'

'You do. I know you do. You're hearing them even now. It's a tinny sound because they're not dead yet but they will be.'

That shiver crossed his shoulders again. Crispin leaned in. 'Stay away from me.'

'I'm not lying.'

'You're mad.'

'Am I?' He scratched his chin through his unkempt beard. 'Aye, maybe so, maybe so. But you know I'm not lying. Listen to the voices of the dead. Listen and hear.' He pointed a dirty finger at Crispin's face and stumbled away.

Unnerved, Crispin watched him go. It was a madman's ravings but, even so, he couldn't help but feel something in his prophesying voice. Something he did not want to hear.

He shook it loose. He didn't need the distraction. Between Philippa and this book, he had enough distractions to last a lifetime.

He hurried on and, taking a shortcut back to the Shambles at the mouth of another alley, he found his way barred again, this time by *two* men.

He tried to skirt past them with a polite, 'I beg your mercy.' But when they stepped back into his path, he squared his shoulders. 'Is there a reason you are preventing me from proceeding, gentlemen?'

And they were gentlemen, from the sheen of their velvet cote-hardies to the fit of their stockings. The dark-bearded one huffed a breath. 'We want a word with you . . . Crispin Guest.'

Crispin eyed them both, noted that they both had swords. 'State your purpose then.'

'You must come with us.'

'Indeed. Where?'

'Don't ask questions. Just comply.'

'I'm rarely in the habit of complying when two churls greet me in an alley—'

The punch to his jaw was unexpected. He landed on his arse. Raising a hand to rub at his chin, he felt blood. Sticking his tongue out, he licked it away from the side of his mouth. 'You shouldn't have done that.'

'You'll get more of the same if you don't do as we say.'

Crispin took his time getting to his feet and wiping the dirt from his cote-hardie. 'You should apologize to me.'

The men looked at one another and laughed. It was true that they were both taller than Crispin, and wider across the chest and shoulders. A wiser man might have been intimidated. But at the moment, Crispin was more angry than wise.

'I said . . .' Crispin slowly drew his sword with the whisper of steel on leather. Even in the shadows, the sun caught an edge and sent a shard of light over the men's faces. 'Apologize!'

In answer they drew their own weapons.

'If that's the way you want it.'

Crispin didn't wait. He charged them, arcing his blade toward their shins. They blocked his sword with their own in a clash of metal and sparks. Stepping back, Crispin assessed. Out of the corner of his eye, he saw people fleeing near the alley entrance. No one wanted to get in the way of a sword fight.

Crispin wiped his other hand over his mouth, swiping the blood away. 'What is your game?' he asked the men. 'Who are you and what do you want?'

'Our master wishes to speak with you.'

'And he would do so from the edge of a blade?'

'If necessary. We were told to bring you to him . . . upright or limp.'

'And who is your master?'

The clean-shaven man only grinned. He lunged and Crispin parried the sword out of the way. A sword came at him from the other direction. Crispin slid around the man and spun, slicing outward with his own blade toward the bearded man.

Steel caught sleeve and flesh. The man's cry was almost anti-climactic. Crispin turned and caught the sword from the other with his own and struck hard, slapping it away.

Crispin was already winded. He hadn't done such swordplay in a while and he was older than these two. If he had been practicing every day as he used to do, as Lancaster had, he would be in fine shape. As it was . . . What he couldn't do with strength he'd have to do with cunning.

He went on the offensive and slashed again at the bearded man's shins. Tactical and expeditious in battle, any knight feared to be laid low by a cut to their legs. The man backed away, parrying the blows away with his steel.

Clean-shaven tried to approach Crispin from another angle but Crispin used the same tactic against him, and he, too, defended his legs, backing away.

There was only one way out of this. Crispin kept Bearded Man back with wild swoops of his blade, while he kicked dirt up into Clean-shaven's face. The man took but a moment to wipe at his eyes, but that was all Crispin needed to spin and force his blade up to the man's neck. Clean-shaven froze.

'That was a wise decision,' said Crispin, close to his face and trying not to pant. Bearded Man stopped his approach. 'I won't have any compunction about killing your companion,' he told the other. Crispin pressed the edge of the steel that much more into the man's fleshy neck. Clean-shaven cringed but forced himself not to move a muscle.

'Drop the sword.'

Clean-shaven did so with an echoing clang.

'Now you,' said Crispin to the other. But Bearded Man did not seem as anxious to comply. 'Do you care nothing for your compatriot?'

Bearded Man scowled. He hoisted his sword, changing his grip on the hilt. Suddenly, he heaved it forward toward Crispin.

'God's blood!' Crispin ducked, using his sword to bat it away from his head. The flying sword rang against the stone wall behind him.

When he looked up again, Clean-shaven had managed to slip away and was gripping his sword in his hand again. And his angry grimace showed no quarter. Without looking away from Crispin, Clean-shaven kicked Bearded Man's blade toward his companion, who picked it up.

Crispin blew his fringe away from his eyes and crouched, his sword at the ready. 'That didn't turn out as I expected.'

They both swung. Crispin ducked and darted toward the opening of the alley. Footsteps behind told him all he needed to know.

He ran harder, glanced back. Yes, they were hot on his heels. *Damn!* There would be no point in stopping and turning to fight. Perhaps in another day when he was at his peak, but that day had long passed.

'Get out of the way!' he cried to the people on the street in front of him. He waved his sword and they screamed, falling to the sides. If he could get enough in front of his pursuers, get to a roof somehow, he could drop down on them. But for now, running was his only course . . . and he was already tired.

He wove in and out of backstreets and closes, but always he heard their footsteps ringing out and echoing off the shopfronts and houses hard behind him.

Someone dumped their rubbish out the window, barely missing him, but it landed on his foes. He heard their curses and their slowing steps. He sent up a prayer of thanks to that unknown woman.

He turned a corner and made a dash for the main road. And it would have gone well for him if that barrel-shaped carriage hadn't suddenly pulled into his way.

He tucked his sword to his side, cast his arm over his face, and hit the canvas side hard enough to tear it.

He landed with a thump on the carriage floor, somewhat amazed that he had survived intact. When he looked up, he wasn't so sure his survival was worth it.

The Duke of Lancaster crouched beside his mistress Katherine Swynford, and they were both staring at Crispin with widened eyes.

FIVE

'Crispin!' cried Lancaster. 'What in hell—?'

'My lady, my lord, I beg your mercy—'

'John,' said Lady Katherine soothingly. Her jeweled hand rested on his arm.

The driver must not have noticed Crispin's untimely arrival, for the carriage continued on, rocking roughly over the parts of the road laid with cobbled stone. Neither did the retainers on horseback leading the carriage notice the unwanted visitor.

Crispin got up off the floor, struggled to sheath his sword in the tight quarters usually preserved for wealthy ladies, and sat on the cushioned seat opposite.

'Well?' said Lancaster testily.

'I . . . I didn't know this was *your* carriage. It was merely . . . opportune.'

'There is blood on your face,' said Lady Katherine. Her eyes, as always, were kind and concerned.

He wiped at his mouth again. 'Yes. Well, that's what comes from someone striking me.'

Lancaster huffed. 'And well deserved, I imagine.'

'No, Your Grace. Not in this instance. I was surprised by two men who meant to do me harm.'

'So it's just another day of the week, eh, Crispin?'

He managed a crooked smile. 'Just so, my lord.'

'Hush, John. Can't you see that your Crispin is hurt and in danger?' She leaned toward him. 'It is fortuitous that you should have . . . well, dropped in unexpectedly. What can we do to help you?'

'My dear!' Lancaster objected.

But Lady Katherine brushed him aside. 'Do you need our help, Crispin?'

He looked from her pale countenance with her expressive hazel eyes to that of Lancaster, dark brows furrowed, dark beard emphasizing his scowl. 'If I might impose . . .'

She sat back. 'But of *course* you can.'

'My lady,' said Lancaster carefully.

'John.' She rested a hand on his. It was a simple gesture, one that Crispin had not seen before. Always in the Lancaster household, Katherine was near, for she had been the governess to his daughters, who had now been married for some time to Spanish and English lords. But she had been discreet in Lancaster's presence at court and at his estates. She had kept to herself, as far as Crispin could remember. Lancaster had spent time with his wives, and Crispin had only seen those gentle family scenes, all the while knowing Lancaster would escape to see his mistress. Obviously, she had not kept entirely to herself, for she had several children by him, long after her own husband was dead. Bastards, but welcomed into the family. Even Henry was friends with the oldest half-brother.

Crispin had always been a sputtering fool in front of Lady Katherine, even as recently as a few years ago. And it was only now (was it maturity or the fact that he loved another?) that he realized that his enmity toward her had always been jealousy. Jealousy of Lancaster that such a beauteous and courteous woman should relegate herself to the background of his life, and yet be at his beck and call. At last, Crispin could admit with some embarrassment that he had been besotted of the lady himself since he was a young man. He felt a surge of pride that he had finally shed it from his person, like an old ram relieved of its fleece. He glanced up at her anew.

'I . . . don't know that you can help me beyond spiriting me away as you have done. I was outnumbered.'

'I don't remember that being a hindrance before,' said Lancaster, sitting back. He still clutched Lady Katherine's hand.

'I am somewhat older than I was in those days that you knew me, Your Grace. And considerably more winded.'

Lancaster smiled. 'So are we all.'

'But how can we aid you?' said Lady Katherine.

'Truly, you have done enough already, my lady.' He grabbed the torn canvas that covered the window and doorway, drew it back, and peeked outside. The men were long gone. They would not follow such a carriage. Not if they valued their lives.

Lancaster smoothed his beard. 'Then where can we drop you off?'

'In such a hurry to rid yourself of me, my lord? We've scarce laid eyes on one another for some months.'

'And you very well know why.'

'Where do you go?' Crispin asked.

'We are heading out of London for Sheen. The queen is ill. Richard is moving the court to get out of London and escape the plague months.'

'Of course. I am sorry to hear of the queen's ill health. She was kind to Jack.'

'And do you still harbor that miscreant?' said Lancaster.

'That and more. Jack has a wife with two children and one coming soon.'

'Good God! You don't say.'

Katherine beamed. 'That is blessed news. Give him my regards and tell him I shall pray for him and his.'

'I shall. He will be pleased to hear it. He often remembers you in his prayers.' He turned to Lancaster. 'And *your* prayers too, my lord?'

'You're still a knave, Crispin.'

How he longed to tell Lancaster of his own son. He'd understand, having bastards of his own. But he feared for the news to get out, to hurt Philippa and her standing. He clamped down on his words and kept them close.

Lancaster grumbled and finally leaned forward on his elbows. 'So what trouble this time, Crispin? Why do you have need to flee?' He squinted at the sword that his son Henry had given to Crispin.

'I don't know how much to say. An object has fallen into my hands. To what purpose, I am uncertain. But I have discovered it is dangerous to . . . certain philosophies and that powerful men would wish its destruction.'

'Then destroy it.'

'I am not certain that this is the best course. *All persons ought to endeavor to follow what is right, and not what is established.*'

'You have the nerve to quote Aristotle to me?' He sat back. 'You will do as you always do, Crispin; ignoring the good advice of others.'

'The simplest way is not always the best, my lord.'

'It is when caught up in a maze . . . as you seem to be. Again.'

Crispin nodded. Hadn't Lancaster benefited all these years with taking the sane course, the logical way? He was the wealthiest man in England, through careful plotting and planning. The best strategist, the best warrior. He married well. And he had kept his head during the worst of the treason against King Richard, a treason that Lancaster himself had engineered to ferret out the disloyal, a plot that Crispin had been caught up in.

'I know, my lord. But . . . I am a man who thinks too much.'

Lancaster's smile was bittersweet. 'So you are.' He studied Crispin a long while. Lancaster was ten years his senior and Crispin was nearing his fortieth year. It had been a while since they had been in one another's company. He gazed at Lancaster just as long as Lancaster gazed at him.

After a time, Lancaster said quietly. 'Have a care, Crispin. If you find yourself cornered by the Minotaur, get word to me. I will send you a Theseus.'

Crispin bowed. 'Thank you, my lord. And now, I must take my leave before I end up in Sheen. I doubt His Majesty will be glad to see me.'

'Indeed he would not.' Lancaster pushed aside the curtains. 'Here is good enough. We are about to meet the Strand. Good luck, Crispin, and God's blessings on you.'

Crispin smiled. 'And to you, and you, my lady.' He bowed to her, cast the canvas aside, and leapt to the road, the driver never aware of his coming or going. He watched the cart amble away. The knights leading the carriage never turned their heads.

Pivoting back toward London, he set out.

What Lancaster said made sense, of course. He had no doubt that those men after him had something to do with the Judas Codex. But what, and who was their master? Crispin had a niggling sense in the back of his neck just who it might be, yet the notion seemed outlandish. But, of course, it was no more outlandish than it had been twelve years ago.

He stopped and turned again. He didn't have the book on him, so what would be the harm in consulting with Abbot William now? He set his jaw and headed toward Westminster.

It took no time at all to reach the abbey. He rang the bell to the cloister and stood as he had done for many years now, awaiting a monk to take him to see the abbot. What did the monks think of his trespass? he wondered. Did they view him as a distraction for their abbot?

Brother John Sandon arrived and said nothing as he unlocked the gate. 'Do you need an escort, Master Guest?'

'No, Brother. I know the way.'

The monk bowed and watched as Crispin headed down the arcade toward the abbot's lodgings.

He knocked at the abbot's door, and heard the abbot call out, 'Come!'

Pushing open the heavy oak door, Crispin looked around. Abbot William sat beside a harper. The abbot held a goblet of wine, and with eyes closed, seemed to contemplate the music.

Crispin coughed into his hand.

'Yes, Brother?' said the abbot without opening his eyes.

'It is me, Abbot William. Crispin Guest.'

The abbot jerked in his seat and snapped his eyes open. 'Bless me, so it is. Come in, Master Guest. My friend,' he said to the harper. 'We will continue this later. Please excuse us.'

The harper stopped plucking and rose. He bowed to the abbot and then to Crispin before he made a quick exit.

Abbot William smiled. 'It is good to see you, Crispin. How goes it?'

'Fair, as always, my lord. But there is a question I have been pondering and I thought it best to come to you, since you are openminded on an extraordinary number of topics.'

The abbot narrowed his eyes and looked Crispin up and down. 'Am I? I'm surprised you didn't mention how unmoved I am by flattery.'

'That was certainly my next comment, my lord.'

Abbot William chuckled and rose. He walked to the sideboard and poured them both wine. 'You're a knave, Crispin Guest. Has anyone ever told you that?'

'Remarkably, I was told that very thing not more than a quarter of the hour ago.'

'I shouldn't be surprised.' He handed Crispin a goblet and they both sat before the hearth that had been allowed to go cold in these warmer months. The windows were open, letting in a breeze.

'I am surprised to find you here,' said Crispin. 'Is not the court moving to Sheen for the summer to escape the plague?'

'I have not been called. His Majesty prefers Dominican confessors beside him.'

'The queen is ill.'

'Oh?' The abbot ran a hand over his lower lip. 'I shall pray for her. She is a kind and generous lady. She tames the heart of the king.'

'Indeed she does.'

'But certainly you did not come all this way to discuss the queen?'

'No.' Crispin toyed with the goblet before setting it down without drinking. 'A book has come into my temporary possession.'

'A book? I would be anxious to see it. Do you have it with you?'

'No. I thought it best to keep it . . . elsewhere. It is a . . . troubling book. Very old. I would beg your opinion on it.'

'I suppose I can offer what I can, not having seen it.'

'Well . . .' Crispin rose and paced before the hearth. 'I fear it may be a blasphemous book. But it also might be of grave importance. I have thought of destroying it—'

'And perhaps you should. If it is a blasphemous book and turns souls away from Christ, then it has no place among God-fearing people.'

'And yet it is not mine to destroy.'

'That matters not at all. You are doing a service to the one who owns it.'

Crispin brooded, staring into the cold ash of the fireplace. Hastily he turned, regaining his seat, and leaned in toward the abbot. 'Is it true that our early Church fathers argued about which gospels would be included in our New Testament? And that there were many more than the four we know well today?'

The abbot's plain and solid features sobered and he placed his goblet on the table between the two chairs. 'Who has told you this?'

'A scholar. He explained how the gospels were discussed and decided upon, just as our creed was argued and decided upon at the Council of Nicaea.'

The abbot shot to his feet. His hands moved in agitation as

he took his turn to pace. 'What manner of "scholar" has put these notions in your head?'

'Are you saying that the Council of Nicaea did not discuss—'

'Yes, yes! Of course they decided. There were heresies everywhere. They *had* to come up with a universal creed.' He faced Crispin. 'But the gospels are the gospels. There are no others.'

He had seldom seen the abbot in so intractable a mood. A man who spent his time awaiting popes and cardinals certainly must know this from that. But, in this, Crispin wasn't so sure that the abbot knew his history. Or would admit to it.

'Hmm,' said Crispin.

'What is this book you have?' said the abbot, in an accusatory tone. Crispin had never heard such or had it directed toward him. At least, not for some years.

'It is another gospel.'

The abbot threw his hand in a careless gesture. 'Nonsense.'

'I'm afraid it is true. It is written on something called papyrus and in a language called Coptic.'

The abbot's eyes enlarged. 'What did you say?'

'I had a translator read it to me. It isn't very long. But I have it on good authority that it is quite old.'

'What gospel?'

Crispin faced him. 'The gospel of Judas.'

The abbot seldom showed varying expressions. He could show joy, irritation, even a bit of anger, but always it was tempered by his weighted eyes, his unmalleable mouth, and stoicism. But now his eyes bulged, his mouth was set open, his face flushed red. There was something in this exchange Crispin had never seen before. The man could patiently argue any fact brought to the fore without showing undue emotion. Was it Scripture on which he drew his line in the sand?

'And how, pray, could Judas write a gospel when he was dead?'

'And dead in two ways, wasn't he?' said Crispin. 'By hanging and then by his belly breaking open in a field? Which one is correct, do you imagine? Neither, perhaps?'

The abbot nodded. 'Blasphemy is insidious. It crawls into the dark spaces of our minds and hearts, makes us question.'

'There are inconsistencies in the gospels, my lord. Surely *you* have noted them too.'

The abbot drew himself up. 'You must bring this . . . this *book* at once to me.'

'And why is that, my lord?'

'So that I may dispose of it and its heresy forthwith.'

Crispin took a breath. 'I do not think that wise.'

'See how the blasphemy infects!'

'On the contrary. *It is the mark of an educated mind to be able to entertain a thought without accepting it.*'

'Do you have the temerity to quote a pagan to me now?'

Crispin slowly rose. 'The temerity? Indeed, my lord. For I have always found value in the philosopher's point of view, be they pagan or Christian father.'

The abbot shook his head. 'Crispin, you go too far. One day you will find yourself on a heretic's stake if you are not careful.'

'God forbid. I see this subject is one that is not available for your usual judicious debate.' Bowing, Crispin headed for the door.

'Now . . . one moment.' The abbot straightened his robes, took a deep breath, and in moments comported his face as it usually was, with unambiguous languor. His hands folded together in front of him. The pace of his speech was careful and considered. He was again the abbot Crispin had known for some years. 'You are right. I was too hot-tempered on the subject. I have always been a man steadfast in the Church. I have sparred with some of the greatest minds of Europe, with popes and their cardinals. My speech has always been measured with poise and deep deliberation. I don't know why I attacked you and your . . . your opinions on the matter.'

'It is a deeply disturbing notion,' said Crispin. 'I don't mind saying that the gospel – or whatever it would be called – burdened me with a wild array of thoughts on the subject, on the history that we know . . . or *thought* we did. But to also discover that only four gospels were chosen out of many . . . One has to wonder as to the deciding factors. You and I both know that a single pious man can be a saint. But two can be a synod. And in that, agendas and factions can be formed. You can't tell me your many journeys to Rome were merely for questions on running this abbey. They must have skimmed along the razor's edge of politics. The popes of Rome seethe with it.'

Abbot William lowered his head as he strode across the room. A breviary sat open on a stand and he lifted a hand to briefly touch it. 'There is much truth to what you speak,' he said softly. 'Then what would you have me say, Crispin? Do you want me to evaluate this . . . this *gospel* of yours?'

Crispin wiped at his brow. 'I . . . don't honestly know. If it is truly as it says, then I realize it is a very dangerous book. I have already been accosted by two men attempting to take me to their unknown master about it. At least, I am fairly certain that was their aim.'

'Crispin.' Now there was concern in his voice. 'You didn't tell me this.' He seemed to noticed Crispin's bruised lip for the first time. 'Are you . . . are you hurt?'

'No. Only a thick lip for my trouble.' His tongue found the sore spot once more. 'I was able to escape them. This time. But they won't give up.'

'Then wouldn't it be the saner option to turn over this book?'

'It is not mine to give. It was handed to me anonymously. For what reason? I can scarce imagine. That is the greater mystery to me now.'

'I see. It is honor that keeps you from your Christian duty.'

'*Is* it my Christian duty? We follow the teachings of the Church and we are taught that thus it has ever been. But that isn't quite true, is it?'

'You speak like a Lollard.'

'And yet I am not. I do follow the teachings of the Church. Gladly. But I do not wish to be martyred in it.'

'Then give up the book, Crispin. Hand it over to me. And I shall dispose of it if doing it yourself is not to your liking.'

'If that is the course I decide upon, Lord Abbot, then I will do as you say. But *until* I am satisfied, I think I shall keep it a while longer, if but only to discover why it was put into my hands in the first place.'

'To tempt you. As it has.'

'The Devil has far better ways to tempt me and lead me astray. In this, he is doing a poor job.'

'You jest inappropriately,' said the abbot with a scowl.

'Do I? It is only to keep fear at bay. The Devil and I have

danced long ago and he is not finished with me yet. But I don't
think his hoary hands are in this. At least . . . not yet.'

'Then you've already decided. Why come to me and trouble
my soul over it?'

'I didn't intend that. I merely wanted sound advice. I suppose
I got it.'

'You received emotion and the weight of the Church, I'm
afraid.' He bowed his head and sketched a cross over Crispin.
'May God go with you and make straight your path.'

'Amen.' He bowed but, before he took his leave, he glanced
back. 'Lord Abbot, might I beg a favor of you?'

Abbot William shook his head vigorously. 'I will not house
this book of yours. Do not ask me to.'

'No, my lord. I merely ask that you make no mention of what
I have told you today. Lives may depend on it.'

The abbot considered and finally nodded. 'I would see you
and yours safe. But,' his taut cheek twitched, 'be swift in your
investigation. For I will not wait forever. I would see proof that
the book was destroyed.'

'Will my word be good enough?'

The abbot deliberated more, and finally – and reluctantly, it
seemed – nodded.

Crispin made his way absently back toward the Shambles. But
something made him turn up Chauncelor Lane before reaching
London's walls. He wanted to see the bookseller again. To thank
him, to maybe find out how much he was asking for that book
of Socrates. Perhaps he could save a few farthings or two, set
them aside.

He found the bookseller's stall between the buildings and
knocked upon the door. Waiting, he glanced along the lane.
Someone always seemed to have a bundle they were carrying,
or the women were burdened with yokes on their shoulders,
balancing buckets full of water. It was just as busy as London
proper.

There was even another preacher – another Lollard, he noticed,
when Crispin could hear the man's words. The crowds seemed
equally divided over what he had to say.

He valued Lancaster's opinions and counsel. But he could not bring himself to believe as the man did on these theological matters. Was Crispin merely being a prude? He'd been accused of such before. And after what he had seen of the wealth of churches and churchmen, it did seem the wiser course to not leave the temptation of greed to priests and bishops by allowing them to own property, and to keep their hands out of politics. Weren't the popes a long line of oligarchs rather than humble saints?

Crispin turned away from the man and his preaching and leaned toward the window to look inside the bookseller's shop . . . and saw books scattered along the floor. He hurried to the door and tried it but it was barred. He didn't hesitate to jump up on to the windowsill and climb inside.

'Master Bookseller! Are you here?'

Books and scrolls were all taken from their shelves and flung across the floor, the table, any surface. Crispin's indignation rose as a fury in his chest. So much so that he almost missed the shoe under the table. When he bent to look, there was a foot inside the shoe, and a leg, and the bookseller's body, lying beneath the table, covered in books and scrolls.

Crispin knelt and touched two fingers to the man's throat but couldn't find a pulse.

SIX

Crispin waited outside the shop for the sheriffs. Sir Richard Whittington arrived first and he even smiled upon seeing Crispin. He dismounted and handed off his reins to his attendants. He had a pleasant demeanor with light brown hair and beard.

'Master Guest,' he said politely. Crispin knew he was a wealthy mercer who also lent money to the king. He could afford his magnanimity. No, that wasn't fair. The man also spent his own money on a hospital and drains in Cripplegate. As far as Crispin was concerned, the man was owed his exalted place.

Crispin bowed low as he used to at court. 'My lord.'

'What has transpired here, Master Guest?'

'Alas. A murder of a bookseller.'

'And you were the First Finder?'

'I had the misfortune to be so.'

He went to the window and looked over the sill, studying the room and the feet of the merchant under the table. He rubbed his beard. 'Now that's a pity. Did you know the man well?'

'I did not. In fact, I do not know his name, but have since been told when I called the hue and cry. His name is John Suthfield. I purchased a book from him once.'

'Indeed. What book?'

'A book of Aristotle.'

'Ah yes. I have been told of your love of the philosophers. How does it go? *Honors and rewards fall to those who show their good qualities in action.* A very Christian thought from a pagan, is it not?'

'True. I suppose a wise man is wise no matter the age, even before Christ was born.'

'An interesting thought. You're just the man for such a conversation. But I gather you'd rather not go to Newgate for a friendly discussion. You could come to my shop.'

Crispin hedged. Whittington noticed and cleared his throat. 'There's no need, Master Guest. I get your meaning. Ah, here comes my associate.'

Where Whittington was congenial, Sheriff Drewe Barentyne was not. It wasn't that he was outwardly antagonistic toward Crispin. He was simply gruff to everyone, solemn and quiet. That kind of man was hard to read, for he might wear a gruff exterior but remain introspective inside his thoughts.

'What's ado, Sir Richard?' he said, staying on his horse.

'A dead merchant. Murdered, so Guest says.'

'Murdered? How?'

Crispin stepped forward and bowed, not quite as courteously as he had for Whittington. 'Cudgeled, my Lord Sheriff. And his shop ransacked.'

'Ransacked? Looking for what? His gold?'

Barentyne was a goldsmith, so perhaps he could be forgiven for thinking in those terms. But Crispin had no intention of divulging the true reason: that the culprit or culprits were looking for the book that was in Crispin's possession. He said nothing, and to Barentyne it was enough.

'Little for us to do, then, until the coroner arrives, eh, Sir Richard?'

'You go on, then. I'll stay a while.'

Barentyne, a man of slightly darker hair than Whittington, with a more pronounced nose, looked Crispin over. He'd seen him many a time, dealt with him, but still harbored his suspicions of Crispin, likely those suspicions that had been passed on by the former sheriffs, and their predecessors . . . and theirs. Crispin bowed so as to shoo the man away that much quicker, which Barentyne did by turning his horse and cantering up the lane back toward London.

Whittington sighed. 'Barentyne likes that he was elected sheriff but isn't interested in the office itself. I, on the other hand, find it fascinating. I suppose that is why you have set yourself up as this Tracker. Will you investigate?'

'I feel compelled.' And guilty for bringing death to the man's threshold.

'And yet you will go uncompensated. I tell you what, Master Guest. I shall pay you your fee, for I consider it a benefit to the citizenry of London that you do this service.' He reached for his pouch and pulled out some coins. 'Will this do?'

'Lord Sheriff, it is too much. I earn sixpence a day . . .'

'It is no matter. You are good for it. And if you find the culprit within days, then keep the sum and I shall call upon you for more service. Is that fair?'

'More than fair, my lord.' He bowed again and took the coins.

As they waited for the coroner, Crispin began to worry. If these men – whoever they were – suspected that Crispin had the book, then they well knew where he lived, and that made Jack and his family vulnerable. His tapped his finger on his dagger hilt in agitation.

The deputy coroner soon arrived, took Crispin's statement, and with the assurance of the sheriff, Crispin was finally allowed to go.

Once he turned the corner he ran. The more he had been detained, the more concerned he became about Jack's safety. Maybe he could have counted on Whittington's help. Or maybe not. After all, he had not told him what the culprits were looking for, and once he had, well . . . If the abbot's attitude was anything to go by, the sheriff might think he deserved his fate.

He made it to the Shambles and, despite his lungs burning, he continued to run, pushing passers-by aside to get to his lodgings. When it was in sight, nothing seemed amiss, but he would not be satisfied until he could get inside.

He made it to the granite step, grabbed the door handle, and flung it wide.

Isabel startled at her seat. Helen suckled at her breast while Jack was feeding Little Crispin with a spoon.

Jack set the child down from his knee and rose. 'Master? What's the matter?'

'I want you to pack up your family and send them to the Boar's Tusk.'

'Why?'

'Your prediction has come true. The bookseller is dead. Murdered.'

Isabel released a harsh gasp and hugged tight to her child.

'Madam,' he said, addressing her but looking aside as she pulled the girl from her breast and righted her chemise. 'There is danger for you here. Until we find the men responsible, you cannot stay.'

Jack gave his wife a searing look. 'You heard him. Bundle what you can and get yourself away to Gilbert and Eleanor's keeping.'

'Will you not accompany them?' asked Crispin.

'They will be fine on their own away from here. I'd rather stay and help you, sir.'

Isabel hadn't waited. She busily wrapped the baby and hurried upstairs to bundle their few necessary possessions.

When she reached the door, Jack kissed her farewell, kissed the top of the baby's head, and ruffled Little Crispin's ginger hair. 'You watch out for your mum, me lad.'

'Da!' he cried. And then the boy turned to Crispin with arms up, wanting a lift. Crispin was unable to resist and lifted the boy in his arms.

'You heard what your father said, boy. Take care of your mother and sister. We'll see you soon.' Without thinking about it, he kissed the boy and lowered him to the ground. The child immediately took his mother's hand.

'We'll get a message to you,' said Jack in the doorway. He watched her go down the street and then surveyed the lane up one side and down the other. He seemed satisfied when he drew back in, closing and locking the door.

'That was stupid of me,' muttered Crispin. 'I never should have allowed all this. I forgot that there are others depending on me to keep them safe.'

'It's just our vocation, sir. We do get ourselves into trouble.'

'But your family. I would never see harm come to them! I would die first.'

'And me, too, master. They'll be safe with Gilbert and Eleanor.'

Crispin huffed and took in the small room. All that he owned. At least, before the quarterly rent was due. 'Where is it hiding, Tucker?'

'In my chamber, sir. Under the bed. In the floor.'

'Let's leave it there for now. You'll sleep in my room. I'd not have your throat slit in the mid of the night.'

Jack touched his throat. 'Much obliged for that, sir.'

'It is most imperative that we discover who gave me that wretched book and who wants it.'

'Maybe I should go to the Boar's Tusk, ask around. See if anyone recognized the man.'

Crispin nodded. 'Yes. Do that. Do not be distracted by your family.'

'Never, sir. Not while I'm on duty, so to speak.'

'Then get you there. I will do my own asking to see if I can discover the man behind the henchmen.'

'What henchmen?' asked Jack.

'I encountered some men in an alley. They didn't want to take "no" for an answer.'

'Who were they?'

'I don't know, and I don't know if it has to do with that damned book or some other thing.'

Jack frowned. They both had enemies because of the work they did. But his frown soon changed to a determined demeanor. 'Have a care, master. I will hasten back as I may.'

Once Jack left, Crispin brooded. Someone had plainly seen Crispin at the bookseller's. They had reported that he had showed the man a book. He raised his head. That meant, if they had followed Crispin . . . other lives were in danger.

He took his cloak and hurried out the door, locking it behind him. He ran toward Wood Street, looking for the tiny barber's shop. The door was closed and Crispin tried the door. Locked. He pounded on it. 'Master Pardeu! Open up. It's Crispin Guest!'

No answer.

He went to the window and pried open the shutters. They weren't barred. He had only to throw them open to stand on the sill when he stopped. The man lay on the floor, his room ransacked.

He had just enough time to call the hue and cry, told the first man he encountered his name and that he would return, before he set off to Westminster at as fast a trot as he could.

He reached the street of the goldsmith, found the shop, and burst in. Matthew Middleton was slumped over his table, a knife in his back. The room was in shambles, but no gold was taken. None that he could see.

Crispin sat on a stool, staring at the man. This was his fault.

Three men were dead and it was his fault. He hadn't been careful. He hadn't been discerning. Was he getting too old for this tracking?

He crossed himself and clasped his hands together in frustration. Or was it a prayer? *Why, Lord? Why punish these for my shortcomings? It wasn't their fault. It was mine.* He was glad to get to the Tuckers in time. He'd never forgive himself if . . .

He dared not think it. But think he must. Who had ordered such cold-blooded killing? Someone with wealth who could hire men for such a task. Someone with influence to get away with it. Someone with an interest in that book. But why? Why would they be so hungry to get it? It had no power like a relic had. Yes, he admitted it at last. Some of the relics he had come across did seem to have some kind of power. Hadn't he experienced it just a few years ago when Little Crispin was born? That relic of a saint that would not seem to leave him alone? But this book had not that kind of power. Its only power was to create chaos, to make a man think as Crispin had done. And who would despise that . . .

'The Church,' he said aloud. Someone in the Church. And perhaps . . . someone he had met before. And looking at Matthew Middleton brought all those memories back, memories he and Jack had tried hard to forget.

Crispin rose. Yes, he'd have to give the hue and cry again, but like the last time, he could not waste his time waiting for the sheriff or the deputy coroner. Again, he told the first man he saw of the circumstances, he told him his name and that he should notify the sheriffs, and then he left. He had to get word to Lancaster, get his help. But God help him, the man was in Sheen with the king. And there was no way Crispin could possibly go. Could he send someone? It would take too long. He'd have to figure this out on his own. But how?

'Think, Crispin.'

But there was nothing. Grumbling to himself at his helplessness, he pushed on but raised his head when he heard a commotion. He trotted forward and encountered a crowd.

'It's that Tracker,' someone said, and Crispin got in close to eavesdrop.

'He's a heroic one,' said his companion. 'Stopped a thief in his tracks only yesterday, I heard.'

'Better than the king's men when it comes to keeping the peace.'

'Aye. He used to be a knight. Committed treason, though.'

'And he still lived? That's a miracle.'

'Aye, the good Lord was saving him for a higher purpose, I've heard tell.'

'Imagine. And him a knight and all.'

Red-faced, Crispin pushed his way through and saw a man very like himself handing over a pouch to a grateful shopkeeper. When the shopkeeper offered a few coins in return, Crispin's double bowed to him, waved to the cheering crowd, and set out down the road. The crowd dispersed and Crispin elbowed his way forward. He wasn't about to lose the man this time.

Crispin threaded his way between stray dogs and shedding work horses tethered to carts. The man turned a corner but, before Crispin could reach him, a broken cart blocked his way. With a muttered curse, he climbed over it, hopped down to the corner, and looked up the street. The man was nowhere to be found.

'Damn.'

Someone tapped his shoulder and began jabbering before Crispin turned.

'It's all well and good that you catch these cutpurses in the street, my good sir, but I still need you to find the gold my nephew stole from me.'

Crispin stared at the round-bellied man in the merchant clothes of long gown and draping hat. 'Are you speaking to me?'

'Yes, by the Devil, I am! You promised to do the job a sennight ago and I have heard precious little from you ever since.'

'Sir, I beg your mercy,' he replied with a brief bow, 'but we made no such agreement. In fact, this is the first I've heard of it, and I've never set eyes on you before.'

The man stared with mouth ajar for a moment before he burst into laughter. 'So I see. You will have your jest. But . . .' He sobered quickly. 'I must have my gold. You promised to, er . . . procure it.'

'I did?'

'God's teeth, man. Are you soft in the head? Of course *you*.'

'The Tracker? Crispin Guest?'

'Who else stands before me?'

Who else indeed. Crispin scowled and jerked his head over his shoulder, seeking but not finding the miscreant he had been after. 'I . . . apologize, good master. I've had a lot on my mind of late. You must see my man at my lodgings on the Shambles . . .'

'Oh no. I told you before that I could not be seen.' He glanced around cautiously. 'That you would . . . take care of this business forthwith.' He whispered the last with a grimacing wink. 'You only needed to make certain my nephew was out of his premises for the day.'

Crispin leaned in. 'Do you mean *burgle* him?'

The man made placating gestures, shushing all the while.

Crispin drew himself up, fitting his thumbs in his belt. 'I am *not* a burglar.'

'Hush, sir. I beg of you . . .'

Crispin walked forward, forcing the man to walk backward. 'And further, if I ever intimated that I was, then I must have been out of my head. If you'd pay for my *lawful* services, I suggest you go to the Shambles to the old poulterer's. Now. Begone!'

The man sputtered and blinked. 'But . . . I already paid . . .' he said feebly.

Crispin had already turned his back on him and walked away. Of all the damned nerve! He would have to stop this knave once and for all, and quick, before he soiled what was left of Crispin's reputation.

He stomped back down the street until he pulled up short. Someone was standing in his way. Reaching for his dagger was a gut reaction.

The man stepped out of the shadows, the same man who had delivered that damned book to him.

SEVEN

Crispin finished the movement of drawing his knife. 'You!' The man took a step back and raised his empty hands. 'Please, Master Guest. Be at peace.'

'Be at *peace*? When three men are dead because of *you*?'

'Master Guest. Please. We must talk.'

He looked down at his blade. He wanted more than anything to thrust it deep into the man's gut. But with a heavy sigh he sheathed it with a snap and scowled. 'What have you to say to me?'

His hood still shadowed his face but Crispin could see the blond hair, the beard. 'Only this. That I knew you would protect the book, because it surely needs protection.'

'It's blasphemous.'

'It may well be. But it is also another facet of our Lord.'

'Who trusted Judas.'

'He trusted them all. And Saint Peter denied ever having known him.'

'Make your point.'

The man, fair of face with blond hair that curled under his ears, was dressed in another blue houppelande. He glanced around. 'Master Guest,' he said quietly, 'may we go somewhere to talk? To your lodgings, perhaps?'

'If we must.' Without another word he stalked ahead and only flicked a glance over his shoulder to see if the man was following him.

They made it to the Shambles and Crispin quickly unlocked his door. 'Get in.'

He had forgotten how hastily Isabel had left. A pot of something congealed near the fire. The baby's cradle lay disturbingly empty. And there were cups on the table and a bowl of cold porridge where Jack had been feeding his son. The sight of it made Crispin angry again, that his . . . his *family* could have been caught up in this, could have been hurt or worse.

He spun on the man. 'Explain yourself.'

'Master Guest, I represent a most important personage. My name is Hugh Ashdown, and though I am not a monk, I live the life of a religious.'

'Who? Who is this personage and why should you wish to preserve a blasphemous book?'

'It isn't blasphemous to the one I follow. It can be a most important book to understand our Lord, to see the greater mystery of Him, to delve deep into the unknowable of God.' He shook his head. 'Sometimes the message is difficult to understand fully. It is not for every man to be able to discern all the mysteries. But there are some who can. Still there are those in the Church who seek to destroy any other message they do not understand. They call them heresies and move to root them out without question. It was from those men I sought to protect the text. From one man in particular.'

'And who is that?'

'A bishop from Yorkshire, who has worked many years in this rooting out of heresies of both books and men. He works secretly with his own henchmen to do his work.'

'I have met those men. They killed an innocent bookseller, a barber, and a goldsmith for no other reason but that I brought that book to them.'

'He is ruthless, Master Guest. Bishop Edmund Becke would see the one I follow quieted.'

Crispin turned his thoughts over. 'I have encountered this bishop before as well.'

'Have you? Somehow that doesn't surprise me. Then you know he poses a threat to the greater wisdom of God.'

'I don't know about that, but he is a single-minded man. I met him some twelve years ago in less than ideal circumstances.'

'Is the book protected? Do you have it still?'

'I do. And I know what it says.'

'May I . . . see it?'

Crispin narrowed his eyes. 'It is safe.'

'Ah,' said Ashdown. 'Well then. Surely you must realize that you are in danger as well. Perhaps it might be best if I take it off your hands.'

Crispin got in close. 'And so you knew this would happen. My whole household has been interrupted and endangered. Why did you bring it to me? Couldn't *you* protect it?'

'Alas, no. Bishop Becke has been on my trail.'

'And now he is on mine.' His glare didn't seem to have any effect on the mild-mannered man. 'Are you, too, a Lollard? London seems to be lousy with them of late. Like the plague.'

'Not quite a Lollard. Not like your own Lancaster.'

'Do not speak of him. I will not allow you to speak of him.'

Ashdown held up his hands again in surrender.

'I remind you,' growled Crispin, 'that what I do, I do for a fee.'

Ashdown observed Crispin mildly a long while before he reached for his scrip. 'I have been authorized to pay you. How much?'

'How much is a man's life worth?'

'Come now, Master Guest. There are sacrifices that must be made for the greater good.'

'Allow a man to decide whether he'd like to make those sacrifices.'

Hugh sighed. 'How much, Master Guest?'

'Half a mark.'

Hugh brows rose, but he dug into his bag and pulled out the coins. 'I was mistaken in thinking it was . . . six pence a day.'

'The price went up.' Crispin snatched the coins and shoved them into his own scrip. 'Now. This personage. What is so special about him? Is he a lord?'

'No. The humblest of people. But you will see. You will be visited shortly.'

God's blood, he thought. Just what he needed. More foolery coming to his doorstep.

The door slammed open and Jack stood on the threshold, his dagger in his hand. 'Master, are you well?' he asked suspiciously, looking over the stranger.

'For now. This is my apprentice, Jack Tucker. And this, Jack, is Hugh Ashdown, the knave who gave me that damned book.'

'Oh *is* it?' With a scowl to match Crispin's, Jack slammed his knife back in its sheath and stalked up to the man. He was several inches taller and he used it to his advantage. 'What you go and give that book to my master for? There's been murders because of it.'

'As I was explaining to your master, it was necessary to make certain it wasn't destroyed. The other men . . . I am sorry.'

'Oh, you're sorry, are you?' Jack didn't seem to have any intention of letting up. 'And what about us? My master and me, getting thrust in the middle of it. My wife and children had to flee this place!'

'And I am heartily sorry for that inconvenience, Master Tucker. But I felt it must be done.'

'Why?'

Ashdown raised his hands to fend them off. 'All will be explained when I bring the one whom I follow.'

Crispin stepped up beside Jack. 'And how do we know we can trust you?'

'Well . . . you will have to go with your heart, Master Guest.'

I'd rather go with my blade, but he didn't say it aloud.

'Do you ever intend to tell me of this "one whom you follow"?'

The man smiled, irritating Crispin all the more. 'In time, Master Guest. I have come to you so that you would not waste precious time looking for me.'

'And now that I've got you, what shall I do with you?'

The man measured him and appeared not to like Crispin's expression. 'As I said, Master Guest, I mean no harm.'

'And yet harm you have done. And what about me and mine? Shall this bishop come to my doorstep and hunt me down?'

'I hope not, Master Guest. For the meantime, I think I have redirected his cause.'

'Oh? What other poor unfortunate do you plan to have killed?'

The man lifted an indignant shoulder. 'Truly, Master Guest. I was given to understand you were from nobility and expected more courtesy from you.'

Incredulous at the gall of the man, Crispin could only stare.

'God's blood, man!' cried Jack, pouring all of Crispin's own indignity into his words. 'Master Guest owes you no such courtesy. And neither do I! Innocent men have died. We might be next.' He turned to Crispin. 'Do I have your permission, sir, to throw this whoreson out?'

'By all means.'

The man had time to take only one step back before Jack grabbed him and shove-walked him to the door, which Crispin promptly opened for him. With a last hard push, Jack tossed him over the threshold. The man tumbled over the granite step and out into the mud. The hog-seller across the way brayed out his laughter, as did others milling along the lane.

Jack enjoyed their jeers for a moment more before he slammed the door and threw the bolt. He brushed his hands together. 'That's him told.'

'Thank you, Jack.' Crispin moved to the window and peered at the man through a crack in the shutter. He brushed the mud from himself as best he could, looked back forlornly at Crispin's lodgings, and trudged away.

'So you found him before I did,' said Jack.

'He found me.'

'And who is this "one that he follows" or some such knavery?'

'I don't know.' He sank down into his chair and stared at the naked hearth.

Jack began to clear the spoiled food and crusty pot. 'What of the one who is after us and killed them men?'

'That is our old friend Bishop Becke.'

Jack stopped and whipped around. 'The same from . . .'

'Yes.'

'Blind me,' he muttered, continuing his cleaning.

It had been a while since it had been him and Jack alone. He watched for a few moments as his apprentice fell back into old habits of cleaning and preparing food. He almost missed those times when it was just the two of them, but with an unexpected pang in his chest, he realized he missed Isabel's humming, Little Crispin's battles with imaginary foes with a stick as a sword, and even Baby Helen's crying, for she giggled almost as much.

'I'll make it right again, Jack, and then your family can come home where they belong.'

Jack smiled under his shoulder. 'Ah, you miss them too.'

'I do. It's foolish of me to deny it.'

'You are a good master, aren't you?'

Crispin threw a spoon at him.

Crispin didn't know what steps to take next. Maybe he should have given it back to Ashdown when he asked for it, but Crispin hadn't liked the strange look in the man's eye. Maybe Crispin should just destroy the book himself and be done with it. He'd been paid more than adequately for watching it. But what if that bishop needed proof? He mulled it, turning the cup of ale Jack had provided him with, spinning it again and again without drinking, watching the damascene foam on the surface rock back and forth.

A knock sounded on the door.

Both on alert, Jack was first at the door with his knife drawn. He looked back at Crispin for permission, and Crispin gave him a nod.

'Who's there?' Jack called.

'Master Guest! I am here. Please open the door.'

That sounded like . . .

'It's Christopher Walcote,' hissed Jack over his shoulder. 'What shall I do?'

'Let the boy in.'

Crispin stood, straightened his clothes, and then felt foolish for it.

Jack opened the door, and the young boy who looked so much like Crispin that Jack shook his head, strode in. A servant was with him, looking about anxiously toward the street.

Christopher bounded forward right up to Crispin and closed his arms around him in a hug. Crispin stood limp-armed, staring down at the boy, at the top of his head covered with a fashionable hat.

'I'm so glad to see you again . . . and that you are still my friend.' He looked up, gray eyes ablaze with warmth.

'Master Walcote,' said the servant fretfully. 'We should not be here among . . . these people.'

'I am not just anyone, sir. I am Crispin Guest, the Tracker, and I am a friend of Master Walcote here . . . and his parents.'

'Yes, well . . . Master Walcote was not to stray far from home today. He said he had your permission—'

Crispin looked down and Christopher wouldn't meet his eye. 'Were you not to send a message to me first? What if I had been out? I very often am.'

'I had to take a chance. It's been so very long since I've seen you, Master Crispin.'

'Only this morning. Well . . . I shall forgive you this once, Master Christopher, as long as you send that missive the next time.'

'There will be a next time, then?'

'We shall see.' He noticed the servant eyeing the two of them. He turned his back on him. 'Tell your servant to await you outside. Make sure no one disturbs us.'

Jack sensed what was needed, grabbed the man, and pushed him through the open door. 'Just out here, my lad.'

'But I don't think—'

'And that's right and proper for a servant.' Jack waved at him and closed the door. He blew out a breath as he leaned against it.

Crispin looked to Jack for help.

'Perhaps Master Christopher would like to handle a sword, master. The proper way to handle a sword comes before using one.'

The boy clapped his hands. 'Oh, yes! I should like that.'

But before Jack could grab his sword, hanging from its place by the door, a knock sounded a second time.

Jack scowled and yanked open the door. 'Didn't I tell you to wait outside . . . oh!'

A man in livery stood on the threshold. Crispin stood to attention when he saw it was the Duke of Lancaster's arms. 'I'm looking for Crispin Guest.'

'I am Crispin Guest,' he said, stepping forward.

The servant handed Crispin a sealed parchment, bowed, and pivoted out of the doorway. Walcote's servant watched him go and looked back hopefully at Jack before Jack shut the door on him once more.

Crispin used his fingernail to snap the wax seal. As soon as he opened it, he saw it was written in the duke's own hand.

> *God have mercy, my dear Crispin,*
> *The queen is dead. His Majesty, mad with grief, has burned down the palace at Sheen. The court ran for their lives. Make certain you stay out of Westminster. Your life will be in danger. The king will brook nothing from you or even word of you.*

He didn't sign it but he didn't need to.

'What's it say?' said Jack.

'The queen is dead.' And even as the words left his lips, every bell in every church in London began to toll.

EIGHT

'Blind me,' said Jack, crossing himself. He bowed his head, a tear in his eye.

Crispin knew the queen's kindness to Jack. She had saved his life from Richard's wrath. Who would save them now?

'He doted on her,' Crispin said softly. 'She was a kind and gracious lady. I shall never forget her bravery and generosity toward you.'

Jack sniffed, rubbing his nose.

'I don't understand,' said Christopher. 'What's happened?'

He could scarce believe he had forgotten Christopher was there. Crispin crouched before him. 'Our queen has died. She was the mother of England. That is why the bells ring.'

Christopher's eyes enlarged. A child is full of empathy and it was clear the boy likened this mother to his own. Those eyes became glossy. 'I should go home.'

'Yes, I'm afraid you should. There will be another time, Master Christopher.'

'Yes. I must stand with my father and mother at this sad time.'

Spoken like a courtier. The boy wasn't all that far from it. His father was an alderman, might even be knighted someday. It made Crispin burn with a sudden flash of envy.

Jack opened the door. 'You!' he called to the servant.

The man scurried to reach the door.

Crispin rested his hand on Christopher's shoulder, feeling the warmth . . . and the boniness. He was but a small boy, after all, and boys were little sticks. He longed to hold him, to crush the boy against him. Reluctantly, he said instead to the servant, 'Come. Take your master home. This is not a day of revelry. For the queen is dead and England mourns.'

The servant looked up to the steeples and the bells tolling and grimly took his charge.

Before Christopher could be led away, he turned back. 'I will come again, Master Crispin.'

'Yes. Do that. But send a message first *asking* to come.'

He watched the boy go with sadness at his absence, at the lost years, at the death of the queen.

Jack was reading the rest of the message that Crispin had left on the table. 'Blind me. His Grace is right. You'd best lay low. There's no telling what the king would do to you.'

Crispin nodded, thinking. And hadn't Crispin's own manor been burned to the ground? Not by his hand, but he was still responsible. Yes, he'd rather it burn down to ashes than let another live there. Perhaps that is what Richard thought. He'd rather not see their home without his beloved wife, for they had been as close as man and woman could be. And yet they had no heir.

They'd have to find another wife for him. If not and he died without an heir . . . Crispin scarce wanted to think of what would come of that.

'I can't sit around here, Jack.'

'Then what are we to do? We mustn't make a fuss.'

'The king has his own worries. He'll never spend a moment thinking of me. But I won't sit here like a boar in a trap, waiting for this bishop to pounce. I want to find him, get it over with.'

'But master, what if his plan is to arrest you?'

'I'd like to see him try.'

'This is what I meant by "fuss", sir.'

'You're coming with me.'

Jack took a mere moment to contemplate that. He seemed more relieved that he would be there to monitor Crispin's activities. It was almost amusing.

They set out on to the Shambles. Jack sighed. 'I miss me wife.'

There hadn't been a moment in their marriage when she wasn't with child. 'She has only just left not more than a few hours ago.'

'Do you suppose it will be long? Her having to be away?'

'I hope not. I've become used to better cooking.'

Jack looked around. 'Where are we going anyway?'

'I haven't the faintest idea.'

They both fell silent, until . . .

'You're trying to draw him out, aren't you, master?'

'I had hoped. I assumed he had men watching our lodgings.'

'Should I . . .' Jack was cautiously glancing over his shoulder. 'Should I be prepared or . . .?'

'Be prepared . . . to be *un*prepared, I suppose.'

'Master Crispin, there is one thing I can always count on with you.'

'And what's that?'

He laughed in spite of the worry on his bearded face. 'I'm never bored.'

Despite what Crispin said about looking unprepared, Jack kept his hand on his dagger hilt. Crispin noticed he'd done the same unconsciously to his own dagger.

They walked the streets of London, watching as the news spread of the queen. Citizens came out of their houses and shops to stand with others, talking fervently. Others wept, crossing themselves. Every now and then, people would lift their tear-stained faces to the steeples and the cascade of tolling bells. Some didn't talk at all but looked on at their neighbors with grim faces, some even muttering over rosaries.

'Why did she have to die?' asked Jack softly beside him. 'I prayed for her every night.'

'Was not your prayer for her soul? And surely these prayers and her deeds sent her to Heaven all the sooner.'

'Aye, that's true. But we needed her here. That the king should burn down his palace! What's to stop him from burning down all of London?'

'His ministers and lords. Gaunt and Bolingbroke.'

'Master,' Jack said quietly after a pause. 'What makes some women strong and some succumb? I . . . I pray each time my Isabel goes to her childbed. The lass is strong and came through it twice and I pray she will a third time. But I worry.'

'Jack,' he said, laying his hand on the man's shoulder. 'You have nothing to fear. She *is* strong. And you are a reverent man. What would all of us do without your prayers?'

'But that's just it. I prayed for the queen . . . and she died.'

He had nothing to say to that. It was for theologians to banter about, not a disgraced knight. He was the last person on earth who deserved Jack's devotion, or anyone's. It was best not to think too hard on it.

The strangeness of the streets – when all the citizens were out and speaking to one another, and commerce had ground to a halt, with nothing but the bells to cover the city like a shadow – the whole of it struck Crispin bluntly, as when the death of King Edward III fell upon London. It had been a strange, sad time.

Amid the muffled silence, the sound of a cart churning down the street with the heavy footfalls of a draft horse fell hard on Crispin's ear like an instrument out of tune. And before he could turn, he reckoned what it was.

The driver was the same man from all those years ago. More gray in his hair, perhaps, but with that same still and stoic face. He wore no livery and pulled slowly on the reins, with arm muscles flexing under a studded leather tunic, until the heavy, covered carriage halted. The carriage's sides bore no arms, gave no clue as to who might be inside. But it didn't need them.

Crispin took a breath and stood slightly in front of Jack out of habit, even though the man could well take care of himself.

A flap on one of the carriage's windows lifted, and an arm beckoned. Crispin made eye contact with Jack before stepping forward.

He stopped before the carriage and waited. A familiar voice came from behind the curtain. 'Get in, Master Guest. And . . . Master Tucker.'

'God's blood,' Jack gasped behind him.

Crispin swept his sword scabbard back, ducked, and climbed in. Jack followed. They sat on the cushioned seat opposite the man Crispin remembered as Bishop Edmund Becke.

His hair was light in color, his eyes blue, with a gaze that ran rampant over the two of them, ticking off details and filing them away. His face still seemed young, as young as Jack's, but it had seemed as young the last time. One of those faces that seemed perpetually youthful, Crispin supposed.

With some unknown signal, the driver pressed on, and Jack jerked forward, nearly pitching to the floor. He righted himself with an embarrassed fidget of his hands and braced his foot forward against the wooden floor.

The bishop surveyed them both with a mild expression. Gloved hands pressed together like a prayer, but the fingers teased at his shaven chin. A ring glinted from one of the fingers and Crispin's gaze was caught by it for a few moments.

Becke smiled. 'Has it truly been some twelve years ago, Master Guest?'

'Yes. Since you attempted to get your hands on some parchments from some Jews doing no harm. Did you ever find them?'

Becke frowned. 'Oh, I think you know the answer to that.'

Crispin kept his steely gaze steady on the bishop.

Becke changed tack. 'You have a new ornament since last we met, Master Guest. A sword.'

Though he now itched to, Crispin didn't touch the sword nor look at it. 'Yes.'

'Bestowed upon you by the Duke of Lancaster's son. A proud moment that must have been.' A Yorkshire lilt to his speech. Crispin remembered it but said nothing. He worked at keeping his breathing even. He refused to look surprised by Becke's revelations.

The sharp eyes turned toward Jack. 'And Jack Tucker. My, my. You were a mere lad the last time I set my eyes upon you. Look at you now. A man.'

'And fully capable of defending my master.'

Becke's eyes lit before he laughed.

Crispin laid a hand on Jack's knee, hoping it conveyed to his servant to keep himself in check.

'Of course you can defend your master. And have. But you need not worry over that today.'

Crispin sat back, resting his shoulders against the seat. 'I wonder if you haven't heard the news, Your Excellency. That the queen has died.'

'Alas, yes. *Requiescat in pace.*' He crossed himself lazily as he tilted his head, listening to the bells. 'Unfortunately, my work cannot wait.'

'Your work?'

'Oh come now, Master Guest. I can tell by the look in your eye that you fully expected to see me. You know my work.'

'I have interfered with it before.'

Crispin was pleased by the sudden flattening of the man's expression. 'Indeed you have.' He rubbed the thigh where Crispin had sunk in his dagger all those years ago. 'I have not forgotten.'

Crispin smiled. 'Good. Why do you concern yourself with a book that no one can read?'

The first sign of emotion crossed the bishop's face. He placed both gloved hands on his thighs and bent forward, eyes spearing Crispin. 'Someone, somewhere *will* be able to translate it. And then the blasphemy will spread and infect. Order, Master Guest. We must keep order or our Christian society will surely collapse. Would you leave us to the mercy of infidels and idolaters?'

'If you haven't translated it, then how do you know what it says?'

He smiled and leaned back. 'I was curious to see you two again. My curiosity is now satisfied. Where may I drop you off?'

Crispin folded his arms over his chest. 'Why kill the men who merely looked at the book?'

With a flick of his lash, he deftly sidestepped the question. 'Can I tell you my theory? This might intrigue you. There are men – and women – who would see the dominance of the Church dwindle. They question the sacraments, they question the hierarchy, they even question the Scriptures . . .' He shook his head. 'You cannot have order on earth as it is in Heaven if such persists. God does not wish for us to question His anointed. He does not wish us to disrespect those He puts above us, both pope . . . and king.'

'But does not God give us mere mortals our free will, to seek and find?'

'Wait, Master Guest. You have not heard my theory.' He paused, body rocking with the lumbering wagon. 'In my theory, I see free will as the key to open the door to the Devil, to let Hell in. And each turn of that key widens the portal, and those that question become drawn to the pit ever faster. They willingly do so in the guise of this "free will". You see, God tests us, Master Guest, as he tested Job. Some say that Job well deserved to push God aside. But what is the alternative? Damnation. A fiery eternity. And for what? Free will. Free will is not free thought. No, my friend. There is no true free will but the holiness that is God and His Word and His Holy Church. These are set in stone and must not veer neither to the left, nor the right. There is only one path. It is straight and narrow.'

'Interesting. But you fail to take into consideration whether a book or two – or a man or a woman's faith – can bring a sinner *to* the righteous path. This book you seek can transform the mind to make all that might be indistinct clear. Isn't that worth championing?'

'You don't understand the sinner, Master Guest, being one yourself.'

'Are not we all sinners, Excellency?'

'Some more than others. The book – for I know what is in it – is dangerous to the mind.'

'I know what's in it, too.'

Jack gasped beside him. Too late. The die was cast. Crispin waited to see how Becke would react.

He slowly nodded. 'I suspected that once it was in your hands you would allow curiosity to get the better of you. Enough to seek out what it said. Alas, Master Guest. It is your doom.'

'I don't feel particularly doomed by it. Nor does it take away my faith. But you're right in that it does make me question the haughtiness of the Church. That only four gospels would be "chosen" among many more.'

Becke frowned. 'You see. You are already infected. But I knew that a traitor would be. You moved against God's anointed in our good King Richard and you blaspheme each time one of God's relics comes into your unbelieving hands.'

'I beg to differ. The relics – whatever they may be – come into my hands *because* of the sins of man. I make all right again. A pity that you and your philosophy cannot see the truth of it.'

'Yes. A pity.' He turned to Jack. 'You're a pious man, Tucker. Your immortal soul is threatened by standing beside this sinner.'

'I'd rather stand beside him in Hell then leave him behind to reach Heaven.'

Crispin stared. Jack's lip trembled but he had no doubt the man meant what he said. Crispin's chest panged with discomfort. He would never stand in the way of Jack's salvation.

Becke said nothing, but his mild expression had vanished, replaced with a slight grimace. He moved the curtain flap and whistled to the driver. The cart lurched to a halt. 'I'll let you out here, shall I?'

'I'll burn the book if that's what you want.'

'Oh, it is what I want. But that will not be the end of it.'

'You would burn me, too?'

'Not as yet, Guest. But I don't trust that you will burn it. Give me the book. And I'll trouble you no more.'

'And if I don't?'

'Then trouble awaits. You can get off here.'

Crispin rose, keeping his shoulders stooped from the low ceiling. But he didn't immediately leave. Instead, he leaned toward Becke. 'You cannot stomp on an idea, Excellency. Once the idea is out in the world, it is like the bee that flits from flower to flower. It cannot be stopped. Ideas are what keep mankind from stagnating in a rotten pool. *It is not once nor twice but times without number that the same ideas make their appearance in the world.*'

Becke was unmoved. He merely sat and stared blankly at Crispin.

Crispin grunted his displeasure and cast the curtain aside to leap to the ground. Jack followed and the carriage driver did not hesitate to move it along.

They watched it go.

'We should have slit his throat while we had the chance,' said Jack.

Crispin nodded. It might have been better if they had.

They found themselves on the Strand, nearly to Westminster, and now they had to walk all the way back. It was late afternoon. Sunset was yet hours away, but it had been a wearying day with one thing or another assaulting them. And little rest they'd get this night with the bishop's men after them.

Nothing was spoken between them as they walked, each deep into their own thoughts. It wasn't until they were in view of Newgate that Crispin spoke. 'I suppose it doesn't matter in the scheme of things whether Bishop Becke gets his book to destroy or not. It is childish of me to hold on to the thing when, in the end, I know it must be burned.'

'But it's like you said, sir. The idea of it is already in the world. I don't suppose it does matter if the book is destroyed.'

'I suppose it's . . . it's just giving in to *him* that leaves a bad taste in my mouth.'

'Me, too, sir.'

They walked along Newgate Market where it turned into the Shambles. The sight of a mounted man in livery, holding the reins of another's empty horse, slowed them. He was standing before their door.

'God's blood, what now?' hissed Jack.

Crispin moved cautiously forward; when they got to their front step, the man merely looked at them but made no move toward them. Crispin pushed open the door and saw a tall figure standing before his cold fireplace.

He turned.

'Your Grace,' said Crispin with a bow.

John of Gaunt, the Duke of Lancaster, flicked his gaze around the room. And before Crispin could ask, the duke stepped toward him and narrowed his dark eyes. 'No nonsense from you, Crispin. I've come to hire you . . . to solve the murder of the queen.'

NINE

'But,' sputtered Crispin, 'you told me the queen was ill.'
'Yes. But there is reason to believe that she was poisoned.'

'And . . . what reason is that, my lord?'

Frowning, Gaunt reached into the ornate pouch hanging from his belt and passed a parchment to Crispin. Opening it, Crispin read:

> *It is foolish to ignore the Lollard treatises. To save England*
> *from the fools in Rome, the old ways must make way for*
> *the new. Those who stand in the way must die. The crusade*
> *begins!*

Crispin turned the page over but found nothing more. 'Where did this come from? To whom was it sent?'

'It was found in the queen's bedchamber. No one knows whence it came. But, of course, the chamber and all around it was razed.'

'Does the king suspect that this was not her rightful death?'

'No. And I would not burden him. He is . . . quite out of his head at the moment. But *we* must know.'

'Yes.' Crispin looked at the parchment again. 'It isn't a precise threat. And the court does allow the presence of Lollards.' He stared pointedly at Gaunt.

'The king does . . . reluctantly these days. And we are ever grateful for what grace he allows us. But if these rogue Lollards are responsible for the queen's death, then his tolerance will come to a swift close.'

'It would.' Crispin walked slowly across the floor. 'My lord, I feel it will be necessary to investigate personally at court. And I think that we all can see the futility in that.'

'I have brought you livery. You can wear a hood and disguise yourself. And I will personally watch over you and your proceedings.'

'You will . . . assist me in investigating?'

He seemed to huff at Crispin's choice of words but settled his face blandly. 'I see no way around it.'

Crispin had to admit that the thought enticed. Then he looked at Jack. 'Jack, I need you to stay here and guard the . . . the object.'

'Of course, sir. What shall I do if . . . if Ashdown returns?'

'Turn him out. And keep a sharp eye out for the bishop.'

'Right, sir.' He bowed to the duke.

Gaunt said nothing as he led the way out of the house. But when they were standing on the granite step, he turned to Crispin. 'An interesting if not cryptic conversation.'

'I have . . . discreet doings to attend to.'

'Strange personages? Bishops? You do move along an odd chessboard.'

'By necessity, Your Grace.'

Gaunt nodded and turned to his retainer. 'Be so good as to give your livery and your horse to Master Guest here.'

'My lord?' He exchanged glances with Crispin.

'Make haste, man,' prodded Gaunt.

The man let go of the other horse's reins, which the duke took up. He dismounted and shrugged out of his tabard and reluctantly handed it to Crispin. Crispin pulled it down over his head, straightened it, and pulled his hood up. He mounted and looked down apologetically toward the man. 'Much thanks.'

Gaunt bent down and spoke briefly to the man before turning his horse and setting out. Crispin followed.

'Besides this note,' said Crispin after they had wound down London's streets heading toward Newgate, 'have you any reason to believe the queen's life was at stake?'

'There are always rumors, threats. Nothing to take seriously.'

'And why the queen? Why not the king?'

'He is well guarded.'

'There must always be an instance or two when he is not. If this did happen at court, any courtier could have laid in wait.'

He gave Crispin a wary glance. 'You seem to have thought this out.'

'Take no offense by it, my lord. If I plot and scheme now, it is to discern what an assassin might attempt.'

'If you say so.' He bounced lazily with the horse's gait and said nothing for a time, until: 'I see your lodgings have improved. There was some discussion about where you lived. Some seemed to think you could now be found on Bread Street.'

Crispin huffed. 'That was . . . an aberration. Some knave is impersonating me.'

'Impersonating *you*?'

'Yes. Some sort of scheme, no doubt, to get money out of the local merchants. I haven't yet caught him . . . but I will.'

'God's blood,' he laughed. 'I would like to see that!'

They chuckled together as they used to do. Though Crispin felt that pang of regret that their camaraderie was only temporary, it didn't seem to hold the sting that it once did. He was glad of it. And he reckoned it had a lot to do with a herd of Tuckers awaiting his return.

'I will need to speak with her ladies. I take it they are still at court.'

'Yes,' said Gaunt. 'I don't know what will be done with them. They are being kept out of the king's eye. He weeps at the sight of them.'

This human side of Richard gave Crispin pause. He'd only known his pettiness at the merest slight, his vengeance, and perhaps even a bit of envy of his boisterous cousin, Henry of Bolingbroke.

'And the physicians attending her. Will they speak to me?'

'I shall make them do so.'

'Is it possible it *was* an illness, my lord?'

'It's possible.'

'When I speak to the ladies, it might be prudent to have Lady Katherine accompany me. Will she allow that?'

'I'm certain she will.'

Crispin brooded over many things: the problem at hand, the book that lay hidden in Jack's chamber, and always, *always* of Philippa. Before he could stop himself, he blurted, 'I have a son.' He would have thrown his hand over his mouth if he could have. But once begun, he couldn't stop. All his self-admonitions fell away. 'He is ten now.'

Gaunt slowly turned to look at him. Those scowling eyes softened. 'A son?'

'Yes. A . . . a bastard. On a woman I . . . I have long loved.'

That arrow hit true, for Lancaster's face was nothing if not sympathetic. 'Ah,' he said quietly. 'I must speculate that since *you* are not married . . . the *lady* must be.'

'Yes.' The expelled word was a balm to the tightness that had bored into his chest. It had wound tight over the years and speaking of it did lessen its tension. 'She is a prominent woman, married to an alderman.'

'I see. And do you dally with her, Crispin?'

'No, my lord. She was not married at the time. I would not burden her so now. But we do burn.'

'That is right and proper. It doesn't do to cuckold a man who doesn't deserve it.'

'He knows nothing of it. He even claims the boy is his.'

'And that is as it should be. He'll be safe. He'll prosper.'

'I know.'

Gaunt reached out between them and their horses and patted Crispin's leg. 'A wealthy man may dally. A poor one does not have the luxury.'

Crispin gritted his teeth. 'I know.'

'How does he fare? Does he look like you?'

Crispin couldn't help but smile. 'He looks too damnably like me. If you saw him you would know instantly. I'm sure I looked much like that at ten.'

'I should like to see him sometime.'

'That's probably unwise.'

'Probably.'

'I promised to teach him arms practice.'

'What? You are speaking to the boy?'

'I could not help it. He was accused of murder and I . . . I exonerated him.'

Gaunt was staring at him. Crispin could tell out of the corner of his eye, but he would not look at his former mentor head on. 'God's blood and bones,' said Gaunt. 'Perhaps you *were* set to a higher purpose. Have you ever considered, Crispin, that had you not been sent from court and become this Tracker, he and many other innocents might have died?'

Crispin shook his head, unable to speak. The thought was too frightening, too close to home. The notion that he needed to be brought low in order to reach the heights was too big to comprehend. Such things happened to martyrs, and he was nowhere close to a saint.

'All the lives you've saved,' Lancaster went on, thoughtfully. 'All the justice you have meted out. None of that would have happened without you. Have you ever thought about it, Crispin?'

'No.'

'Well do so. It may lessen the suffering.'

'I have come to an understanding after all these years, my lord. I am . . . content.'

Gaunt's head jerked sharply. 'Are you indeed? Ah, Crispin. I am glad to hear it. There have been many nights when I . . . well.' He swallowed. 'I have done much penance for all I did to you, my friend.'

'I have forgiven you.' He surprised himself when he said it. He hadn't known he had.

Gaunt smiled, raising his head as they cantered toward Westminster. 'And now more justice to serve,' he said quietly, as Westminster Palace came into view.

Crispin pulled his hood close and kept his head down. They moved into the courtyard and dismounted. Men took their horses to the stables, but there was much more chaos than Crispin had anticipated. Not only were there the returning carts from Sheen, but there were scores of woodworkers and masons working on the great hall. Crispin had heard that the master mason Henry Yevele, who had worked on Westminster Abbey, and the king's master carpenter, Hugh Herland, were erecting a new roof and windows. The whole was in a mess of dust, workmen, timbers and beams, and ropework throughout. Crispin followed behind Lancaster as they worked their way through the maze of what was left of the great hall.

Gone were the pillars that held up the roof. Now there were temporary struts holding aloft great carved beams with the faces of angels. The stairs were moved, the windows were different. When it was complete, it wouldn't be recognizable from the hall Crispin had known and had dined in.

It seemed that stewards were busily hushing the workmen and the call had gone out that the work was to stop for a time in deference to the death of the queen. Masons and carpenters were packing up their tools, moving tables piled with more tools and measuring devices. The aproned men gathered in groups, discussing it all, perhaps wondering when the work – and their pay – could recommence.

But besides the milling workmen, there was no raucous talk or laughter among the courtiers. Those standing about did so solemnly and talked in quiet, even reverent groups. Yes, this was much like when the old king died. Thankfully, Richard was nowhere to be seen.

'Where to first, Crispin?'

'Perhaps it is best you not use my name, my lord,' he said quietly. 'Call me . . . Jack.'

Lancaster smiled. 'Very well . . . *Jack*. Where shall we go first?'

'Let us call on the king's physicians.'

They made their way through the grave crowds and came to St Stephen's Chapel, the doors to which were guarded by knights. Crispin peeked over their shoulders through the open doors. The queen was lying on a bier, draped in finery and lit by candles at the four corners of the resting place, and a figure – the king – knelt before it, head crushed under his arms as he wept.

'How long has he been thus?' Crispin whispered.

Lancaster ushered him away. 'Ever since we returned. She's to be moved to Westminster Abbey. But he won't allow anyone to enter the chapel.'

Crispin moved hastily away from the door, though he needn't have worried; the king would never notice. 'One of his intimates must help lure him away. Or . . . you.'

'I am not one of the king's favored intimates these days.'

'I am sorry to hear it.' *And shocked*, he thought to himself. Surely Richard's uncle was one of the most trusted men in the realm.

'Let us go,' Gaunt said gruffly. They moved through the corridors to Lancaster's apartments. His wife, Constance of Castile, had died only a few months ago. Crispin expected that all would still be draped in black, but this was not so. Lady Katherine had been discreetly moved in and the windows had been thrown open, with garlands of flowers draping over their casements instead.

Both his marriages had been done with an eye toward dynasty. With his first wife Blanche he had attained his title of Lancaster and its lands, and from Constance, he gained a claim to the throne of Castile – though that claim and subsequent battles in Spain ended without a good result.

Yes, a fresh breeze had entered with the scent of blooms throughout. Crispin had never experienced the like in Lancaster's lodgings. It was Lady Katherine's doing, surely. Crispin wondered if the duke dared marry her. Could he hope to finally marry the woman he loved? He was the richest man in England. He could certainly afford to. Perhaps he had made his intentions known to the king, but would Richard give his permission?

Oh, to be a wealthy and important man again.

Crispin did not see her, but she was probably in his wife's old quarters. It wouldn't do for visitors to encounter her on first glance in the antechamber.

'I will call for the physicians to meet us here.'

'My lord, I shall – at some point – have to view the body of the queen.'

'I doubt Richard could be torn away.'

'This is monstrous.' Even Crispin had to sympathize with the king and his loss.

Lancaster unbuttoned his cloak and laid it aside. Crispin stilled. 'My lord, where are your servants?' He wondered if *he* shouldn't have helped the duke as he used to do.

'I sent word that they should . . . er . . . disperse, anticipating your arrival.'

'You were that certain I would come.'

He only smiled in answer. 'Why don't you pour us some wine, Crispin. I mean *Jack*.'

Crispin did as he was told and went to the sideboard. The fragrant golden wine was likely from Flanders. He brought the finely embellished goblet to the duke. Crispin expected him to send a servant for the physicians straight away, but he didn't. He sat on a fur-covered chair, stretched his long legs before him, and enjoyed his wine. He gestured vaguely to the chair beside him. Cautiously, Crispin seated himself, goblet in hand. Why wasn't the duke hurrying to the task he'd set Crispin upon?

'The years have been harsh to you, Crispin, but you have made the best of them. You have a loyal band of people surrounding you.'

And how did the duke know who surrounded Crispin? He had to acknowledge that Lancaster probably had spies.

He sipped his wine. 'I have done what you trained me to do. What was the alternative? To surrender? To lay down and die?'

'I never expected you to.'

'I garnered too many friendships to allow that to happen. And, of course, Jack Tucker. He reminded me of my own humanity. That boy – that *man* – was responsible for bringing me back to myself.'

'I shall be ever grateful to him for that.'

Crispin settled into the chair, leaning back, studying the wine shimmering in the silver goblet. 'Of late, it hasn't been a bad life. I even have some coin set aside. And Jack and his family will care for me in my dotage. If I *reach* old age, that is. It could have been far worse.'

'I am heartily glad to hear it.'

'And it's certainly been interesting. Far more interesting than merely copying out documents. Did you know I was briefly a clerk? But of course you did. No, I would say it's been . . . satisfying.'

Lancaster turned away. He reached a hand to his face but Crispin didn't see what exactly he was doing.

'I cannot lie,' said Lancaster, still turned away, speaking into his hand, 'I feared what would happen to you and was powerless to interfere. I . . . I hadn't been brave enough.'

What was Crispin to say to that? If Gaunt had reached out to Crispin, he would have been accused of treachery, even treason. He had already been accused by certain members of the Privy Council and others who whispered in the corridors of Westminster. He had a dynasty to see to. A son, his heir, and many others depending on him. In the end, Crispin couldn't begrudge him.

'I have already forgiven you, John. There is nothing more to say on the matter.'

Gaunt turned. His eyes were wet. 'Even as a child you were always the serious one. How I longed to put a smile on your face. I tried mightily for years.'

'I am what God has made me out to be.' He took another sip

of wine and set the goblet aside. It was good to sit with his old mentor, good to remember how it used to be. But those were long-ago days, and they were both different men now. 'And more often than not, you *did* manage to put a smile on my face. In your household I felt safe, and loved, and nurtured. What more could an orphan boy want?'

John nodded. He looked as if he would say more but stopped himself. He leaned back and stared at the tips of his boots for a time until he rose and stepped toward a door to an inner chamber. He rang a small bell there.

A servant appeared, never glancing toward Crispin. He bowed.

'I want you to collect the queen's physicians from every corner of the palace they might be. Bring them all here as quickly as possible.'

The servant bowed and left.

'It might be advisable,' said Crispin, 'to find any Lollard sympathizers who are not among the men you know well. I should like to study them.'

'Good advice.' He rang the bell again and a different servant appeared, an older man. 'You are to find any Lollard men you are unfamiliar with. Speak with Thomas Clanvowe, for he will know this information. Make certain to tell him you come direct from me. Seek out their names and report back directly. Take any servant with you whom you trust if you need them. Make haste, man.'

The servant bowed as if he were called upon to spy every day for the duke. It might be that he was.

Crispin sighed. 'If only I had such resources. But then, I would have to charge more for my services.'

John looked at him before he laughed. 'What would you call yourself then? The Lord of Trackers?'

Crispin smiled. 'I quite like the sound of that.'

They seemed more companionable now. More comfortable with one another. Crispin told him tales of some of his adventures, and John would shake his head in surprise, digging deeper to get at the juicy details. Then John would tell Crispin of his battles in Spain, and Crispin, sitting at the edge of his seat with a longing to have been with him, made noises of sympathy when it all seemed to go wrong for his mentor. John told him that once he had returned from Spain, the king had begun treating him differently, more distantly. Something had changed but he hadn't known what. But to break the morose fugue in the air, he told Crispin an amusing story that made him laugh out loud.

Crispin was enjoying himself. It had been many a day since he had been in the company of those in his class. Society, he realized, was a strange thing. He had been cast away from this for so long he had supposed he was used to the underclass of London, and yet he wondered why, over the years, he had felt more adrift than not. After all, by his count, he had lived almost as many years outside his social strata than in it. He knew this was where he belonged, but also knew that it was not to be. He liked his new friends – the solid Gilbert and Eleanor Langton, the studious lawyer Nigellus Cobmartin and his lover the lively John Rykener, and faithful Jack and his family. But it always seemed to him temporary, as if he were waiting for something else. Perhaps that 'something else' was Heaven. He could only hope.

His musing had made him miss the last thing John had said to him, and he avidly watched him laugh with silent amusement. It was good to see him laugh, good to see him with Lady Katherine as he had seemingly always longed to do.

A knock on the door made them both sit up and reminded them where they were and what they were supposed to be doing. Crispin rose, straightened out his tabard, and stood off to the side as any household knight would.

The servant had returned with three black-robed physicians, not a one of them under fifty years old. Long beards all, with gray hair hidden under merino caps.

They bowed to the duke but seemed perplexed as to why they had been called to present themselves to him.

The first man introduced himself as Robert Gaswyne, the second as James Trentham, and the third as Edwin Sackford. They were interchangeable in Crispin's eyes, at least on the outset.

'All of you cared for the queen,' said Gaunt as he studied them, as if he were looking over his troops.

They nodded humbly, two with hands to their hearts, the last with a sniffle of pity.

'This man,' and he gestured toward Crispin, 'Cr— Er, Sir Jack, will be asking you questions and I expect you to answer him with the truth, as if you were speaking to me.'

He stepped back and allowed Crispin to move forward. He bowed to the physicians. 'My good sirs,' he began. 'Is it your contention that this was a natural death?'

They glanced at one another in silent consultation. The first man nodded sagely, as did the second, but the last one put a hand to his cheek and buried his lips within mustache and beard.

'You, sir,' said Crispin. 'Master Sackford, is it? Do you believe otherwise?'

'I wish I could agree with my colleagues, Sir Jack. But alas. The queen, God rest her, was suffering from stomach pain and lethargy while here in Westminster. These symptoms grew only more acute when she arrived at Sheen. The carriage ride was no doubt most uncomfortable for a woman in that state. But we were not in the carriage with her.'

'Were her lady's maids with her?'

'Yes, Sir Jack. It was not our place to ride with her. But when we got to the palace—'

'Now, now, Master Sackford,' said the second gentleman, Trentham. 'She seemed merely tired. Tired at our fussing. She was in her *monthly* condition,' he said confidentially.

'I have been attending Her Majesty for years, my good Trentham,' said Sackford huffily, grabbing the front of his gown with both hands and rocking importantly on his heels. 'And she never appeared thus during her menses. I tell you she was ailing greatly.'

'So it was established,' said Gaswyne, stroking his beard. 'She was in her menses but something else was afoot. I warned that it was the plague.'

'The sweating sickness, surely,' said Trentham.

'Absolutely not,' said Sackford.

'Gentlemen,' said Crispin. This was getting them nowhere. Each one seemed to have his own diagnosis. 'Is it your opinion – as a supposition – that the cause could possibly be intervention by . . . other means? Poison, for instance?'

Gaswyne shook his head vigorously. But Trentham and Sackford put their heads together, discussing it back and forth in Latin.

Crispin waited, flicking a glance once at Gaunt.

Trentham shook his head sadly. 'Do you contend, sir, that this was an unnatural death?'

'We merely wondered,' Crispin said judiciously. 'There are enemies at court.'

'But . . . to kill the queen!' said Sackford in hushed tones.

'Is it within the realm of possibility?'

Sackford glared steadily at Crispin. 'It is true . . . that there are enemies at court.'

God's blood. Did the man recognize him? By the look he was giving Crispin, he didn't doubt it. He pulled his hood closer, uselessly.

'But not in this room, sir,' said Lancaster, stepping forward.

Sackford acknowledged the duke's defensive posture, flicked a glance at Crispin once more, and shrugged. 'There is the possibility, given her symptoms and sudden turn for the worse.'

'Out of the question!' Gaswyne insisted.

'Not so far out of the question, Robert,' said Trentham. 'But unlikely. How would it have been administered?'

'Her ladies. At table. In her garderobe. A pinprick from a passing courtier.'

Lancaster pulled himself up tall. 'You seem to know a great deal about this, Sackford.'

'Only as close confidant to Their Royal Majesties. For I must be made aware, mustn't I?'

Lancaster snorted. 'That sounds more like the Florentine court than England's.'

'We must talk to her lady's maids,' said Crispin.

'Very well. You,' said Lancaster to the physicians. 'You will not repeat what you were asked today . . . or by whom,' he said pointedly to Sackford. 'I would be very displeased if this got back to the king. And you *don't* want to displease me.'

The men received the message with stark faces. They reasoned that they were dismissed and turned to go in a huddle, keeping close like black geese.

Lancaster ran his hand through his still thick hair and frowned. 'Those bumbling arses. Do you suppose they know aught of what they are saying?'

'Medicine is an imprecise science, my lord. Three men, three opinions.'

'Then you must talk with the lady's maids.'

'And where can they be found?'

Lancaster searched for a servant in the room and found none.

'You've sent them all away, you know.'

'I know that,' he said testily.

'Perhaps . . . the queen's chamber? I can go—'

'*We* will go.'

Crispin smiled. Like the old days.

As they moved through the apartments toward Lady Katherine's lodgings, Crispin said quietly, 'Do you know of a bishop from Yorkshire – a Bishop Edmund Becke?'

Lancaster paused at the door. 'I have heard the name.'

'And do you know his cause?'

'He has many causes.'

'His main cause is to root out heresics, be they Jew or Christian . . . or Lollard.'

Lancaster angled his head and smiled. 'I know.'

'He is . . . after *me*.'

'Is he?'

'Yes. I am in possession of a book—'

'Crispin, Crispin. How many times must I tell you . . .'

'As many times as I must tell *you* that I am caught in these webs for good or ill. A book came into my hands. Whether heresy or not, I leave that to theologians . . . if it can get that far. He wants it destroyed. I am loath to do so.'

'These are the troubles that put you so untimely in my carriage?'

'They are. Three men are dead because of it. Because of me.'

'Because you sought knowledge. I know I taught you years ago not to be afraid of that search, no matter the cost.'

'The cost, this time, was not mine to spend.'

'You see it that way, but it is not so.'

Crispin's anger bubbled over. 'I *led* that man to them. They *did* die because of me.'

'Be that as it may, what is your course of action?'

It was that same tone Crispin knew well from some twenty years ago, that Socratic mien that so annoyed a younger Crispin. 'I haven't yet decided. I'm supposed to meet an "important personage", the reason the book was spared. Who that may turn out to be is anyone's guess.'

'And here I have stolen you to do this minor task.'

'Minor? Shall we seek out Lady Katherine?'

'Yes.' He knocked on the door and a servant answered. The man said nothing as he led them forth into an inner chamber where Lady Katherine received them.

'I've been waiting.'

'Crispin – I mean *Sir Jack* – wishes to speak with the queen's ladies. Are they in her apartments?'

'Or very near them. Shall we go and see . . . *Sir Jack*?'

TEN

C rispin acted as he had years before as their household knight, leading them through the corridors to the queen's chambers, not very far from Lancaster's. A guard stood at the arch and came to attention when he noticed the duke.

'We are looking for the queen's ladies,' asked Crispin. 'Are they still lodged here?'

'They have been given no orders contrary and so remain,' said the guard, trying to see into Crispin's shadowy hood.

Crispin gestured toward their female companion. 'Lady Katherine wishes to . . . consult with them.'

'They are in mourning.'

'As are we all.' Crispin waited. The guard could plainly see the duke and Lady Katherine and knew he couldn't stop them.

'The king does not wish for visitors,' said the guard half-heartedly.

'We are not "visitors",' said the duke in his most imperious manner.

The guard said nothing but turned, knocked, and then opened the door. 'Enter,' he said and then stepped aside.

Crispin entered first, looked around, and saw no one in the antechamber. When he approached the door to the queen's inner chamber he found it locked. He turned to Lady Katherine.

'Madam, will you . . .?'

Her gown was as rich as any duchess's, a deep blue of a soft material, tight on her arms and buttoned up to the elbow with silver buttons. The fur trimming it was black sable, and she wore the horned headdress and veil that the queen had caused to be fashionable. She looked every inch a queen herself. It sparked that stab of regret at how the wheel of life had turned, how Lancaster had not been king, how Crispin had not enjoyed a life with him. But it was more pinprick these days than dagger point.

'My ladies,' she said, her face close to the door. 'It is Lady Katherine Swynford. I have come to talk to you.'

There was a rustling within. A chair scraped. A whispered word. Then, 'We are in prayer,' said a heavily accented voice. The same accent as the queen's.

'It is very important. And it would be a service to our dear queen.'

The woman behind the door sobbed and spoke in that foreign tongue. But after a pause, the key turned in the lock, and she opened the door.

A plump woman, older than the queen by several years, with a tight starched headdress, peeked around the door. When she spied Lancaster, she threw her hand over her mouth. Lady Katherine reached out and grabbed her hand before she could disappear behind the door again. 'We wish to ask questions regarding the queen's last days. Dear Markéta, can you and your ladies speak of it?'

'But the king . . .' she muttered behind her hand.

'This is the king's uncle, as you know. And this,' she gestured toward Crispin, 'is the master of the queen's Goat.'

Puzzled at first at such a distinction, Crispin soon remembered that this is what the queen had called Jack when he was a prisoner of the palace and had stumbled upon Queen Anne in distress. She had called him 'Goat' because she had discovered him climbing over the garden wall. He had done her a great service, and in return she had saved his life.

By the look on Markéta's face, she well remembered the incident from some six years ago.

Lady Markéta scoured Crispin's face – as much as she could see under the shadowing hood – and stopped her sniffling. She pressed a cloth to her reddened eyes and nose. 'You are Goat's master?' She lifted her eyes to Lancaster, took in the august company, and remembered at last to curtsey. She opened wide the door. A little shrine had been set up to St Anne – the queen's patron saint – with candles and flowers. The other ladies – some seven of them – had been kneeling and rose, straightening out their gowns. They each clutched ornate rosaries.

Lady Markéta gestured toward Crispin. 'This is Goat's master. He wishes to speak with us.'

They leaned their heads together and whispered, snatching glimpses at Crispin. He heard the word 'Goat' several times.

Finally, they broke apart, and with reddened eyes with dark circles around them, they stared at him like frightened birds.

'My ladies,' he said with a bow. 'I wish to enquire about Her Majesty's illness. Was there . . . anything unusual about it in your reckoning?'

A young woman who looked very like the queen with her small chin, creamy skin, and pale blue eyes, closed her hands in prayer. She spoke softly in accented English. 'It came on her suddenly. So very suddenly.'

'My lady . . .'

'Alžběta,' she said.

'Lady Alžběta, was this unusual?'

'Yes. Had it been the sweating sickness as one of her physicians said, surely we should be ailing as well.'

'And *are* any of you ailing?'

They all shook their heads.

'Now, think carefully. Did any of you eat or drink the same as Her Majesty? Off the same plate, out of the same cup or flagon?'

Again, they exchanged glances. An English woman shook her head. 'We never did that, sir. My lady, my poor lady, she had her own plates and cups.'

'And the food. How does it come? A servant brings it from the kitchens, no? Does she have tasters?'

It suddenly became evident where Crispin was heading with his questions. Some of the ladies threw hands over their mouths. Others began to weep again.

'But that cannot be!' cried Alžběta. 'You are saying that our precious Lady Queen was . . . poisoned!'

'It is a possibility.'

'No,' said Markéta. 'No, it was an illness. She was a frail creature. And we all took such very good care of her.'

Crispin pulled the folded parchment from his pouch and opened it. 'Have any of you seen this before?'

The English lady stepped forward. 'Yes. It was I who found it. I sent it to Lady Katherine.'

'And just where exactly was it?'

'It was in her chamber at Sheen. It was on the coffer beside the bed.'

'Had she seen it?'

The lady shook her head. She was gowned in rich velvets. Her veil was black. 'When I saw it, I immediately took it and hid it.'

'What do you suppose it means, demoiselle?'

The other women didn't appear to know the contents of the parchment and looked on curiously.

'It seemed to be a Lollard threat. But of its nature I couldn't make it out.'

The English lady seemed to want to say more, but Markéta put a hand to her shoulder and she lowered her face and said nothing.

'If any of you should think of anything that might be pertinent,' said Crispin, 'please do not hesitate – whatever the hour – to come to me in the duke's apartments.' He bowed to them and led the way out of the chamber, where the ladies locked it again.

They returned to Lancaster's rooms and settled into the antechamber. There, Lady Katherine attended the duke as if she were already a wife. It was pointless to think otherwise of her, for this she was for all intents and purposes.

'It is late and I've kept you from your supper,' said Crispin, pushing the hood back off his face.

'But you must be hungry, too,' said Lady Katherine. 'Come. Sit with us and sup.'

'I *am* feeling somewhat . . . hollow,' he conceded.

Servants brought food, and Crispin broke bread with his long-time lord, something he hadn't done in over seventeen years.

'I was grateful to be in your household,' he said between bites. He didn't know why he felt compelled to share his innermost thoughts, but now seemed as good a time as any. There were likely fewer times for him to actually be in Lancaster's company as the years tolled on. 'I felt it was my home, more so than my own manor in Sheen.'

'And you were very like a son to me,' John admitted. He smiled and then pushed at Crispin, nearly knocking him from his chair. 'You were my practice son, at any rate.'

'I'm certain Henry appreciated it.'

'He did. But more than once, he tried to blame you for something *he* had done.'

'God's blood! The knave.'

'Oh, but Katherine saw it all, didn't you, sweeting?'

She kept her eyes downcast and nibbled on a piece of bread smeared with softened cheese. 'I refuse to say,' she said. When she raised her eyes, there was a distinct twinkle there.

Crispin sighed. 'I miss it. But it's not all tears. Jack and his are my family now. I do not regret keeping him in my life. And I have a son. A son I cannot acknowledge, but a son nonetheless.'

By Katherine's unsurprised expression, he surmised that John had told her. She leaned in toward the table. 'I think it a good thing that you are in contact with him. A man must know his sons.'

'It is vanity that makes me want to tell him . . .'

'Vanity. Perhaps. But you loved his mother.'

'I love her still.'

'A chaste love from afar, then. A man who grows up to know he was born of love, not of duty . . .' Her voice choked and she brought a hand to her mouth. John looked fondly on her but with a bit of chiding, too. Most men couldn't afford to marry for love. An arrangement was always necessary. Even Jack weighed his prospects, even though he was taken by Isabel at first sight.

It was only now that John could marry for love . . . in his fiftieth year.

Even Katherine could see the foolishness of her statement. She waved her hand before her face, but not before Crispin saw the tears rimming her eyes.

She put her hand on John's. 'A mother must never say that she favors one child over another, but here, in the confidence of this company, I can say that the Beaufort children are my pride and joy.'

John looked at her with such tenderness that Crispin had to turn away. Crispin was nearly forty. Maybe there was still time for him with another woman. If only he *could* open his heart. Maybe . . .

Katherine wiped at her eyes and laughed. 'Emotions have run high this day. And it has been a very long one. Forgive me, Crispin. But I've always thought of you as family, as my lost son.' She wiped at her eyes with trembling fingers. 'I think it time I retire. You must think on it, too, John.'

'I may have more to do this night.'

She rose and leaned forward, kissing his forehead.

John of Gaunt, the great warrior and lord of Lancaster, blushed. She said her goodnights and disappeared beyond a door.

Crispin and John looked at one another before the duke stretched. 'I almost forgot we fled for our lives today. The court is still in disarray.'

Crispin sobered. 'I still need to see the queen's body.'

'God's teeth, Crispin. Is there no sacrilege you will not perform?'

'You know I must.'

'I doubt the king has left her.'

'Perhaps he can be lured away. Perhaps his confessor . . .'

'If I can get that damned Dominican Alexander Bache to do my bidding.'

'*Can* you?'

John sighed. It *had* been a long day. So much had happened to both of them. It would be good to put it to bed. Crispin was weary as well, but he couldn't afford to lay his head down just yet.

'I will do my damnedest. I'll return anon.' He rose – joints audibly cracking – and left the apartments.

Crispin had little to do but tidy up. After a time, a young page entered and nearly pushed Crispin out of the way to clean up after the supper. Crispin stepped back and allowed him. After all, this was the boy's household. It wasn't Crispin's any more.

He walked to the window as the page piled high the dishes on a tray and, rattling all the while, left the room. Crispin looked out through the diamond-panes. Night had fallen, and thistle-sharp stars twinkled above the rooftops of Westminster. He hoped, perhaps even prayed, that the queen's death was not by misadventure. God knows what Richard would do if it were so. But more than that, over the years Crispin had seen firsthand what murder did to the families. These weren't faceless strangers and a mere puzzle to solve. Those who were nearest to the victims suffered greatly, especially when the murderer was a family member, as was so in Philippa's case. There was nothing akin to that sorrow. He would not wish it on anyone. Even Richard.

It might have been an hour. It might have been longer. Crispin spent his time between the window and pacing across the floor. At last, the door opened and revealed Lancaster.

'Richard's confessor was able to lure him away to his chamber. We have very little time before he returns. Make haste.'

Crispin threw his hood up over his head again and followed his mentor out into the corridor once more.

Quiet had descended on the palace. Not the earlier quiet of people murmuring as they mourned and wondered about the future. But the quietude of courtiers who had gone to their beds, as Crispin longed to do. And as John, no doubt, desired to do as well. He noted their shadows cast by lamps in the corridor niches; John's taller to Crispin's slightly shorter. Was it a sin to enjoy this as much as he did? He and Lancaster . . . he and *John* were together again, doing the important work they used to do. But he dared not prolong it. He had a course to follow and a job to accomplish.

They made their way through archway after archway and finally to the chapel. Knights guarded the portal but, on recognizing the duke, they let them pass. When Crispin lived in the duke's household, he never realized how much the duke's presence or name literally opened doors that otherwise would have remained shut. How well he learned *that* over the years.

The chapel was dark except for the candle sconces at each corner of her bier. Shadows of the canons of St Stephen's College paced up in the watching loft above the rood screen. The painted walls and statues were now muted by shadows and gloom. It seemed no longer a place of celebration, but of death and fear.

He looked upon the queen laid out in the finest samite, with a long white silken veil covering her face and head and draped all along her body, ending over her slippered feet. She looked tranquil, as if in sleep, as she should have been, not taken so young while the blush of youth still tinted her cheeks. Now it did not. She was as pale as alabaster with all life gone from her. Entombed as she surely soon would be, she would diminish in size even more, shrinking away from light and health and all that was life itself.

He felt John at his shoulder and, without speaking, he gently lifted the veil. Her face was still peaceful, though wore that waxy, relaxed look of the dead, where drooping muscles no longer kept the face supple. If she had died of plague, there was no sign of it. Could she have died of the sweating sickness? He had no way of knowing. But had she ingested poison? There were signs that could tell him.

He leaned over and smelled her mouth. Of course, she had been prepared for burial and so any signs of foam or poison on the mouth might have been washed away. Otherwise, her face showed no sign of poison from enlarged and darkened veins. He reached and gently pushed open an eyelid. He knew that sometimes poisons colored the whites or caused the veins to darken or freckle the eye. But her eye showed no signs of any of that. Instead, they were pale and milky, and saw no more.

He glanced once more at the doorway before he took her hand. The joints were stiffening. She had barely been dead some six or so hours and the stiffening rigor had begun. As best he could in the dark, he examined her fingers for signs of poisoning. Some poisons could darken the fingers . . . but there was no sign of it here.

Gently laying her hand back on her chest, he set the veil back in place. There was nothing here that he could see. Her ladies would have known if there were any other signs of assault, a knife wound or a bruise on the head. They had been the ones to prepare her, no doubt.

Crispin turned to John and shook his head. Lancaster nodded and turned to the door. Until he was stopped by a commotion there.

'No! I will go back to my wife! She is alone. I must not leave her alone in the dark.'

Crispin's breath caught. Richard! Gaunt heard it too, and yanked Crispin behind him, just as King Richard entered the chapel.

ELEVEN

Grateful for the darkness and his sheltering hood, Crispin still hadn't got his breath back. He stood behind Lancaster, head down, trying to slow his breathing that seemed much too loud.

Richard jerked to a halt. Crispin saw only his long-toed shoes. For some reason, his eye fixed on the intricate embroidery there.

'Uncle,' he gasped. 'You . . . your presence startled us.'

John bowed low and Crispin followed suit, keeping his head down, keeping his body in the shadows. 'Forgive me, Your Majesty. I . . . I only wanted to offer my prayers for our Lady Queen.'

Richard tried to hold it back, but a gut-wrenching sob escaped him. He threw his arm over his eyes. 'She's gone! She's gone.'

John hesitated. For anyone else, he might have opened his arms for an embrace. But Richard – who thought himself sacred as one who was anointed by God to his throne – did not give himself to such human interaction.

Richard dragged himself unaided to the bier and knelt. He put his forehead to the edge of it and wept.

John watched him for a moment – helpless – before he bowed again and backed away toward the chapel's door.

'Your man,' said the king, raising his head. His face was wet and puffy from crying. 'Leave him here to keep watch of us. We fear . . . we fear to be alone.'

John stopped. '*I* will stay with you, nephew,' he said softly.

'No. You must get your rest. Leave your man only.'

John's stark expression must have matched Crispin's own. 'But, er . . . I would be glad of it. To stay with you, sire. We are blood, Richard.'

'Leave your man. Do as I say . . . Lancaster.'

Richard's words brooked no dispute. There was nothing they could do. John cautioned with his eyes and Crispin acknowledged it with a nod.

'You must get your rest, Your Majesty,' said Lancaster.

'In time, Uncle. In time.'

There was nothing more John could do. He seemed as if he was trying to stall, until Richard turned to him again with a hooded expression that left no doubt. He bowed again, and left Crispin alone. With the king.

Slowly, he turned to Richard.

'Stay and watch with us, man. Keep watch of your queen.'

Crispin nodded and stepped back into the shadows, his left hand resting on his sword hilt.

For a long time, he watched Richard weep, cursing himself for getting into this situation.

It might have been an hour that Richard kept his vigil. Crispin's back ached from standing in one place unmoving for so long. There had been a time when such things were easy. He'd stood guard many a time outside Lancaster's pavilion when ready for a battle. But that had been long ago.

At last, after another half an hour had passed, Richard took a shuddering sigh and crossed himself. He lifted an arm. 'Help us up.'

Crispin eased a breath over his lips and stepped forward, taking the king's arm and bracing him as he rose. Richard was older since the last time he'd seen him. He was twenty-six now. He'd been king for nearly seventeen years. His face seemed sallow, but that could have been from his day of weeping. A soft trimmed beard and mustache of a light brown color were the only prominent features on his face. His whole manner was always effete, but Crispin knew he often marched ahead of his troops to distant places, though he did not fight himself. He thought of a younger Richard, the vindictive man, the spoiled prince. Had he changed? Of course, it hadn't been that many years ago that Henry Derby had accompanied other great lords of the realm with an army to demand that Richard put aside his favorites and rule as he should. Was Richard behaving himself now? Was he ruling as a king?

Richard leaned over and massaged his knees and thighs. 'We are weak in her presence. We have always been weak with her.'

Crispin said nothing as Richard contemplated her body before raising his eyes to his chapel. 'It is a fine place. But she must rest in Westminster. She deserves more than this humble chapel.

She was a queen and must rest with the other kings and queens of England.'

Saying nothing, Crispin stood as still as possible.

Richard turned sharply toward him. His eyes were red and puffy. Crispin lowered his head. 'You are a good and faithful knight, sir. Tell us your name.'

God's blood, he raged in his head. Should he lie? He had to lie, but could he disguise his voice? 'Jack,' he said, in as gruff a voice as he could muster.

'Jack?' Richard scoffed. 'What sort of name is that for a knight? Our uncle certainly chooses the most unusual courtiers to surround himself with.' Crispin hoped that would be the end to the conversation and Richard's talkativeness would soon pass, but it was not to be. 'How long have you been our uncle's man?'

Clearing his throat, Crispin attempted a deeper timbre. 'Thirty-four years, Your Majesty.'

'Thirty-four years. That's longer than we've been alive. Thirty-four years of faithful service. And yet, we don't recall a knight such as you at court.'

Crispin didn't reply, but Richard would not let it go.

'Eh? If not at court, where have you been?'

What could he say? The more he spoke, the more likely the king might recognize his voice. There was nothing for it. Better to be on the offense. He dropped down to a knee and bowed his head.

'Well, what's this?' said the king.

'Forgive me, sire.' He used his own voice this time.

'Forgive you? Forgive you for . . .'

Crispin waited. It was only a matter of time. He'd either live through this or he would not. Time seemed to pause as Richard worked it out.

'*Guest!*' he spat.

'Forgive me, Your Majesty.'

Richard trembled. His breath came hard and swift. Lunging forward, he grabbed the hilt of Crispin's sword and yanked it from its sheath. When Crispin looked up, Richard had taken it in both hands and swung his arms back, winding up for the blow.

It was as if life itself had begun to slow. A moth hovered near one of the candles, bobbing close to utter destruction before weaving away, and Crispin seemed to see each flap of its delicate wings, one after the other; seemed to hear them as a soft, slow patter. The many carved saints around them appeared to pause, to glance in their direction, pondering what the mourning King of England was about to do. Crispin could hear his own breath ease in and out of his nose in great gusts, and his heartbeat – perhaps the last strokes of it – thumped in a quickening staccato.

But the longer Richard kept the sword over his shoulder, the more his face – so red and enraged at first – slackened. All at once he let the sword drop from his fingers with a loud clang to the Purbeck marble floor.

The guards at the door jerked their heads to peer inside. But all they saw was their king standing before a kneeling man. They exchanged glances with one another and, not knowing what else to do, slowly turned away.

Richard's anger seemed to have gone. But he glared at Crispin uncomprehendingly. 'What are you doing here, Guest? Why in Christ's name are *you* here?'

'Forgive me, Majesty. But I . . .' He glanced at the queen, and though it wasn't the whole truth, it was certainly part of it. 'But I . . . wanted to come. I had to pay my respects to our queen.' Remarkably, tears welled in his eyes. It was the truth. He had been grateful for her intervention, for she had spared Crispin once, too. 'I never meant for Your Majesty to see me. I grieve that my presence has harmed you now.'

Richard sagged. He watched Crispin's tears for a moment. 'You loved her too,' he said softly.

Crispin wiped his face and nodded.

Richard sighed and rubbed his forehead. 'What am I to do with you, Guest? You show up at the most inopportune times.'

'I am sorry, Your Majesty.'

'Of course you are sorry.' He walked unsteadily away, veering toward the bier, then away from it. His hand covered his mouth, stroking the mustache, then the trimmed beard. 'The entire realm is sorry,' he said into his hand. 'They all loved her.'

'Yes, they did. They still do.'

'Oh, Guest, Guest.' Richard's voice fell soft and slow amid the echoes of the chapel, gently bouncing off the cold painted stone. 'We were so young then. So . . . inexperienced. We never expected Father to die like that . . . We weren't expecting to be king so soon.' His shoulders lifted with his sigh. 'We needed help of trusted men, trusted knights. Our uncle was there, of course. We knew that he was versed in what a king should do, should say, how he should act. There were tutors . . . so many tutors.' He gazed at Crispin with glossy eyes. 'We would have been overjoyed to have *you* serve at our side,' he said. There was an unaccustomed tenderness to his tone, something Crispin wasn't used to hearing, especially when directed toward him. 'To be a knight of the court,' the king went on. He even smiled. 'Do you remember when Henry and I were young and we enjoyed many an entertaining hour in your company?' He cocked his head, shaking it slowly and frowning at Crispin. 'You had no idea how much I . . . *loved* you, did you?'

Crispin's jaw slackened in shock. If Richard were to don motley and dance for the court, he couldn't have been more surprised.

Richard chuckled bitterly. 'You never knew that, I'll wager. That I loved you and looked up to you. You who were merry and full of mischief and so very clever. I could never be that clever. Or so very full of mischief. No, I had to behave. I was to be the heir . . . and then suddenly the king. But oh! Such a horseman you were! How I loved riding with you. I learned much about my own mount; more from you than from my many governors.' The king's smile faded as the memories, no doubt, dimmed. He stiffened and drew himself up. 'I was hurt by your treason.'

Crispin lowered his head again. Shame suddenly washed over him. When Richard took the throne, he was the same age as his son was now. And Christopher had been just as hurt by Crispin's seeming betrayal by ignoring him for the last two years.

'It is a poor excuse to say I was young and didn't know the extent of my . . . my betrayal,' said Crispin. 'But the truth of it is I wasn't that young. Not young enough. I . . . I didn't know . . . didn't realize the full extent of the hurt I caused. I am sorriest for betraying your trust, sire.'

The king leaned over, resting his hands on his knees, to look Crispin full in the face. 'Are you truly sorry? Are you? Today is a day of penance. Would you swear it in the presence of our gentle queen?'

'I do so swear it, Your Grace.'

He studied Crispin, brown eyes roving over his features beneath its hood. 'Why must you be so contrary?' He sniffed, wiping the royal hand under his nose. 'You swore an oath to me and then you broke it.' He shook his head. 'A knight should never do that.'

Crispin drew a trembling breath. 'I know, Your Grace.'

'Look at you. You are more knightly now than you ever were at court. It drapes about you like a mantle. Not many men can do that, Crispin. I wish . . .' He raised his gaze to the chapel's vaulted ceiling again and wiped at his eyes. When he looked down at Crispin again, they were dry. 'My wife the queen urged me to forgive you.' He shook his head. 'But I can't. You must understand. I can't.'

'I know, sire. You have no reason to forgive.'

He straightened. 'Have I not? Do you still plot treason, man?'

'No, sire. I am loyal to the crown.'

'To us?' He beat his chest. 'To Richard?'

He could almost hear the little boy in that plea. 'Yes. To King Richard.'

A tear ran slowly down the king's cheek. It wasn't for Crispin, he was sure of it.

'To the prince I once was? To that boy?'

Crispin lowered his face again.

'I wish I could believe you, Crispin.'

Crispin stared at those embroidered slippers again. 'So do I.'

Richard almost laughed. 'You are still and always will be an impudent fellow.'

'So I have been told.'

'Ha! By your lord of Lancaster, no doubt.'

'And many others, sire.'

'He smuggled you into our court.'

Crispin hesitated.

Richard waved him off. 'You need not answer. Your fabric betrays you.'

He looked down at the tabard with Lancaster's arms.

'Under our nose. At our most vulnerable . . .' Richard wrung his hands. 'So many times you could have killed us. Even in this past hour, you could have killed your king whom you betrayed with treason when we were but a child. Why did you not?'

'It was never my intention . . .'

'You are under the eyes of God here, Guest.' He stretched his arm to encompass the chapel. His hand gestured finally to the crucifix above the rood. 'Best not to lie.'

'I am not lying, Your Grace. It was never my intention to do your person harm.'

'Only depose us.'

Crispin said nothing. They both knew the truth of it. Still on his guard, Crispin's shoulder muscles tensed.

Richard seemed to relax. He even rested his hand on Crispin's shoulder, still kneeling as he was. 'How we wish you could have been loyal to us,' he whispered. 'We would have laid honors upon you. Made you a favorite. I'm certain of it. You are so loyal to our uncle. Why not to Richard?'

Did he want an answer? Crispin pondered what he could say.

'But that time has passed,' said the king regretfully. His hand fell away and he wandered toward the south wall. With his back to Crispin, he said, 'You may return to our uncle. Try not to let us see you again.'

'Sire.' Relief flooded his whole body. Crispin rose unsteadily and bowed.

'You're getting old, Crispin.'

He paused. 'Yes, sire.'

'You can thank your mentor for that.'

'Yes, sire. And you . . . for your mercy.'

'Yes, mercy.' He seemed to contemplate the far wall, when suddenly he spun and faced Crispin anew. 'Do you think I *wanted* to execute you?'

It had never occurred to him before. But now he saw the truth of it and felt a renewed warm wash of shame in his heart again.

'Don't forget your sword, Guest. Since my cousin Henry saw fit to give it to you, you might as well keep it.'

'Your Majesty.' He bowed and backed toward the archway.

'Pray for our queen, Guest.'

'Every day, Your Grace.'

'Good. That is good. Good man.'

The king seemed to have expended his conversation, so Crispin knelt to retrieve his sword and sheathe it. He edged further toward the entry, pivoted, and hurried away.

'God's blood,' he whispered, finally away from the guards. He crossed himself and sent his grateful thanks heavenward.

He'd barely gone a few steps when someone hissed at him in the shadows.

'Psst! Goat's master!'

When he looked harder, it was one of the queen's English ladies. 'There is something I wish to say to you,' she whispered.

TWELVE

'**M**y name is Lady Agnes. I have been the queen's attendant since she came to this country. I know everything about her.'

Crispin studied the sweet, oval face of the woman before him. She was swathed in a cloak and hood and held that hood close to her face. 'The note you showed us,' she went on. 'It made no sense if it was a threat against our dear Queen Anne. Because, you see, she asked for and was given—' She stopped and looked both ways up and down the corridor. 'She was given,' she whispered, 'a Bible . . . in English. She learned to read it.'

'A Lollard Bible?' said Crispin.

'Yes. She was a friend to them. She often calmed the king when he began raging against it. He had not in the early days. He knew many of his lords sympathized with Lollard teachings. Now he is not as gracious.'

'Then the queen knew Lollards and received a Bible from them?'

'Yes. It would have been a great crime indeed if a Lollard had plotted against her, knowing well how she stemmed the king's wrath on them.'

He nodded. 'I see what you mean. Thank you for this information. Did she have any enemies in other quarters?'

'No. I can think of no one who harbored ill will toward her. As you know, she was kind and gentle.'

'Yes. I have never heard an unkind word about her.'

'I knew I had to tell you. I believe the queen died of illness, just as the physicians said. There is no cruel cause here, good master.'

'I am beginning to see that, Lady Agnes.'

She clutched at her hood and glanced up the corridor again. 'And Master Goat. Does he fare well?'

Thinking of Jack made him smile, and he needed to smile just then. 'He does indeed, fair lady. With a wife and children. He has always been my faithful man.'

She seemed to brighten. 'Ah. That does my heart good. I shall tell the others. We worried so about him.'

'You need never worry over him. God shines his blessings upon that man.' He thanked her again and allowed her to make her way down the corridor without him. He waited a moment more before he set out himself to return to Lancaster's apartments. When he turned the corner, the man himself was pacing. He whipped around at Crispin's step.

'God be praised,' he gasped and rushed toward him. He took Crispin by his shoulders and drew him into an embrace.

Surprised, Crispin allowed it, face thrust against John's shoulder. John pushed him back to look him over. 'You are alive!'

'There was some question about it at the time,' he answered.

'Come inside.' He ushered Crispin beyond his door and through to the antechamber. 'What happened?'

Crispin gestured toward the wine on the sideboard and John granted him leave. He poured two generous goblets. 'Mostly, I stood guard.' He handed John one while he gulped at his own. When the wine settled in him he released a sigh. 'But then he spoke to me and I had to answer. And then I felt it was useless to hide who I was.'

John's eyes were wide. 'He . . . knew?'

'Yes. And though I thought he would kill me, he soon abandoned that idea. He told me things . . .' Even now the king's voice played in his head. The plaintive sound of it, as if he were ten years old again. He drank the wine. 'I feel the worse for my part in his betrayal.'

'You felt your cause was just.'

'Yes. But I never thought beyond it. I never imagined that it might mean Richard's death. And that should have been foremost in my mind.' He knocked back the rest of the wine, hesitated, then returned to the sideboard to refill it. 'I was at the top of my strength then, John. Lord of Sheen, a burnished knight, a strategist on the battlefield.' He shook his head and drank. 'How young and foolish I *truly* was.'

'How truly *all* of us were.'

'He said he had loved me. And I never knew that. In my pride, in my arrogance . . . I never knew.'

John remained quiet as Crispin slowly sloughed off the prickly emotions as the wine settled within him. 'I, er, also encountered one of the queen's ladies when I left the chapel. I am becoming more convinced that this death was . . . a natural one.'

'Not murder?' John fell hard into his chair. 'Thank God for that. Do you still need to speak to our Lollard courtiers?'

'I would still speak with them. On other matters. But this matter can be put to rest.'

'Thank you, Crispin, for your work. If the king only knew, he would be grateful.'

'Let us all make certain that he *never* knows.'

They both lifted their goblets to that.

Crispin slept heavily in one of the niches set aside for pages. He thought he would find it hard to sleep in such cramped quarters, but as soon as his head hit the pillow, he was out until morning.

He stretched, feeling the cricks in his back. As Richard had told him, he was old and felt it. He asked one of Lancaster's grooms for shaving things but, knowing who he was, the groom offered to do it for him.

With a face clean and shaved, he greeted his hosts once more. Though there were servants around them, John chose to serve Lady Katherine himself, bringing her tidbits to eat and poured her warmed wine.

It was almost as if Crispin had never left them all those years ago. Almost.

But then it was back to the business at hand. Thomas Clanvowe, a Lollard but one of the king's men, sent a message to Lancaster, telling him he would meet with him. And so Crispin and Lancaster waited. It was mid-morning when Clanvowe arrived.

He was brusque, with a dark head of hair and a trimmed beard and mustache. He was richly attired as Lancaster was. Crispin knew that he had joined the king's household only a few years ago and had married one of the queen's ladies. He was from Herefordshire with important connections there.

He greeted Lancaster, and then turned a stern eye toward Crispin.

'I know who you are, Crispin Guest,' he said without preamble. 'I know the duke and so know of you. You are an enemy of the king.'

Crispin girded himself.

Clanvowe's expression softened. 'But your family is Welsh, as are mine, and so, as a fellow countryman, I extend my hand.' He did so and, without hesitation, Crispin took it. 'I understand, Your Grace, that you have a question for me and my compatriots,' he said to Lancaster.

The duke reached into his pouch and unfolded the parchment, handing it to Clanvowe.

Clanvowe read it and lowered the parchment. 'What is this?'

'This was left on the queen's bedside at Sheen,' said the duke.

'And it follows that Lollards are responsible for her death?'

Crispin gently took it back from him. 'I hope you could tell us otherwise, my lord.'

'That is a foolish supposition. The queen was a friend to the Lollards of court. No one would dare touch her.'

'Yes,' said Crispin, handing the note to John. 'I have already discovered that.'

'You're that Tracker in London they speak of, aren't you, Guest? You ferret out criminals.'

'I am and I do.'

'Good. Glad to see your training is not going to waste. But . . . I have heard another rumor among my friends both in and out of court. These rumors travel quickly. You seem to be in possession of a . . . a book.'

John narrowed his eyes. 'What have you to say on this matter . . . that involves several deaths?'

Clanvowe's smile was grim. 'Only that such books can be dangerous. That some would gladly free it from Master Guest's hands for their own purposes. And . . . that he should be very careful.'

'Do you know a Bishop Becke?' Crispin asked, keeping a tight lid on his ire.

'I've heard of him. He's no friend to the Lollards.'

'He's no friend of mine either. And he, too, knows of the book.'

'Then beware. When he strikes, you will not know it until you fall to the ground a corpse.'

'You are indelicate, sir,' said John. 'The queen lies in the chapel.'

Clanvowe bowed. 'I apologize. I did not mean to injure your sensibilities.'

Lancaster put a hand to his hip. 'The *queen*, sir. Whatever you think of me, the king is still my nephew. It would be a shame should the information reach him that one of his rising courtiers had been tactless on the matter.'

Clanvowe changed tactics and set his features more congenially. 'Forgive me, John. I'm afraid emotions are running somewhat high.'

'Indeed, they are. Have a care. I might not always have defended Lollards, but you know I am one.'

'I know. I merely wished to warn your . . . your pupil, here, that it is known what is in his possession.'

'Such a well-known book,' said Crispin, 'and in an incomprehensible tongue, too. Curious.'

'It was known before *you* got a hold of it, Guest. If I were you—'

'Alas, you are not.'

He seemed to be struck mute for a moment . . . before he laughed and nudged Lancaster. 'Your protégé.'

Lancaster said nothing.

'I've seen a great deal of Lollards lately,' said Crispin. 'On the streets of London, preaching. Am I to be careful of Lollards, too?'

'For this book, yes.'

'Why in hell would a Lollard want to be seen with *this* book?' said John. 'Don't they fear enough trouble when caught with an English Bible?'

'Well, I am not so entrenched in Lollardy that I am in the midst of the cabal – if it could be called such. But I have heard rumors that this book is desired among those who lead.'

Crispin shook his head. 'I can't imagine why. And they've killed the only man likely to be able to translate it in London.'

'They?'

'Becke's men.'

'Becke doesn't care to translate it. He only cares that it is destroyed.'

'What have you got yourself into, Crispin?' said Lancaster with a frown.

'Too much . . . as usual, my lord.'

There was little left to discuss. Clanvowe bid his farewells and Crispin knew his time to depart had come. He turned to Lancaster regretfully. 'I should be going too. I do not think you need fear that the queen died by misadventure.'

'That is good, Crispin. You've done well.'

Crispin looked down at his tabard. 'If I may keep this, Your Grace . . .'

'I believe I gave you one before.'

'I was careless with it.'

'Hmpf,' grunted the duke.

'It will help me leave the palace, at any rate.'

'You are the most charmed man alive, Crispin.'

'Am I?'

'You should have been dead a thousand times over by now.'

He chuckled. 'I have a very weary guardian angel, my lord, that is the truth of it.'

'If you must leave then have a care. You are in our thoughts and in our prayers. And tell that man of mine that he can stop guarding your Jack.'

Crispin hadn't known what Lancaster had said to the man from whom he had got the tabard, but now he was more grateful than ever for the duke's intervention. 'That was kind of you. Thank you.'

'I know how you dote on that boy. Reminds me of . . . well. Of the two of us.'

Crispin could only nod. He was afraid his voice would betray him.

Lady Katherine was either listening at the door or had a sense about these things. She appeared in the doorway just as Crispin was taking his leave.

'You are leaving us?' she said.

He bowed. 'Yes, my lady. Always with regret. But I have other business to do.'

'Your conclusion is resolved, then. The queen died of a sickness?'

'As near as I can conclude. Be at ease on it.'

She sighed and crossed herself. 'That is good news – among all the bad.'

'Yes. Well, it was good to see you both. I thank you for your hospitality.'

'God be with you, Crispin.' She took his arm, drew him in, and kissed his forehead like any mother would. His throat tightened for a moment, for it had been many a year since his own mother had given him her blessing . . . but he sobered quickly when he felt a pouch pressed into his hand, a pouch of coins. He was about to object when she gave him a tender look that stilled his tongue. Well, if she wanted to be his mother, he supposed he'd have to indulge her.

He bowed again, clutched the pouch tight in his hand, and left them.

He made his way alone through the still mourning court, where courtiers wore solemn faces and conferred with the canons of St Stephen's in the corridors. The scaffolding and ropes were still present in the great hall but no workmen were in sight. With impunity by virtue of his tabard, he made his way out the doors of the palace and into its courtyard.

And when he passed through the gates he came to halt when he noticed a beggar, the one who had accosted him before, sitting outside the gate, seemingly waiting for him.

THIRTEEN

Crispin grabbed him by his disgusting coat and dragged him to his feet, shoving him against the wall. 'Why do I see you at every turn?'

'Do you think I am following you, Master Guest? I just have to prick me ears for the voices of the dead to find you. They surround you.'

Crispin released him and frowned. The dead. Yes, he was surrounded by the dead. The deaths of his parents, those that died in the conspiracy that had failed to execute him, the dead of London who fell into his path. He did not like the images that grew in his head of the dead surrounding him. 'You are a mad old man. I say again, stop following me!'

But even as Crispin stalked away toward London, he heard the beggar's steps behind him. He whirled. 'Do you have a death wish?'

'Ah, a death wish. Now there is some strange language. No, no, I have no wish for death, not as yet. But I tell you, from what I hear – that constant chatter – that it isn't so bad to die. No, not at all. It is just that those that die from murder are the saddest, sorriest voices you'll ever hear.'

'I praise God that I do not.'

'Do you? Well now. It is a gift and a curse. For I hear them at night when I rest me head. And there's been many a time I've pleaded with them to stop.' His eyes seemed suddenly demented for a moment. He smacked his skull a few times. 'But blind me, they don't. They don't stop neither day nor night. They plead. They call. Do you *not* hear them?' He appeared annoyed that Crispin did not share in his madness.

'No. Away with you.'

'You pulled your sword on me once. Would you hear *my* voice in your head?'

Crispin thought of drawing his sword . . . and then left it alone. He didn't like the idea that he *might* start hearing these voices.

'What do you want of me?' Crispin dug into his pouch and took out some of the coins that Lady Katherine had given him. 'I'll pay you to walk away.'

The man never even looked at the coins, some of them gold. 'I don't want your money. I can't use it. I want . . . I want . . .'

A man on a horse rode hard, kicking up mud between them. Pedestrians jumped out of his way. Crispin stepped back, but once the rider was gone, so was the beggar. Crispin searched both ways on the wide avenue, but the man was nowhere to be seen.

'Perhaps I *am* losing my mind,' he muttered, stuffing the coins away, and heading toward London.

When he arrived at the Shambles he noticed Lancaster's man, dead asleep and standing up, leaning against a wall opposite Crispin's lodgings. Crispin strode up to him, tapped him on the shoulder, and smiled. The man sputtered awake and made a move to draw his sword.

With an appeasing hand, Crispin shook his head. 'You have done your duty, and I thank you. His Grace the duke told me to tell you that you may return to Westminster.'

The man straightened his clothes and smoothed out his hair. 'Where's my horse?'

'Oh. I didn't think to bring it with me.'

The man sighed wearily. 'Very well, then.' He eyed the tabard that Crispin had taken from him and wasn't about to give up. 'God keep you, Master Guest.'

'And you, sir.'

He watched the man walk away for only a moment before he proceeded to the poulterer's shop. He unlocked the door and walked in.

'Who's there!' came the cry from above. Jack was at the landing with dagger in hand. 'Oh! It's you, sir.' He scrambled down the steps and sheathed his dagger. 'Well? What happened?'

'The queen died by sickness.'

Jack sagged against the table. 'That is a relief. There would have been holy hell in the streets had any other verdict been reached.'

'Yes, I am glad of it, too. Oh, and Jack. The queen's ladies wished to give my salutations and good prayers to my "Goat".'

Jack did not smile as he expected him to. Instead, a sadly

tender expression stole over his features. 'Aw, now. It makes me sad, thinking of the poor queen, bless her soul. But them sweet sentiments and soft memories I take very kindly. Very kindly indeed.'

Crispin nodded and took out Lady Katherine's pouch and handed it to Jack. 'Courtesy of Lady Katherine Swynford. Put it in our retirement hoard.'

'Hoard, is it?' Jack grumbled. But when he looked inside the pouch he whistled. 'Blind me. Maybe a hoard after all.' He went to the loose board behind the stair and secreted it among the other coins and baubles he and Crispin had managed to save.

'Any trouble while I was away?'

'There was a man outside watching the place. I kept my eye on him.'

Crispin laughed. 'And he kept his eye on you. He was Lancaster's man.'

'Oh, that's a fine thing! Someone could have told me.'

'I'm sorry.'

'I'm just glad to have you back in one piece, sir. If you had run into the king, I feared I'd never see you again.'

'As it happens . . .' he said, hanging his hood and cloak on a peg. He slipped off the tabard and carefully laid it in a coffer. '. . . I did. We have come to an . . . understanding.'

'Eh? And Richard didn't kill you where you stood?'

'He almost did. Ah, Jack.' He sat, fingers drumming at the table. 'It is all far more complicated than I ever imagined. I felt sorry for him. He loved her dearly.'

It was all on Jack's face. He would not ask for details and Crispin would not give them. It *was* far more complicated than ever *he* imagined. Had Richard's fondness for him truly saved his life? Perhaps appeasing his uncle only served as a convenient excuse. And now that feeling of guilt would not leave him. He pondered the mystery that was Richard Plantagenet. He thought him a spoiled child, tending to tantrums, and when he got older and was king, his opinion on the matter hadn't changed all that much. To suddenly discover that Richard *loved* him, had, in fact, *wanted* to save him, threw all his memories of him to the winds.

Jack thankfully awoke him from his guilty musings. 'Is it safe to bring Isabel and the children back?'

'I don't think so. As long as we are in possession of that book. Apparently, there are Lollards abroad who also want it.'

'Blind me. Why would any of them want that book?'

'It is a puzzle to me as well, Jack. But there are men who would wish to contemplate it, as I have done.'

'I don't see that it does anyone any good. It's already killed three men.'

'We are in agreement, to be sure. And, I have come to the conclusion that I must tell the sheriffs . . . well. What can I tell them? That a bishop is on my heels, that his men slaughtered those innocents on Church business? What would they say to that? What could they do about it? Sue to the Church? It is a complete muddle.'

'Sheriff Whittington was good to you, sir. You must tell *him* something, at least.'

'You're right, of course. The truth is often the best. Let him sort it out.'

Jack kicked at an ashy stick loosed from the hearth. 'It all don't feel right, does it, master? We usually catch the man and the sheriffs scoop him up. And then that's that. But here we are at loose ends.'

'Yes, it does trouble me. I . . . I don't know what to do, what to feel. And then there was this damned beggar following me, talking nonsense of hearing the dead and why didn't I hear their voices too.'

'What's that? A beggar who hears voices? Well, there's something new,' he said derisively.

'It wasn't just voices but particular ones. The murdered ones, he said. That they were all around me.'

Jack shivered and crossed himself. 'He's just mad . . . isn't he?'

'Yes. Yes, of course.' Crispin hunkered down in his chair. Was he listening to the silence, straining to hear those voices?

'The sheriffs, sir?' Jack reminded.

Crispin nodded and rose. 'Yes. I must go.'

'And I suppose . . . I must stay here.'

'The book needs guarding.'

'Shouldn't we just surrender it to the sheriffs and let them sort it?'

Jack wore such a hopeful expression that Crispin nearly gave in. He wanted Isabel and the children home almost as much as

Tucker did. But there was an itch at the back of his head that told him he mustn't give it away. Not yet. Perhaps he *was* meant to destroy it as he had done all those years ago with the Mandyllon, that bit of cloth with Christ's face upon it. Maybe some things were meant for the ash heap. Maybe some things were too dangerous. But damn it, *he* would decide, not some vile priest.

'For now, Jack, let us keep it safe. But for God's sake, if it comes down to you or the book, choose yourself, man. I can't do without you.'

Jack perked. 'Aye, sir.'

Crispin walked out the door and headed down the Shambles, trying to organize his thoughts. He'd tell the sheriffs everything. He'd tell them about Bishop Becke's quest, about his murderous henchmen, about the man who gave him the damned book to begin with. He prayed that Sheriff Whittington was there. Crispin was certain *he* would understand all.

Vaguely, he was aware of London's citizens who had gone back to their normal lives; the women carrying water in bougets over their shoulders, boys playing with sticks and skittles along the lane, girls sweeping the front steps of their shops, and men calling loudly about their wares. After all, even though the queen still lay in a chapel in Westminster, life for the rest had to go on.

Smells of cooking fires mingled with horse droppings – and he deftly stepped over a fresh pile of warm oxen's dung, ringed by flies. Nimble cats trotted along the edges of houses, and birds twittered or called from the rooftops. It was London as it always was. And, as always, none of them had a clue as to what secret thing was transpiring all around them.

He thought about the queen, of Richard's surprising confession, of Lancaster and Lady Katherine. There was always more below the surface than he would ever fully understand. And though he had enjoyed his brief time with Lancaster, he found himself surprised that he had been anxious to get home. And 'home' had come to mean the Shambles.

'Curious,' he chided himself. When had it happened? Perhaps some years ago when a red-headed boy had shoved his way into his life. He smiled thinking of it. But lost that smile when he thought again of the queen and now his dread duty ahead.

The great gate of Newgate loomed ahead. The crenellations along the top speared the sunshine, as if there was no misery within, as if the very nature of what it represented had anything to do with sunshine and fresh air. Crispin had been a prisoner there, not once, but twice. And walked away. Twice.

The bailiffs were not there under the dark arch, but the blond-haired page Rafe was, and he took one look at Crispin, turned, and led the way up the stairs.

The boy said no words to him as he bowed to Crispin and left him at the entrance to the sheriffs' chamber. Hamo Eckington, the clerk, was absent, and so Crispin cautiously moved forward, straining his neck to see around the corner. Sheriff Whittington was standing at the grilled window, looking out to the street. Crispin stayed in the doorway, loath to make himself known, until Whittington said, 'Come forward, Master Guest. No need to stay within the shadows.'

'I beg your mercy, my Lord Sheriff.'

'You need no mercy from me, Master Guest.' Whittington never turned away from the glass. 'I saw you coming down the lane. Isn't it a beautiful day?'

'Er . . . yes, my lord.'

'But I suppose . . . you have unpleasant tidings to impart.'

'It is my burden to bear.'

Whittington chuckled, cocking his head to get a better view out the window. 'I have served nearly a year as one of the sheriffs of London, Guest. And do you know what that year has taught me? It has taught me that there are men who will commit crimes, and men who will not. Some very heinous crimes indeed. Drink has much to do with the everyday criminal, the man who stabs the one he drinks with, or the man who kills his wife or his wife's lover . . . or both. But then there are other men, like you or me. We would never commit the crime, would we? Oh, we would defend ourselves or others, and that is right and proper. But we would never conspire to kill our neighbor or even a fleeting acquaintance, or any other soul. Why is that, do you suppose?'

Crispin shook his head. 'Character. Character does not only belong to those with breeding, my lord. Good character is conferred on the lowliest of peasants. God grants certain men and women this character and no trial of Job will see them change their minds on it.'

Whittington turned then. 'But treason, Guest?'

'Ah,' said Crispin, pressing his hands together before him. His thoughts suddenly fell on Richard and the private words he had spoken to Crispin. 'A man swears an oath and finds he must break it for the greater good. Those men are given their just reward.'

'But not you.'

'Oh, Lord Sheriff, I *was* given what was my due. Though I was not executed as was the right of the king and of justice, but instead exiled into London to make my way as a disgraced man with only the coat on my back. It was designed to set me low and it did. How it did. Do you think I was lucky? Do you think I was blessed?'

'I . . . don't know. I don't know you. But I think I know your character.'

They looked at each other for a moment longer before Whittington sighed. 'You've come to tell me about those murders, haven't you, Guest?' He moved away from the window at last and seated himself behind the table on a large chair. He did not entreat Crispin to sit.

'Yes, my lord. I feel . . . I feel I should tell you the entire tale.'

'Oh? There is more to dead men in London and Westminster?'

'Much more. It began yesterday. A man came to me in the tavern I favor and gave me a parcel. I did not know the man nor the nature of the parcel.'

Whittington sat back, blinking, with a curious expression on his face. He looked as if he might interrupt with a question, but instead fell silent, listening.

'I naturally took the parcel home and discovered that it was a book. A book I could not translate.'

The sheriff sat forward, hands on his table. 'What did you do then?'

'I took it to a bookseller for help.'

'Ah, a wise move . . . Wait. The bookseller. The one—'

'Yes, my lord. He could not translate the text, so I took it to a . . . a man I knew in Westminster, a goldsmith . . .'

'The next one to be murdered? Oh, Master Guest.'

'Yes. And he recommended I take it to a certain scholar he knew, who was a barber by trade.'

'A scholarly barber? You do know the most intriguing people.'

'So I have been told. This scholar understood the writing. And told me that the book itself, that likely began as scrolls that were put into book form, was very old. And then he told me what the text said. It was written in a language called Coptic, something the early Christians in Palestine used to speak and write.'

'The devil you say. Fascinating.' Whittington put his clasped hands to his mouth, leaning on his elbows.

'Yes, and this text was in fact a hidden gospel. The Gospel of Judas, as it turns out.'

Whittington fell back in his seat, mouth open. 'Blessed Lord.'

'A most unusual text with an unusual philosophy. Not as we were taught in our catechisms.'

'Bless me,' whispered the sheriff.

'I could see instantly that this was a dangerous book and those in the Church would certainly move to suppress it.'

'I should think so! Did you burn this heinous book?'

'Lord Sheriff, in my prudence, I did not think it was my book to dispose of. After all, I was told to keep it safe. And so I did. But then . . . I met up with a man I had known from years ago. A certain bishop from Yorkshire, a Bishop Edmund Becke.'

Sheriff Whittington slowly rose. 'Becke?'

'You . . . know of him, my lord?'

'Good God.' He rubbed his bearded chin and returned to the window. 'He is a dangerous fellow, Guest. You don't wish to tangle with him.'

'How well I know it. But his henchmen have been busy, both in London and in Westminster.'

The sheriff pivoted to face him. 'You mean—'

'I am very much afraid so.'

'Damn the man. What wretched folly is here? Master Guest, I don't know what to say.'

'I only wished to apprise you of these facts, Lord Sheriff. To make you aware of what has been transpiring.'

'And what of the book? What have you done with it?'

'I feared for the safety of my household. I sent my apprentice's wife and children away. Bishop Becke wants me to surrender the book to him.'

'And what will you do?'

'I . . . suppose I must. I have no alternative. And now, Lord Sheriff, what will *you* do?'

'Me?'

'I have told you my lengthy tale to attest to the murderers of those three men, to tell you who they were and what were the circumstances. Are you going to arrest the bishop's henchmen and this bishop?'

'Well, these men I shall certainly apprehend. But as to the bishop, I'm afraid we cannot possibly touch him. He is a cleric, and under the auspices of Rome.'

Crispin slammed his hands to the table. 'He has ordered the deaths of three innocent men! Does that count for nothing?'

'In the eyes of the law, Master Guest, he is under ecclesiastical rule. Not the king's justice.'

Crispin huffed a dissatisfied breath and stalked away from the table. 'Something must be done. We cannot have two laws for our citizens.'

'This has been practiced for a very long time, Master Guest. And I doubt that now, in the state the king is presently in, that any of this will change any time soon.'

'I would see these victims receive their justice.'

'And they will. We will send men to find these henchmen.'

'And if they, too, are clerics?'

'Well . . . you know the answer to that as much as any man, Guest.'

Crispin clenched his hands into fists and stared into the far corner.

'Master Guest . . . I know that this is now your vocation, and a fair one it is, but you must realize, there are limitations . . .'

'I know them well.'

'Then I must ask you to understand.'

'I . . . I do. You have been most generous with me, Sheriff Whittington. Both in my purse and with my person. I am grateful for your time. I would most likely have been less than forthcoming with Sheriff Barentyne.'

Whittington chewed on that thought a moment. 'I appreciate your candor, Guest.'

'What will you do now?'

'Search for Becke's men . . . and bring them in.'

Crispin nodded. It was the most he could hope for. 'And . . . the book. Am I obliged to hand it over to the bishop?'

'Well, in all truth, Master Guest, what else would you do with it?'

The man had a point.

Crispin bowed. 'I am at your service, my lord.'

'Have a care, Guest. God be with you.'

Crispin left Newgate feeling soiled. He hadn't wanted to bare his story to the sheriff but saw no other way to explain it all. He thought he'd feel relieved, but he was far from that.

Grumbling to himself, he heard the murmuring of a crowd. Was it Lollards preaching again? Some other amusement? *Lord, let it be an amusement, for I am in sore need of it.*

When he turned the corner, he saw the gathered people. Two maids were huddled together directly before him. They exchanged hurried words with one another and kept peering this way and that through the spaces between the crowd.

'What's amiss?' Crispin asked.

'Oh, sir!' said one of the maids. Once she got a good look at Crispin her posture changed to something leonine, and she offered a dimpled smile. '*Good*, sir. It's that Tracker. He's done it again.'

Crispin seethed but tried to keep it out of his voice. 'Done what?'

The other maid nearly pushed the first aside to get closer to Crispin, batting her lashes. 'He saved yon woman from losing her purse. Here now. Do you know it's funny. You have the same look of him. Handsome.' She giggled.

Crispin scowled. His double was at it again. 'Which way did he go?'

Both maids pointed over the crowd. 'That way,' said the first.

Crispin pushed them aside, ignoring their squeaks of protest, and threw himself forward.

FOURTEEN

He struggled through the people, their carts, peddlers selling food and trinkets, horses . . . but still he kept the man in sight. He seemed to be moving fast, ducking into the shadows and hurrying to some purpose. Once the lane had eased its traffic, Crispin easily spotted him turning down an alley.

Trotting forward, Crispin came to the alley's dark entrance in time to spy the other 'Crispin' handing coins to a swarthy man with a dirty face and patting his arm companionably. The swarthy man turned and made his way up the alley and around the corner. Crispin's double turned . . . and suddenly faced Crispin head on.

For a moment, the man only smiled and tried to move past him. But Crispin put a hand to his shoulder and shoved him back. Perplexed, the man looked at Crispin a moment more . . . before his eyes widened. He turned to flee, but Crispin had grabbed a good wad of the man's cote-hardie at the shoulder and shoved him back into the alley and against the wall.

Crispin looked him up and down. Yes, his face had a similar appearance with a sharpened nose and rounded jaw. His eyes were gray like Crispin's, his hair black. And though his cote-hardie was nearly the same color as Crispin's, it wasn't nearly as well made and showed signs of grievous wear. His stockings, likewise, were blue as Crispin's but patched.

He wore a sword on his belt, but it was obviously a very poorly made one. Something a mummer might use.

Crispin smacked him into the wall again just for the hell of it. 'Why are you impersonating me?'

'I . . . I . . .'

'Tell me one good reason why I shouldn't beat you bloody.'

'Now . . . now Master Guest . . . I thought you would be flattered . . .'

'Do I *look* flattered?'

'Er . . . no. You don't. I can explain!'

Crispin released his coat and stepped back far enough to glare. 'Well?'

The man straightened his coat, smoothed back his hair. 'You see, a while ago, I was told by people who knew, that I looked like you.' He waited for comment.

Crispin scowled, tapping his fingers on his sword hilt.

The man licked his lips and went on. 'So . . . so I thought that I could perhaps do the same as you. Stop knaves from committing crimes.'

The man's accent was all London, and not from the higher echelons of it. But he appeared to try to cultivate a bit of the palace in his tones. He was attempting to emulate what he thought Crispin must sound like, and that made Crispin scowl all the more.

'You were paying that man in this alley.'

He sputtered and shook his head. 'No, Master Guest, I was not.'

'I tell you what I think you are doing, Master . . . er . . . what shall I call you?'

'I . . . my name is Spillewood. Erm . . . Walter Spillewood.'

'Master Spillewood.' Crispin rested his hand against the wall at Walter's head and leaned in close. He could smell the sweat pouring off the man. 'This is what I think you are doing. I think you and your swarthy friend are deceiving these good townsfolk.'

'Oh, no, Master Guest—'

He was cut off when Crispin grabbed his hair and slammed his head back against the wall, holding it there. 'I suspect that the two of you are making a mummery. Your friend cuts a purse or steals a sack a merchant is carrying and runs off, and then here is *Crispin Guest* sweeping in to the rescue, recovering said thievery and getting a fine fee for it. Have I got it right?'

'Now that's n-not quite—'

Crispin twisted Walter's hair and forced his head back, exposing his neck. If Crispin had a mind to it, he could easily slit the man's throat. 'Have I got it *right*?'

'Yes, yes! Have mercy!'

Crispin leaned in close, baring his teeth. 'You stole my name, knave. My name and my hard-won reputation. What do you think I should do about that?'

'God help me. Have mercy, sir!'

'And if I give you mercy?'

'I won't use your name again. I swear!'

'And stop this deceit at once. I also suggest moving quickly and quietly out of the Bread Street ward. Do you understand me?'

'Yes, Master Guest. I do apologize for using your name, sir. You'll never hear from me again. I swear it! I'll even grow a beard. W–would you like that?'

'I tell you what I'd like. I *do* want to know your whereabouts. I want to know exactly where you are at all times. If you don't get word to me where you next land, I will hunt you down. And you know I can do it. They don't call me the Tracker for nothing. I will hunt you down and cut you from here—' He poked a finger at his throat. 'Down to *here*.' He punched hard with his finger into the man's cod. 'Is that understood?'

Coughing, Walter nodded vigorously. 'Yes, yes. It is most definitely understood.'

Crispin released his hair and stood back again.

The man made long rolling swallows on his stubbled neck. He straightened his coat again. 'Am . . . am I f–free to go, master?'

Crispin delivered a lingering scowl before he swatted his hand in a vague gesture. The man wasted no time and was gone in a heartbeat.

When his running steps could be heard no more, Crispin's mouth curled into a smile. He laughed, listening to its echoes off the alley walls. A ginger cat looked at him curiously.

That had felt good.

He dusted his hands at a job well done and made his way down the lane. The creak of wagon wheels behind him made him walk to the side, allowing it room to pass. Except it didn't pass and continued its slow amble directly behind him.

With a long exhale, Crispin turned. Becke's frowning driver stared down at him as he gestured for Crispin to get in.

Standing his ground, Crispin stuck his fists in his hips. 'And if I don't?'

The driver threw the reins aside, and nimbly leapt down, squaring with Crispin.

'Good,' said Crispin, polishing one fist in the palm of another. 'I think I've needed to punch someone in the face.'

The driver stalked toward him. Crispin gathered himself, waiting, and when the man got close enough, Crispin threw the first punch.

The driver ducked, knee to the ground, and came up with his fist in Crispin's gut. Crispin doubled. Out of breath and wincing, he managed to block another double-handed blow from above. He rolled away and staggered to his feet, fists before him again.

'By the mass, Master Guest,' came the voice from within the carriage. 'Must we endure this savage display of vulgarity?'

Gasping, Crispin finally got his breath back and managed to croak, 'Sometimes a "savage display of vulgarity" is what's needed, Your Excellency.'

'Get in the carriage, Master Guest.'

'I still refuse.'

'Then my man will have to force you.'

'I'm not your puppet. Nor am I at your beck and call.'

'Is that a pun? A very poor one. Get in. I shan't ask politely again.'

Crispin measured the driver, a burly man who seemed ready for anything. And then measured himself, already winded and sore . . . before he straightened and lowered his fists. With a frown, he slowly sauntered to the carriage, keeping the driver within his gaze at all times. The driver's eyes were the only thing to move, watching his every step. It wasn't until Crispin threw back the leather-curtained door that the driver turned and climbed back up to his seat.

Crispin shoved the curtain aside and sat hard on the seat opposite. 'I have just talked to the sheriff,' he growled, 'and they shall apprehend your henchmen forthwith.'

'Oh? And why is that?'

'Because you sent them to kill those men.'

'What men?'

'You know damn well what men: the bookseller, the goldsmith, and the barber.'

The bishop adjusted his gauntlets, never glancing at Crispin. 'Master Guest, that is an extraordinary accusation. What evidence have you to back it up?'

'Their following me, their threatening me . . .'

'Master Guest, I tell you in all honesty that I ordered no such thing. And that my . . . my "henchmen", as you call them, did no such deed. Yes, I have sent them to watch you and only watch you. To compel you to come to me when I desired, but that is all.'

'And I'm supposed to believe you.'

'Believe what you like, Master Guest, but you well know I shall tell the sheriffs what I have told you, and I daresay that they will believe me over you.' He smiled at Crispin then. 'But into the bargain, Master Tracker, it is the truth.' He raised his hand and looked heavenward. 'I swear on my soul to our heavenly Father.'

Crispin frowned. If this were true – and he was still not certain that it was – then those men did not kill the three victims. And if *they* didn't, who did?

He fell back on rudeness as his only weapon. 'What do you want?'

'Ah, Master Guest. What does any man want? What does a man of the cloth want? Peace, faithfulness, God's rule of the earth. What else could there be?'

'Love, charity, humility.'

The spark in Becke's eyes dimmed. 'Is not all that under the jurisdiction of our Lord?'

'Not the way *you* say it. Tell me, Your Excellency, what is the ambition of a traveling bishop? Can he aspire to a higher calling? Cardinal, perhaps? Pope? If his accomplishments reach so far and wide, what heights can he not achieve?'

'I have no ambitions but to be a humble servant of God.'

'Of course. Any cleric would tell me thus. But somehow . . .' He leaned back against the seat and folded his arms. 'I think there is more afoot with you . . . Your Excellency.'

The bishop stopped fussing with his gauntlets and raised his gaze to Crispin's face. 'You are an extraordinary man, Guest. You rose to the heights of court and tumbled down as far as can be, like Lucifer who stood against God.'

'You are likening me to the Devil? That might be apt.'

'And you revel in the comparison. If you must cast stones of humility, cast them first at yourself.'

'I know who I am, my lord. I know my faults and my sins. My question to you is, do *you*?'

'The profundity of this conversation eludes me,' he dodged. 'I have only one simple question. Will you hand over the book?'

Crispin remained stubbornly silent.

Becke whistled for the driver. The cart lurched to a halt. But even as Crispin made to rise, the canvas was thrown back, and the bearded henchmen thrust his head in. Crispin had little time to react before the cudgel in the man's hand struck.

FIFTEEN

Crispin hadn't been knocked out completely. He vaguely remembered falling back in his seat with a bone-jarring headache. The carriage had moved on again and he was aware of a presence beside him. Probably the henchman. But he had little recollection of how far they drove. He seemed to have fluctuated in and out of a bleary awareness.

He understood when the carriage stopped and felt hands on him none-too-gently dragging him out. He was thrust into a chair and bound, but never came fully awake until a bucketful of cold water was thrown into his face.

He sputtered and spit out the foul water and squinted at the bishop sitting sedately in front of him. He wondered blearily if they were still in the carriage, sitting as they had been. But when his eyes were able to focus he flicked his gaze into dark, cobwebbed rafters with the smell of horse dung strong in the air.

To his left, the bearded man who had hit him. He frowned down at Crispin. Elsewhere in the shadows was the clean-shaven henchman. Crispin had little doubt the bulky driver stood guard outside.

Adjusting himself higher in his seat – as much as he could do, tied to it – Crispin settled his gaze on the bishop. 'Was this truly necessary?'

'I tell you, Master Guest,' said Becke, 'that my considerable patience does tire. I want that book.'

'My, my, Your Excellency. I expected better of you. A certain formality and congenial deportment, at least. This "savage display of vulgarity" goes too far.'

The bishop twitched an eyebrow, but it was enough to signal Bearded Man to Crispin's left to draw forward and jab his fist hard to Crispin's gut.

He heaved forward, nearly retching, and gasped for air. The bishop allowed him to recover and sit up again. Glaring at the henchman, Crispin slowly fixed his eyes on the bishop once more.

'Master Guest, I am a reasonable man. But when doing God's work, I cannot, in all good conscience, let anything that may damage the Church slip through my fingers. This book is a danger. *I* know it, *you* know it. There is no use hiding behind your pagan philosophers. Why not save yourself more pain and suffering – which you know I have the patience to mete out – and give me the book?'

Why wasn't he? Wasn't he going to hand it over to him anyway? Why take a beating on a principle? Was it worth it?

He ached. His belly ached, his neck ached, his head ached. It was all so damned foolish and unnecessary.

'You know, Your Excellency, you are right. As much as it *pains* me to say so.' Crispin even chuckled. 'I'll tell you what I will do.'

The bishop guffawed. Crispin giving him orders tied to a chair?

'You will meet me at Charing Cross,' Crispin continued, 'tomorrow at the stroke of noon. And I will give it to you then.'

'Master Guest, must we play these games?'

'My lord, allow me a small portion of my dignity. I am my very word. When I give my oath to protect something, that is no mean thing. My reputation is at stake. If I can seem to *decide* to give it to you at my chosen time and place, can you not allow me that?'

Becke considered, tapping his gloved finger to the side of his face. 'Master Guest, were it any other man, I would *not* allow it. But seeing that it is you . . . yes, I will concede you this. You must have your way, eh? Ah, the folly of a man's pride.'

'I am who I am, my lord. And now . . .' He pulled at his bindings. 'If your man will release me . . .'

The henchman took another subtle signal from the bishop, pulled his dagger, and sliced off the ropes. Crispin rose unsteadily and shook out his hands. When he felt stable enough, he hauled his arm back and swung, catching the henchman in his bearded jaw, knocking back his head. He sank to his knees.

The clean-shaven henchman jerked forward and Crispin pulled his fists up to guard his face.

'Now, now,' said the bishop in a bored tone. Clean-shaven halted. 'Master Guest simply took his due. Let him go freely.

Tomorrow at noon, Master Guest. I shall take it very unkindly if you are late . . . or don't show at all. Very unkindly.'

Crispin rubbed his sore knuckles and gave an abbreviated bow. 'Don't worry. I'll be there.'

Clean-shaven blocked the door for only a moment before he stepped slowly and deliberately aside.

Crispin kept him in the corner of his eye as he passed through the doorway, and then gave a wide berth to the driver who was standing in the stable yard, oblivious to the dung-crusted hay under his boots.

Crispin stood at the gate, assessed where he was, took his time straightening his cote-hardie, his belt and scabbard, before he sauntered away up the road toward London proper, wondering if he couldn't find a handy round stone to heave at the driver's head.

SIXTEEN

He walked back toward the Shambles, rubbing his sore stomach. If Becke's henchmen did not kill those men – and even now he wasn't certain he was ready to completely exonerate them – then who else would have cause to do the deed? Of course, Becke could be lying. But his oath seemed sincere.

'Clerics. Who can trust them?' he grumbled, walking up to his door.

The door opened before he could reach the latch. An anxious Jack stood in the doorway. 'Well, master?'

'Let me in the door at least.' He pushed past his apprentice and sat in his chair before the smoking hearth.

Jack suddenly seized his wrist, looking over the bruises on his knuckles. 'What's this?'

Crispin gently pulled his wrist free. 'A run-in with our friend the bishop . . . and his men.'

Jack ticked his head from side to side and crossed his arms, looking at Crispin like a fishwife.

'There's no need to look at me like that, Tucker. I was his prisoner.'

'Sir!'

'And was let go. Do you want to hear this or not?'

Jack gestured for him to continue.

'Well then . . . I told Sheriff Whittington the whole tale. He said he could arrest the bishop's men but not the bishop. And it was all for naught in any case, for the bishop himself assured me that his men had no instructions to murder our victims.'

Indignant, Jack threw back his head. 'And you believe him?'

'I don't know what to believe. No, that is not entirely true. I think . . . I think I believe Bishop Becke in this. Even after he was a bastard and abducted me.'

'Why in blessed Jesus' blood would you believe him, sir?'

'Because he swore an oath. And . . . as horrendous a man as he is, I don't think he is capable of lying in a protestation to God.'

'Blessed Virgin. Of all the things to believe.'

'I'm to surrender the book to him tomorrow at noon.'

'I don't like anything about that book, sir, but I don't like giving in to that bishop.'

'Nor do I, but I don't see the point in holding on to it.'

'Then why wait till noon tomorrow?'

Crispin smiled. 'Because now it's on *my* terms.'

Jack grinned. 'I like your terms, master.'

Jack dropped on to a chair opposite Crispin. His tall body sagged, and he draped his arms loosely over his thighs. 'If not the henchmen of the bishop, then who killed them men?'

'I don't know. Any ideas?'

'I can't imagine. Except . . .' Jack raised his head. 'The man what gave you that book in the first place. He's sore suspicious to me, sir. What was his game, eh? Give you the book so that Becke will go after you and not him? What's all that about? If he had kept it to himself, no one would have known about it.'

'Yes, he isn't entirely innocent in all this. Well, one thing is done at least,' he said. 'I have torn a strip from the knave impersonating me.'

Jack sat up. 'Eh? You met him, then? What happened?'

'Caught him in the act. It seemed that he hired men to steal purses and goods just so the Tracker could perform his very public and heroic deed. And the victim would be so grateful that they'd pay him on the spot, and then he'd share the spoils with his compatriots.'

'God blind me. That's gall, that is.'

'Yes.'

'And profitable, if his goods were anything to go by.'

'Don't get any ideas, Master Tucker.'

'I wasn't getting any ideas,' he muttered vaguely, eyes alight, no doubt, from memories of Spillewood's hoard.

'I have to give him credit for ingenuity,' said Crispin. 'It was a clever scheme.'

'But no false Jack Tucker, then?'

Crispin chuckled and kicked Jack's booted foot. 'No, Tucker. Your reputation remains intact.'

'That's good.'

They both sat, contemplating their belt buckles, until Jack broke the silence. 'So what do we do now?'

'I suppose we do what we always do. We investigate and ask questions.'

'To the bookseller first?'

'A good idea.'

They both rose and, after locking the door, made their way up the Shambles, first stopping at a seller of meat pies where they each wolfed down their own.

Reaching Chauncelor Lane, Crispin measured the street. He walked up the road and couldn't help but stare at the shuttered bookseller, the only closed shop on the busy lane. Of all the shops, it saddened him the most that this one should be barred.

'A bookseller,' said Jack. 'It's a shame is what it is. Did he have kin, do you suppose? Will it be shut for good?'

'I've no idea, Jack. Let us find out.' He walked next door where a clerk was carefully penning something on a piece of parchment pinned to his slanted worktable. He sat in the wide-open window, no doubt enjoying the cooling breeze.

'I beg your mercy, master,' said Crispin with only a slight bow.

The clerk looked up. He was a young man with spots on his reddened cheeks and nose. His brown hair lay in greasy layers to just past his ears. 'My master is not in,' he said curtly, looking Crispin over before studying Jack.

'I feel I can ask *you* my questions.'

'And who are you?'

'I am Crispin Guest, Tracker of London.'

'A tracker? What is a tracker? Something to do with game-keeping?' He looked Crispin over again and didn't seem to like what he saw.

'I am investigating the murder of Master Suthfield, the bookseller.'

'Bless me.' He crossed himself. 'Such a horrid thing.'

'Indeed. Did you see anything? Note any strangers hereabouts?'

'Everyone's a stranger to me. I'm new to this part of London. I was raised near the Tower. But . . . I remember you.'

'You recall my coming to see him?'

'Yes. You and your man here.'

'And after we left, did you see anyone visit him as well?'

'Now let me think. That was a day ago, wasn't it? The day the queen died. Oh, it was a horrible mess on the streets. People leaving their shops. Everyone walking about in a daze. So much lamentation on the streets. What a terrible thing. First Master Suthfield and then the queen.'

'Yes, there is much to mourn. Still, might someone who seemed to ignore all the lamentation become prominent in your mind?'

He tapped his cheek with an ink-stained finger, leaving a mark just above his jawline. 'A man did come to see Master Suthfield.'

'Just one man alone?'

'Yes, just him.'

'What did he look like?'

The clerk rubbed the side of his nose, leaving a black smear there as well. 'Just an ordinary man. I did not see his face.'

'Young or old?'

'Younger than you. Older than your lad.'

'What was he wearing?'

The clerk shook his head and screwed up his mouth. 'A green coat. Maybe blue. Could have been brown, come to think of it. It was a dark color, in any case. Can't say that I noticed much.'

That is a certainty. Jesu, it's like forcing a horse to talk. 'Did you see him leave?'

'Don't know. Wasn't paying that much attention. When I do the book and sums, I am dead to the world.'

Not as dead as Master Suthfield, Crispin thought with a scowl. 'Well, I thank you, good sir.' He offered only a cursory bow before returning to the middle of the lane.

'That was about as helpful as a boil on me arse,' said Jack. '"The coat was blue, no green, no brown." Jesus wept.'

'*Less* helpful, I should think. There is no way of knowing if that man in a blue-green-brown coat was client or murderer. It's—'

Crispin paused. A woman in a stall across the way was beckoning to him. He walked over. 'Madam? Were you calling to me?'

She was a plump woman, and her crimson cote-hardie had laces up the front instead of buttons, and a good thing it was, for it nearly burst its seams. She appeared to be a seller of baskets.

Her wares were stacked about the doorway and hanging overhead. 'You're Crispin Guest, aren't you? I seen you on Bread Street.'

Crispin bristled. He swallowed down his indignation and said softly, 'I am.'

'Are you looking into poor Master Suthfield's murder?'

'Do you have any information to offer?'

'I'll tell you what I told the deputy coroner. I seen a man go into his shop, and shortly after the shutter closed.'

'But the shutter was open when I spied Master Suthfield's body there.'

'It must have been the wind. For I saw him go in and soon thereafter the shutter was closed.'

'Did you hear anything? An argument? Shouting?'

'No. Naught like that. It was just as quiet as it is now.'

Crispin listened to the commerce of people talking but was not able to discern the words. Carts squeaking, dogs barking, and children squealing and running. It was like any ordinary street.

'What did the man look like?'

'Wore a dark coat. Brown I think it was. Naught special about him.'

'And what did he look like leaving? Did he run away?'

'No, that's the queer thing. He looked like he'd concluded his business and he was on his way.'

'And you saw no one approach the shop after him?'

'Well, the thing of it is, I can't say. I have me own customers to tend to, don't I?'

Crispin looked back toward the shop. She had a clear view of it. 'I see. So you can't be sure if he were the last person to visit Master Suthfield's shop?'

She fiddled with her apron. 'Well, you are correct there, Master Guest. I can't be sure.'

'I thank you just the same, madam.' He bowed and, taking Jack's elbow, steered him back toward the middle of the street.

'Just as unhelpful,' said Jack.

'We know that a man in a dark-colored coat visited him. Let us go to the barber's place to see if a similarly clad man visited *him*.'

'But master.' Jack gestured toward the street. 'Most men have dark-colored coats. Even I do. What would that prove?'

'It proves nothing if we don't bother to ask.'

Jack fell in step beside him toward Wood Street in London proper. Unlike the shuttered bookseller, there was a crowd of people milling in and out of the barber's shop: men, women, and even children. As Crispin and Jack approached, those who noticed elbowed those who didn't, and the conversation, though a low buzz, quieted to a soft murmur before petering out completely. The men stared at him. The women shushed the children standing closest to them and drew them back protectively behind their skirts.

Crispin straightened his coat and bowed. 'Masters, demoiselles, I am Crispin Guest, and I—'

The murmurs began again and two men approached him. 'We are the sons of Peter Pardeu,' said one. The dark-haired men were well dressed like merchants and moved closer than Crispin would have liked. 'We know you, sir,' said the other quietly. 'I am John. And this, my brother William.'

'Masters,' said Crispin with a nod. 'I am deeply sorrowed for your loss.'

'Thank you. You came to see my father on his last day,' said William. 'A shopkeeper to whom you told your name told us.'

'What happened to our father?' asked John. 'We – his friends and family – have come to see his shop, to try to understand who could have done this.'

A flash of guilt assailed him and he felt he could do nothing short of telling them the truth. 'I fear it was because of me, good masters. I asked him to . . .' He paused, deciding not to say. 'He . . . helped me with something most important and I fear he was killed because I came to him with it. I am sorry.'

William looked down at his feet for a moment. 'But . . . he helped you in your important endeavor?'

'Yes. It was extremely helpful.'

'Ah, then. He did not die in vain.'

'I will find his killer, Master William, Master John. I will.'

'We did not doubt it,' said John. 'How can we help you?'

'If any of your people – any of your neighbors – saw anything, anyone, it would help my cause.'

Tired faces searched his. None of his family and what he presumed were fellow Jews had seen anything. They confessed that they didn't work or live on this street.

'But you could ask his immediate neighbor, Geoffrey Little. He spoke to the coroner.'

'And where is he?'

John Pardeu pointed to the shop beside the barber's. It looked to be a cobbler's with a broken shoe for a sign.

'I thank you, Master Pardeu. Please accept our sincere condolences for this tragedy.'

'He lived a good and pious life, Master Guest.'

'Of that I have no doubt.' He bowed and left them for the shop next door. The door was open and so he and Jack walked in. Shoes were stacked up high on shelves. Crispin wondered how the man could ever get to all of them to repair.

The cobbler in question was at his bench, bent low over a shoe placed upside down on a wooden form. He pulled a sharp metal needle through the sole of a slipper and gently pulled the threads.

'Master Little?' said Crispin.

The man startled, pricked his finger, and jumped off the bench. '*Jesu*, you . . . you frightened me! And with what happened to Master Pardeu, well . . .'

'Forgive me. We are here to enquire about that very thing. I am Crispin Guest and this is my apprentice, Jack Tucker. I am called the Tracker and investigate crimes.'

'Bless me, so you do. Crispin Guest, eh? I thought you'd be taller.'

Crispin brushed the comment aside. 'Were you in your shop yesterday when Master Pardeu was murdered?'

'Indeed I was. I heard such a ruckus! I thought the man was destroying his furniture.'

'Did you hear any voices?'

'No, just the ruckus.'

'Did you see anything?'

'See? Oh, no. I stuck to my work.'

'But . . . did you not enquire to see if Master Pardeu needed help?'

'Well . . . Perhaps it isn't a very Christian thing to say, but I simply assumed all was well when the noise stopped. He does do surgeries there, after all. Some men yell like a banshee when he must do . . . things . . . to them.'

'And you never looked? The man was your neighbor.'

He sucked on his sore finger. 'Look, Master Guest. He had his own business to attend to and I had mine.'

'A man is dead, Master Little.'

'And is that any fault of mine? I didn't look, I didn't glance at the window, for what was there to see?'

'A murderer perhaps.'

'And perhaps he would have murdered me.' He sucked his finger again before pulling it from his lips. 'I'm sorry I cannot help you.'

'I am sorry too.' Without another word he spun and left, with Jack scrambling to catch up.

'That's a sorry excuse for a Christian,' said Jack. 'What's this town coming to when the Jew is more charitable than the Christian?'

Crispin thought that he would mourn the bookseller the most, but he found that the quiet little scholar who hid himself as the parish barber was a very great loss. All his learning gone. All his great wisdom. Crispin was suddenly sorry he hadn't treated him better.

'Shall I go to the other businesses, sir?' asked Jack.

'Yes. See what you can find out. Meet me back at our lodgings in about an hour.'

'Aye, sir. I'll do what I can.'

Crispin left him to it. He was discouraged by the lack of information. That damned cobbler had heard it all but did nothing.

He headed home, unlocked his door, and looked around his deserted hall. Nothing looked disturbed and he was satisfied that all was well. With a great sigh he dropped into his chair and covered his face with his hands, rubbing away the cobwebs, when some little weight flopped into his lap. 'Gyb? How did you get in here?'

The cat yowled at him and he set to smoothing his hands over its soft fur, bringing out a purr rumbling from deep within the black and white pelt.

'Have I been ignoring you? I do apologize.'

The cat butted his head insistently against Crispin's hand and he took the hint to scratch the cat's head in earnest.

'Do you miss your tormentor, that little knave, Crispin?' He looked around again at the shadowed corners and the interminable quiet. 'So do I. We must conclude this soon so they may return.'

Gyb seemed unimpressed, especially when Crispin stopped petting. 'What can I do, Gyb? I must solve these murders and avenge these men.'

The cat merely blinked slowly at him and Crispin sighed, laying his head back against his chair. Oh yes, he *was* getting old. Talking to cats, not racing down the street after some knave as he used to do. But these deaths were a heinous plot by someone. And if not the bishop's men – and was he truly ready to give up on them as suspects? – then who and why?

A knock on the door startled him. He gently pushed the cat from his lap and stood, hand on his dagger hilt. There was no point in opening the door if he didn't have to. Of course, in an earlier day he wouldn't have hesitated. 'Getting old,' he grumbled, before standing next to the door. 'Who is there?'

'Master Guest, it's me!'

'Who is "me"?'

'You know damn well. Now open this door!'

The voice sounded familiar. He shrugged and threw the bolt.

The man who had paid Crispin's imposter to burgle for him pushed his way over the threshold.

SEVENTEEN

The man looked around Crispin's lodgings. 'Strange surroundings. Why you should move to the Shambles from Bread Street is beyond my ken.'

'Let us make one thing clear. You hired a man *claiming* to be me. I am the one and only Crispin Guest and I would never have agreed to steal for you.'

'I . . . I don't understand.'

'You've been cheated, sir. Your money has been stolen just as surely as your nephew stole from you. A man impersonated me. I have since put a stop to it.'

The man put a hand to his cheek and slowly sat. 'This is preposterous! I . . . I can scarce believe it.'

'Neither can I. But . . . if you wish to hire me, I'm afraid you will have to pay *me*.'

'Absurd!' He jumped to his feet. 'I won't do it! I have already paid you.'

'You are mistaken. You have paid an imposter.'

The man walked slowly forward, examining Crispin's face from far too close. 'This is . . . remarkable.' He threw up his hands. 'And how by all the saints can I know that *you* are the one true "Crispin Guest"?'

Crispin sighed. He could not fathom how to prove it until he glanced at his sword hanging by the door. He took down the scabbard and drew the blade. Showing it to the nervous man, he explained, 'You see here what it says?'

On the blade was the engraving *A donum a Henricus Lancastriae ad Crispinus Guest – habet Ius –* A gift from Henry Lancaster to Crispin Guest – He Has the Right.

The man read it slowly, lips moving slightly. When he'd finished, his eyes widened. 'Then you *are* the true Crispin Guest.'

Crispin took the blade in both hands. 'Yes.'

'Then damn it all! What am I to do? I've been robbed twice!'

Crispin returned to the scabbard and sheathed the blade. 'I

can help you . . . twice. But I must be paid my fee. Sixpence a day.'

'Less than that scoundrel was charging,' he muttered to Crispin's scowl. He stuffed his hand in his money pouch and withdrew three days' worth. 'Here. I shall be glad to pay it to make two thieves humble.'

He took the coins without counting and placed them in his own pouch. 'And as you now know *my* name, perhaps I should know yours.'

'Edward Howard. I'm a mercer on Threadneedle at Bishopsgate. My nephew is Francis Bastian, my sister's boy. He is a knave, and it was thought that to give him more responsibility was to make a man of him. Alas. It has not. And with *my* gold. He was to deliver it to a vendor of mine but instead he has spent it on himself.'

'Have you told this to the sheriff?'

'My sister would not let me. So I decided to go by more irregular means.'

'I will not steal it for you. I have my honor, after all.'

'Yes, yes.' He waved his hand. 'I can see that. Your blade tells me, at least.'

'Where does your nephew live?'

'With his mother. On Trinity, near Walbrook. Her husband was a furrier.'

'Very good. I shall go to see him and discuss the matter.'

'But Master Guest! He will surely lie to you, dismiss you.'

'You will find, Master Howard, that I can be very persuasive.'

His fleshy face twitched into a smile. 'Oh, I see. You'll rough him up a bit. That boy needs it.'

'I do not think I shall have to resort to violence . . . only the threat of it.'

'Very well. I depend upon you, Master Guest.' He rumbled to the door and cast it open, nearly upending a boy with a dirty face. 'Watch yourself!' he barked to the boy, shoving him out of the way.

Crispin hoped to God that he had never behaved such when he was a wealthy man. Making amends for his client, he reached down and helped the boy up. 'Are you all right there, lad?'

'Aye, sir. Are you Master Guest?'

'I am.'

'I have a message for you, sir.' Out of his grimy shirt he pulled a scrap of parchment and handed it over.

Crispin opened it and read:

> In all mercy and God's splendid grace, I greet you, Master Guest.
> I hope you will be pleased that I am obeying your order to tell you I have alighted on East Cheap.
> In God's humble service and in yours,
> Walter Spillewood

'Speak of the devil.' Crispin smiled, but the boy looked at him askance. He patted the boy's shoulder and reached into his pouch to pull out a farthing. 'For your trouble, lad.'

He took it with widened eyes. 'Oh, thank you, sir!' It was hidden as quickly as Jack Tucker used to hide the purses he cut. Then the boy was off the step and whirring down the Shambles before Crispin could take another breath.

He stepped out, locked his door, and headed toward Trinity. He perused the signs hanging before the shop fronts. A silk merchant. A cordwainer. A tailor. And finally, the furrier. Crispin walked up to the shop and knocked on the door.

A servant answered. 'I am looking for Master Francis Bastian.'

The servant lowered his eyes. Crispin noticed a bruise on the boy's right cheek. 'He is very busy, sir.'

'Is he? Did he give you that?' He pointed to the boy's bruised cheek.

'I'm just . . . clumsy, is all, sir.'

'I'm certain you are. Clumsy enough to let me pass to find him.' Pushing his way through, Crispin looked around the shop, walls hung with furs from a variety of animals. But no customers and no one working on the furs themselves at the empty work-tables. In fact, the place had a shabby air about it, as if it had been a fine place once but now languished under disuse.

'But sir,' said the anxious servant, 'he'll be angry.'

'We'll see about that.' Crispin made his way to the stairs to what he presumed was the lodgings of the family, put his foot on the first tread, and looked back at the servant enquiringly.

The boy nodded and then ducked through a doorway, disappearing.

Once he got to the gallery he began opening doors. He reached what he supposed was a solar, and a plump man in a velvet houppelande trimmed with fox lounged before the window, stuffing himself with sweetmeats. 'What do you want, Hob?' he said without turning toward the door. 'Didn't you learn your lesson about disturbing me?'

'I think he has. And so have I.'

He startled out of his chair and nearly spilled himself on to the floor. 'Who the hell are you?'

Two strides took Crispin into the room and in front of the nephew. 'I take it you are Francis Bastian.'

'What . . . what . . .'

Crispin grabbed him by his fur collar and lifted him up but didn't let go. 'You *are* Francis, aren't you?'

'Well . . . yes, but . . .'

'The nephew of Edward Howard?'

'Yes, but . . .'

'The man who struck that boy downstairs?'

'He . . . he . . .'

Sneering, Crispin looked him over. 'Oh, you are a sorry excuse for a merchant. Yes, I can well see why your business suffers.'

'Unhand me! Who are you?'

Instead of releasing him, Crispin pulled him closer. 'I'm Crispin Guest, and your uncle hired me to get his money back.'

'Y-you . . . you . . .'

'I what?'

'You . . . can't do this to me.'

'I can't? You plainly don't know me, boy.' He yanked the struggling man out of the solar and dragged him to the rail of the gallery. 'You see, if you knew me, you'd know that I was a convicted traitor to the king and prepared to die in a most unpleasant manner. When I was spared, I vowed that I would never suffer fools. And you look to be a great fool indeed, squandering the life you were given, stealing from your own relatives, destroying a business your father built.' He shoved him against the railing and stood over him.

'You can't talk to me like that. I'll call the sheriff.'

'Call him. If you can. Right now, I'm waiting for you to give me the money you stole.'

'I won't give you a farthing. I know who you are, right enough. You're a criminal, a traitor. You belong on the gallows, not in a fine shop.'

'Oh, well, in that case, I shall suffer no more ill treatment if I do this.' He grabbed the man and shoved him over the side . . . and caught him just in time by his furred collar.

Francis yelled murder, and the servants and apprentices at last came running, standing below and looking up with horrified faces at his fat, dangling legs.

'Don't let me fall!'

'I won't,' grunted Crispin, struggling to keep hold of the large man. A ripping noise made the man slip farther. 'Tell me where the money is you stole from your uncle. Come, man. This seam is ripping.'

'I . . . I don't have it any more!'

'That's a pity. You see, I get paid either way.'

'"Either" way?'

'Whether you fall or not.'

'No, no! Someone help me!'

His servants took cautious steps toward the stairs but never hurried about it.

'You can judge a man's actions on how his servants act. See the fruit of your labors.'

'Get up here, you miserable wretches!' cried the red-faced nephew.

Still they lingered at the bottom of the steps. The collar ripped away a few more stitches.

'I think it important for a servant to know his master. The fact that you stole gold from your own uncle who put his trust in you, for instance.'

Francis twisted. 'He lies!'

'Is that so? So your uncle did not give you money to pay his vendors?'

'Well . . . that may be true . . .'

'And they were not paid?'

'These things take time . . .'

The servants still had not moved from the bottom of the stairs, watching the proceedings curiously.

'I haven't got that much time, Master Francis. My hands are weakening and I fear I will soon drop you.'

'My God! My blessed, blessed Jesus!'

'Tell me where the gold is.'

'All right! All right! Lift me up and I will show you. For mercy's sake!'

Crispin braced himself against the railing and heaved him up, scraping Francis none too gently along the rails. He dropped him on the floor in a heap and stood over him, fists at his hips.

Francis breathed great wheezing breaths. 'You're a knave, Guest.'

'That I may be, but I am not a thief.'

He blustered a few more moments, still sitting on his arse, back leaning against the railing. 'For God's sake, man, help me up.'

Crispin yanked the man by his collar to his feet. Francis stretched the cloth away from his pudgy neck and coughed. 'You are rough, sir.'

'Sometimes a man needs to be rough with another to get his point across.'

'So I see.' He straightened his clothes and, with as much dignity as he could muster, stomped back into the solar. He grabbed the chair he was sitting in and upended it. A money pouch was tacked to it below the seat. Tearing it free, he thrust it toward Crispin. 'There! Take the cursed thing. And leave my house. I never want to see you again.'

'I heartily agree.' He saluted with the pouch, pushed Francis aside, and stalked out of the room, descending the stairs.

The servants gawked with mouths agape as he walked by them. He gave them a wink and left the shop.

He hummed to himself as he secured the pouch and adjusted his cote-hardie. Invigorating. That was more like the old days. It was good to know he still could intimidate. It wouldn't do to go soft and appear gelded.

He turned a corner at Walbrook with the intention of moving toward Threadneedle and promptly ran into that damned beggar.

The man grabbed him with his grimy hands. 'Can you not hear the gathering voices, Master Guest? The wailing of them?'

Crispin shoved him away. 'What the devil . . .? What did I tell you, knave?'

'The voices follow you, as they follow me.'

'The only thing following me is you. If I find you again near me I *will* take my sword to you.'

'But Master Guest . . .' He looked far away, above the rooftops and beyond. 'Only you can stop the voices.'

The man was an annoyance, but Crispin's sense of charity was getting the better of him. He remembered all the help he had received when he was first thrust upon the Shambles with nothing to his name. Taking a breath, he said, 'Look, old man. Here are a few coins. Get yourself some food, eh? Go to a monastery and get shelter. The brothers will look after you. I can take you . . .'

He pulled away. 'No one puts Hugo Crouch away.'

'Is that your name? Well, Master Crouch, I wouldn't put you away, but take you to shelter, a place of peace. Then maybe the voices will cease.'

He smiled with what teeth remained. 'You think that will stop the voices, Master Guest? A little food, a roof out of the rain.' He looked upward toward the overcast sky. 'They're on the wind. They come from all over. They never stop. They never stop.'

Crouch's faraway glance suddenly sharpened and he peered at Crispin from under a wild spray of gray brows. 'God does not want the voices stopped for you, Master Guest. God wants you to seek out his own. He wants them precious gifts from the dead to be yours. The holy ones. The dead. Beware. Beware!' Abruptly, he turned and waddled away, tossing his hands up and muttering as he went. People on the street gave him a wide berth and crossed themselves as he passed.

Crispin watched him go, shaking his head. He supposed the man was to be pitied rather than threatened. Only God knew if Crispin wouldn't be a jabbering idiot someday after all his truck with relics.

He cast his thoughts back to that book in his lodgings. Well, it was to be given over to the bishop tomorrow, and good riddance to it. It was no relic, thank God. And why was he so staunch in protecting it? Why had he simply not returned it to Ashdown when he'd asked for it back? Crispin frowned. There was something about the way the man had said it that Crispin had not trusted. When he had given it to Crispin in the first place at the Boar's Tusk, he'd seemed to be a different man with a different character. He had *entrusted* it to Crispin. But when he had asked for it back . . .

'Speaking of suffering fools,' he grumbled. Now it was all too late. He'd promised the bishop and hoped with every hearty prayer he knew that he would never have to see the man again.

'Other people's property,' he muttered, touching the money pouch in his own that he was to return to Edward Howard. Books and coins and relics. What did it all add up to but more trouble for Crispin?

Suddenly he laughed, and then felt like a fool for doing it for little reason and ducked his head at the stares he got. It was just that he realized this was his life, and why not? It *was* better than the death he would have received for treason . . . yet Richard had found a way around that, would have done anything to avoid his execution, it seemed. He loved Crispin, after all. Like a brother? Another uncle? He shook his head at that, too. And then his thoughts lighted on Philippa and his son. They could have lived together. In poverty, certainly, but . . . perhaps they could have been happy. How could he have been so wrong about so many things? Sometimes he felt like a child, disciplined this way and that for not thinking it through. He had thought he was so clever all those years ago. Fate had shown him otherwise.

He asked someone on the street, who pointed out Edward Howard's house, and he stepped up to the door and knocked. A servant answered and had Crispin wait in the entry.

'So soon, Guest?' boomed the voice of the man before he appeared around a corner. 'I warn you, I'll pay you no more than I already have.'

Frowning, Crispin withdrew the pouch from his own and dangled it before the man. 'Your gold, sir.'

'What?' He staggered forward and cradled it in his palms before closing his fingers on the pouch. 'How did you—?'

'I told you. I put the fear of God in him. And now . . .' He bowed. 'We are done.'

'But . . . what of my money stolen from me from that scoundrel who impersonated you?'

'You have your gold, Master Howard, and your peace of mind. Is that not enough?'

Howard seemed to struggle with the idea. 'Well . . . bah! Very well. You've done an exemplary job, Guest. I won't have a quarrel with recommending you.'

Crispin waved without turning and exited, feeling lucky to have got away with a fee for so simple a job.

He looked back at the Howard house, so much like many a merchant's lodgings, and suddenly stood at the crossroad of Threadneedle, Cornhill, Lombard, and Poultry. If he continued down Poultry it would take him down Mercery . . . where Philippa lived. It was the quickest way to the Shambles, after all. At least that's what he told himself. He dared not chance it. At Poultry he cut down to Budge Row and hurried along the twisting avenues until he could get back up to St Paul's. Back on the Shambles, Crispin returned to the poulterer's, just as Jack was coming around the corner.

'Jack, you're back.'

'And you, too, sir. Where have *you* been?'

'I had an encounter from one of my imposter's clients. I fixed his problem and made a shilling.'

'Ah, well done, sir!'

'And what have you discovered?'

Jack stood before the cold hearth and stripped off his shoulder cape and hood. 'Well, I talked to many folk along the street, and they seen naught. Just the regular men along the way. It doesn't sound like the bishop's henchmen, sir. And it don't sound like . . . well, anyone we already know.'

'This is a terrible puzzle, Jack. Could it be that we will never know?'

'Not with you on the trail, Master Crispin.' He sighed, crumpling his hood. 'I wish I could bring me wife and children home.'

'Soon, Jack. As soon as that book is gone from us.'

'Sir, if you knew the trouble we would have with the murders and such, would you have taken on the book?'

'That's impossible to answer, Jack. I . . . feel a responsibility to guard it. Was it worth the lives of those men? Was my own honor worth it? I don't honestly know.'

Jack's mouth twisted.

'And you, Tucker. What would you have done? You'll be a Tracker someday. Men will come to you and rely on your honesty. What would you have done?'

His apprentice jerked to his full height – a few inches taller than Crispin, he noticed. 'Well now. That is a problem for a philosopher.'

Crispin tried not to smile. He would have wagered his whole estate that Jack Tucker would never have uttered those words had he not come into Crispin's life.

'But if I had to choose . . . if a man came to me and told me I'd know what to do . . . Aw, blind me! I would have done what you've done. And that don't make me feel better.'

'It makes *me* feel better.'

'Still, there you were, forced to keep hold of it. Made you keep it for this "important personage"! Well, where is he, eh? For all his words, where, by all the saints, is this important personage?'

A knock sounded on the door. They glanced at each other before turning their faces toward the barred entry.

EIGHTEEN

A knock again.

'Aren't you going to get it?' asked Crispin.

'I . . . well.' Jack rose, straightened his cote-hardie, and walked with all dignity of any steward to the door. He lifted the lock and opened it. 'Who is calling?'

A woman's voice. 'Is this the house of Crispin Guest?'

Crispin twisted in his seat to look. A nun, by the look of her, in a black gown with a long black veil covering the white wimple. He rose and walked to the entry, gently pulling Jack aside.

'Dame,' he said with a bow. 'I am Crispin Guest.'

She smiled. 'Oh, good. May I come in?'

She had a retinue of three nuns and two footmen.

'I have a very small and humble dwelling. Perhaps the footmen and your ladies can wait outside?'

In answer, the other nuns only crowded closer, concern on their faces. 'Or just the footmen. Your ladies are welcomed inside to accompany you. But I . . .' He turned to survey the room he knew well. 'But there isn't enough seating or tableware to accommodate you all.'

'Perhaps,' said Jack, 'your ladies can come through and stay in the back courtyard. There is seating there, with shade and flowers.' He smiled congenially.

The nuns looked to their leader. She turned to them, instructing them to go with Jack. She told the footmen to wait outside. 'All will be well,' she told them.

The nuns moved through. They tried to keep their eyes downcast but they couldn't seem to help but look around at their strange surroundings. Soon their treads quieted as Jack escorted them out the back and closed the door.

The nun walked over Crispin's threshold and stood in the center of the hall, unashamedly gazing around her. 'You must excuse me, Master Guest. You see, I am used to such small surroundings. I don't leave my convent. And this has been a very unusual journey for me.'

'Oh? Whence do you come?'

'Do forgive me, Master Guest. I have not introduced myself. I am Dame Julian. I am usually . . . well,' she chuckled. 'It has been my custom to be an anchoress, but of late, I seem to have no anchor at all. But my convent is in Norwich.'

'You're . . . Julian . . . of Norwich?'

'Yes.' She gave him a beatific smile.

He bowed low. 'Dame, you . . . you honor me.'

'Oh no, Master Guest. It is you who honor me. I have heard of you, you see. A man who encounters relics, who is touched by the hand of God. Well, in my vanity to see such a man, to talk with him, I did, perhaps, a very foolish thing. I asked to leave my cell and come to see you.'

'Me? All the way from a convent in Norwich?'

'Yes. Any man who deals so much in the relics of our Lord's friends is surely someone I had to know.'

'But . . . I could have come to you should you have wished an audience.'

'That is true. But I desired to see where it is you dwelt. You can know a man by his surroundings. How humble or how selfish.' She shook her head, chuckling. 'Surely a vain thing. I will do my penance accordingly.'

'My lady.' He found himself down on one knee to her. 'You should not have come all this way . . . for me.'

'Arise, Master Guest. Please. I am not such a brittle thing that I need your kneeling. Please, sir.'

He rose and stood a bit away from her. Jack returned as she sat. 'Master?' he said warily.

'Jack, see that Dame Julian receives refreshment. Anything she desires. She's come a long way. All the way from Norwich.'

The man was faster on it than he expected. 'Julian of Norwich,' Jack gasped. He bowed. 'My lady, what is your will? W–we have wine. If you hunger, I–I can make you food.'

'Just a little refreshment. Make sure my ladies and my footmen sup first. The road was long. Just a little bread and cheese, if it won't come too dear.'

Jack scurried to do as bid. Crispin sat gingerly beside her. 'What has brought you to my humble home, Dame?'

She laid her hand on Crispin's. There was a strangeness about it, for he had felt the same thing when he had touched a true relic; an odd tingling in his hand and a sense of something unreachable. He did not move his hand away, but longed to and yet, at the same time, would have stayed thus for an eternity.

'There were tales of the disgraced knight who righted wrongs and to whom religious relics came. I wanted to see such a man, to understand him. And then, next I heard, he was in possession of an unusual book that I had longed to see.'

'How could you have heard the latter, for that book came into my hands only yesterday.'

'Strange, isn't it? How these things communicate to us. God hides his secret things from us, but in Him we are made to know them. Through God, through those that know, I have come to hear of your sad history. Our courteous Lord knows of your suffering. In falling and in rising we are ever kept in Him who loves us all.'

He had no voice. His throat was suddenly too hot, too thick to be able to form the words. He merely stared at her hand on his. He knew who this woman was. She was known far and wide as the anchoress of St Julian's Church in Norwich. She lived as a near hermit, in a cell built for her on the side of the church building. She was a holy woman, a living saint, and that she would leave her solitary place to cross England to find him . . . was completely unheard of.

It was obvious that Jack knew of her too, for he stumbled by her, bringing a tray to her ladies out in the back courtyard, but never taking his eyes from scrutinizing her.

'I would bring you wine . . .' said Crispin at last.

'Only water. That will do.'

Reluctantly, Crispin released her hand and rose to fetch a cup of the water they kept in a bucket by the door. He wiped the rim of it with his sleeve and offered it up. She took it with thanks and drank.

He watched her face, determined to remember everything of this encounter. How the wimple, so starched and white, dug into the sides of her cheeks from its tightness. And how pale her skin seemed, with a soft smoothness, though there were wrinkles at her eyes and forehead that peeked from below her bandeau. She was plainly, for all the rosiness of her cheeks, an older woman, certainly older than Crispin. But in her, as he had not seen in clerics very often, was the acceptance without judgment of the man with whom she was speaking. Her eyes lit with wonder at everything she gazed at. He could no more imagine her scolding than the Virgin herself.

'Forgive me, my lady. But what is it you would have of me?'

'I know your soul is troubled, Master Crispin. May I call you so? I feel we are siblings.'

'Of course, my lady. Whatever you wish.'

'Your soul, Master Crispin. You mustn't worry so much over it. You must never fear, for He is here with us, leading us, and shall be until He brings us all to His bliss in Heaven. *Your* soul, as well. Never doubt it.'

It was unexpected. The flush of emotion assailed him and a hot lump in his throat halted his voice. He had worried for the last seventeen years about his soul, knew for a fact that he was bound for Purgatory only if he were lucky. Expected Hell for his betrayal. And yet, such simple words from this small woman's lips calmed his searing soul like no other cleric or murmured prayer had. 'Well, my lady . . . if *you* say so, I have no argument against it.'

'Of course it is so. How silly of you to think otherwise. For we have all sinned, Crispin. Every one of us. Did not Adam, the first man, sin? Our gracious God took the falling of Adam harder than any other creature He created, for Adam was endlessly loved and securely kept in the hollow of His hand. How could you be any less in His eyes?'

'It is hard living in the world, Dame. Men suffer. Men do vile deeds and must be brought to punishment, to justice in this world. It is difficult to understand how God can still love us when we cause such pain and suffering.'

'But you have only to know your own heart, for that is the seed of your soul. As the body is clad in the cloth, and the flesh in the skin, and the bones in the flesh, and the heart in the whole, so are we, soul and body, clad in the goodness of God.'

He shook his head. 'I find that it is so when you say it. But

I fear just as much that when you leave, the truth of that will fade as well. Though tell me, my lady, for I must know. Was it Hugh Ashdown that told you of this book?'

'Yes. I received a missive from him, telling me of you and of London. Tell me, Crispin. Do you have this book?'

He lowered his face and rubbed his hands over his knees. 'In truth, my lady, I do have this book, but I fear it is not something . . . not something that would compare with your philosophy. I fear you have come a long way for nothing.'

'I suppose only I can be the judge of that.'

Jack returned and stood back in the shadows when Crispin looked up. 'Jack, get the book.'

'Get the book?'

'Yes, man, get the book!'

'Right, sir. I'll . . . get it.' He scrambled toward the stairs and took them two at a time.

'While my apprentice retrieves it, I must tell you about it. Then it will be up to you to decide.'

A knock on the door again brought Jack to the gallery railing above. He had pressed the book to his chest but stared at the door. Crispin motioned for him to stay as he was and rose himself to answer it.

When he cast it open, Hugh Ashdown himself was at the threshold.

'Master Guest, please don't throw me out.'

'Give me one good reason why I shouldn't?'

Ashdown glanced past Crispin's shoulder. 'The reason lies beyond your door, sir. For here is my patron lady.' He nudged Crispin aside and stretched on to his knee before Dame Julian. 'My lady, you are here! It's a miracle.'

'Not so much a miracle. Perhaps a bit of the mason's art to free me from my cell.'

'But here you are. And there above, Master Tucker with the book I told you of.'

'Dame Julian,' said Crispin. 'How well do you know this man?'

'He has been in my service for some years, being my eyes in the world. He is sometimes a foolish man, but loyal and faithful to God above.'

This somehow did not fit Crispin's perception of him. He felt he was proud and pompous, but perhaps to Dame Julian he was softer and humbler.

'But how *well* do you know him? Where does he come from? What are his credentials?'

'Crispin, I don't ask a faithful man whence his faith derives. For I know it.'

'Master Ashdown,' said Crispin, bearing down on him and forcing him up against a wall. 'If your patroness were so accessible to you and you had the book, why didn't you merely give it to her yourself? Men have died for your folly.'

Julian gasped. 'Master Ashdown! Is this true?'

'I only had the book briefly. It was given to me with instructions to hand it over to someone who could keep it safe until I could get it to you, my lady. I knew that someone to be Master Guest.'

'But who has died?' she implored.

Crispin bit down on the words he wanted to say. 'The men who helped me to translate it.' He turned back to Ashdown. 'Who gave it to you, Ashdown?'

'I don't know. A lordly man. It was he who told me you would know how to translate it and keep it safe.'

'Describe him.'

'A big man with hair almost as ginger as Master Tucker's, and a little older than him too. I know he was an important man because his own men kept referring to his father, the duke.'

An image of Bolingbroke flashed in his mind. 'Did they call him "Henry"?'

'Why yes. I think they did.'

'Henry Bolingbroke!' cried Jack.

Crispin rubbed his face with his palms.

'Do . . . do you know him, Master Guest?' asked Ashdown.

'Yes, I do. But how I wish you would have simply sent it on to your . . . patroness.'

'My apologies, Master Guest. I see now . . .' He looked around, as if seeing the ghosts of these problems. 'I see now how I have erred. My dear lady, forgive me.'

'I am very distressed that there are deaths associated with this book. Tell me, Crispin. Tell me what the book contains.'

'Simply put, it is a hidden gospel, a Gospel of Judas. Who tells us that he was the closest friend to Christ, not Peter, not John. That he was the only one to understand His true purpose. And that salvation comes from within us, and not through the sacrifice on the cross.'

'You see,' said Ashdown. 'I told you, Dame Julian. It is not a book fit for you.'

'Master Ashdown,' she said softly. 'I cannot judge the worth of the writing until I read it myself.'

'But that is the danger of it. To read it is to absorb its vileness.'

'You think I am incapable of making up my own mind as directed by God Himself?'

Ashdown squirmed, longing, it seemed, to naysay her again.

Crispin wanted to punch him in the face.

Jack descended the stairs, book still clutched to his chest. He walked like a man to the gallows, shuffling along the floor till he reached Dame Julian. He offered the tome to her and she took it, laying it on the table before her. She opened the cover and ran her hand over the rough surface of the papyrus.

'What strange writing,' she murmured.

'I have been told it is Coptic, Dame, a language spoken in the Holy Land by early Christian fathers.'

'Is it?' She beamed and carefully turned each page, poring over the faded ink. With hands laid flat on the pages she looked up. 'Who helped you to translate it, Crispin? One of the murdered men?'

'Yes. He was a barber. And . . . also a rabbi, one of the leaders of secret Jews still living in London.'

'Master Crispin!' gasped Jack.

'My apprentice admonishes me for revealing this dread secret. But I feel I can trust you, Dame, that you will not reveal what I have told you. Nor your man here.'

'This is true,' she said. 'You would not have told me if it were not true. Master Ashdown, I must have your word that you shall never repeat this information. The innocent must not die.'

'I will do as you bid. But . . . my lady, is it not better to flush out these people, to force them to baptism?'

'Master Ashdown, baptism cannot be forced. It is something

freely given. A babe takes baptism as he takes milk from his mother, for it is milk from his Mother Jesus. But a grown man must live in his conscience and cannot accept that which is forced upon him. Speak no more of it, Master Ashdown.'

He bowed and stepped back. Crispin studied his lowered face. He began to wonder if Ashdown had not followed Crispin from bookseller to goldsmith to barber.

She turned again toward Crispin. 'These are strange words from a stranger gospel. But I see no contradiction as you seem to see it, Crispin.'

'Don't you? If salvation comes from within, then there is no need for Church at all.'

'I suppose some might see it that way. But it tells me that only a deeper knowledge of all that the Church teaches, coupled with a deep inner knowing, is what can bring us to salvation. Our Lord's precious blood needed to be spilled for us, so that we might take up all that His Church has given. And this, too,' she said, patting the open pages. 'I should like to get this translated. To understand it more fully. May I borrow this book for a while?'

'I give it to you freely,' said Crispin. 'Only . . . only there is a bishop who seeks the book to destroy it. He does not like these ideas in the world.'

'He wishes to destroy it?' She glanced down at it and closed the cover protectively. 'No. He shall not have it. I will take it. You may tell him so.'

'But . . . my lady, he is a bishop. If he should order you to turn it over to him . . .'

'Oh, Crispin, I don't think he shall ever say so to me. Do you?'

There was something about her. It was as if a glow was shining around her, but it was not so. A trick of the light from the open shutter, perhaps. 'No, my lady. I cannot imagine he would have the nerve.'

'Well, then. It's all settled. Master Ashdown, will you take this and wait outside with my footman?'

He took the book she offered and smiled, passing that smile over Crispin as if to say, 'See? I told you', before he went outside.

Dame Julian reached her hand up to Crispin. He took it, feeling that tingle again. 'And now, Crispin, I want you to hear my words. I have heard of the many relics that have reached you. I have also heard how skeptical you are of them.'

'My lady,' said Crispin, genuinely perplexed. 'How could you have ever heard that?'

'Never mind. Be certain that I have. What I must say to you is this: God does not want us to be burdened because of sorrows and tempests that happen in our lives, because it has always been so before miracles happen. You, my friend, have had your share of tempests. Now you must wait for the miracles.' She smiled again. There was the merest of dimples in one of her cheeks. Without looking away from Crispin's face, she said, 'Master Tucker, be so good as to call my ladies. We must be on our way.'

'Oh! My lady, we can give you hospitality. There is no need for you to rush off. You have not eaten.'

'You are sweet, Master Tucker, but I have so little need of sustenance. And we must hurry back. The masons will have need to brick me up again. I must not be tempted to fly away on another whim as I have. I have a duty to God, after all. But . . . I am glad He allowed me this last time.'

Crispin held her hand as the nuns came rushing back into the hall. He held it still as she rose and walked with him to the door. 'Never fear, Crispin. And his good man Jack. All shall be well, and all shall be well, and all manner of things shall be well.' She gave one more look around his lodgings, sighed, and then passed through the door. The nuns surrounded her, seeking protection like ducklings, while the footmen carried their goods. Ashdown carried the book. They traveled up the road away from Newgate, no doubt venturing through London toward Aldgate, the road to Norwich.

Crispin glared at Ashdown who was in the rear and trotted to catch up. Crispin clasped a hand to his shoulder. 'A word with you, if you don't mind, Master Ashdown.'

NINETEEN

He fumbled with the book in his parcel as Crispin approached him. 'Master Ashdown, I am curious as to your doings once you left me with the book at the Boar's Tusk. Further, I am curious as to when exactly you told Dame Julian of this book and that I would have it.'

The man glanced back at the retreating figure of his patroness. 'I have served Dame Julian for many years—'

'So she has said.'

'The lord who approached me gave me the book, told me of you. We weren't in Norwich at the time, if that is your concern.'

'Henry,' Crispin muttered. That troublesome boy. But he was not a boy. He was a man, with five children already. No, six, for a girl child was born to him just days ago. Crispin had practically raised him in Lancaster's household. They were tutor and pupil, governor and governed, and sometimes rascals together. He had grown into a powerful warrior and statesman, perhaps not as prudent and subtle as his father, but he was someone to be reckoned with. Crispin was proud of him and saddened that he saw him so infrequently. The sword that hung at his hip had been given to him by Henry, and he cherished it, as well as the memory of when he gave it to him. Crispin was a Lancaster man, true enough.

But where in God's name had Henry got that book? And then he remembered that Henry had been in the Holy Land only last year . . .

What did it matter? He'd given it to this fellow to give to Crispin, only to give it back to this damned fellow. And a good jest it was. It had Henry all over it.

'You told your patroness that I would have it and then traveled to London.'

'Yes. He . . . he told me to do as much. I sent a detailed missive to Dame Julian as I left for London.'

'I've no doubt that's true. But why would she come to me?

Would it not have been more prudent for me to come to her? An anchoress, man!'

'It was her choice. We – her nuns, that is – begged her not to leave. But she insisted. It was most unusual. Her nuns told me that once she had heard your name, she made plans immediately. They said . . .' He edged closer confidentially. 'They said that she had had visions of you.'

It was as if cold water had been poured over his head. 'Visions?'

'Yes. Of you. And she desired to see you in person, in London.'

Crispin had been holding his breath. He slowly exhaled, thinking furiously. Visions? Of him? The cryptic and mystical words of Abbot Nicholas as he lay dying spun through his head again. What mischief had God arranged now? A shiver snaked down his spine.

'And so I hurried here on a fast horse, Master Guest. Two days.'

'What? Oh, er. Are they returning tonight? It is a hard road for those on foot.'

'They have horses. And she will stay this night at an inn. I insisted.'

He shook it off. He couldn't afford to indulge in theological meanderings. Not now. 'What inn, Ashdown?'

'The Horse and Dog. On Fenchurch . . . near Lime.'

'I'm glad to know that.' He got in close to the man. 'You have been following me, Master Ashdown. Learning my habits, shadowing me.'

'I–I needed to find a discreet way to get the book to you.'

'Did you also follow me throughout London once I had the book? And to Westminster?'

He looked back again, but Dame Julian and her entourage were long gone amid the many citizens on London's streets. 'Well . . . yes. I needed to make certain that it was safe.'

Crispin scowled. 'And did you make certain that no one else should know of the book?'

'What do you mean?'

Crispin edged closer, his face close to Ashdown's. 'You know what I mean. Did you kill those men for the sake of your mistress, to keep her safe?'

'No! Of course not!'

'Your protestations are weak. I don't know that I believe you.'

'You . . . you must believe me. That was never my mission.'

'But it would keep her safe, keep prying eyes away from her and her purpose.'

'This is a despicable thing you accuse me of.'

'Is it? I happen to think murder is despicable.'

Ashdown said nothing. He swallowed hard while keeping his eyes on Crispin's. 'M–may I go, Master Guest?'

'To the inn tonight, yes. You must watch over your patroness. But I don't want you to leave town.'

'But . . . my mistress! I must go with them.'

Crispin grabbed his coat and dragged him in close. 'I said, Don't. Leave. Town.' He held him a moment longer before shoving him back. Ashdown stumbled, clutching tight to the book.

He nodded and staggered away, glancing back now and then toward Crispin until he disappeared in the crowd.

'You've given him the book,' Jack remarked, leaning in their doorway, arms crossed over his chest.

'I thought it best. After all, Dame Julian requested it.'

'That's all very well, but what will you do tomorrow at noon, then?'

He'd only just remembered his meeting with Bishop Becke and smacked his forehead. 'God's blood!'

TWENTY

'What are you going to do, Master Crispin?'
'I don't know.'
'The bishop won't like that.'
'No, he won't. Jack, maybe it is best to become a tavern keeper after all.'

'Indeed, sir. There's many a time I've thought about it.'

Crispin sat, rubbing his hands over his face, for not the first time. 'I can scarce believe that all that has transpired has happened in only two days.'

'Aye.' He counted it out on his fingers. 'There's the book, there's the queen, there's them murders, there's Julian of Norwich . . . What else could possibly happen?'

'Good God, man, don't say that.'

'Oh, right.' Jack crossed himself and sat opposite, staring into the ashes of the hearth. 'So Henry Bolingbroke gave that man the book. It hardly seems possible.'

'It is strange. But not unlikely. I can well see how Henry would trust me to translate such a book. But why not send it directly?'

'He could have met up with this man at a tavern.'

'Seems awfully trusting of him.'

'I never understood lordly men.'

When Crispin looked up, Jack smirked.

'The queen was not murdered, thank God,' said Crispin quietly. 'And I discovered that Richard . . . had not wanted to execute me.'

'Eh? That is strange. For he always seems angry with you.'

'Perhaps his anger is more frustration. Frustration at my actions, and that I could not see how much I had hurt him. And I hadn't seen it.'

'Now you're feeling sorry for the king.'

'I am. Oh, Jack. Treason is such a bitter betrayal. It is not just the actions of a man to flout the laws of his country, but doing away with the man who rules it. I had never thought of it that way. Not at the time anyway. My sole concern was to get Lancaster on the throne. I never thought that it would mean Richard's death.'

'But it didn't have to, master. He . . . he could have been put away.'

'And be the focus of an insurrection? No. Anyone who takes the throne must be willing to kill the one from whom he took it. It is simple logic and strategy. It is the fallen king on a chessboard. The king cannot be allowed to live. And I, in my youthful arrogance, never imagined it.'

'I'm sorry.'

'Sorry? Sorry for what?'

'That you have had to relive it, sir. Even as an exercise. It must always weigh heavy on you, master.'

'It did. But, strangely, it does no longer. Richard himself lightened my load.' He passed a hand over his eyes. 'Anyway, it was all so long ago. I was only two years older than you are now.'

'God's teeth,' he muttered. It played over Tucker's face; what he might have done in Crispin's shoes. 'I am glad I am not a lord.'

'At the moment . . . so am I.'

Jack looked askance . . . before he burst out laughing.

Crispin let his cheer die down before he said, 'We still have murders to solve.'

'What makes you so certain that the bishop's men didn't kill them men?'

'Despite the actions of the bishop himself, I think he is honorable when it comes to telling the truth.'

Jack made an exasperated sound.

'You scoff, Tucker, but you know how much store I give to honor.'

'Oh, indeed. I know right down to me toenails. But just because you think a thing, Master Crispin, doesn't make it so.'

'You're right, of course. I'm tired. With a murderer still to find.'

They spoke very little, even after Jack cobbled them a supper. They went to their beds in solemn contemplation, Jack sleeping on Crispin's chamber floor at his master's insistence. They arose in much the same solemn way the next morning. Still thinking at the table in the hall, Crispin leaned a cheek on his fist, his legs stretched out before him. His mind ticked from item to item until each connected like a link in a chain. He surprised himself when he jumped up and hurried up the stairs to his chamber. There he grabbed his one and only book, the book of Aristotle that he so prized. With a regretful sigh, he bore it down the stairs and placed it on the table. 'We will need something to wrap it with.'

Jack picked up the thought with the agility Crispin had come to appreciate in his apprentice. 'Oh no, Master Crispin! Not your Aristotle.'

'I've nearly got it memorized anyway. Come now. It will buy me time. Get me that rag to cover it. And some string to bind it.'

As Jack moved to comply, Crispin got his writing things, tore off a bit of parchment with his knife, dipped his quill, and began to write:

> *To the Most Excellent Bishop Edmund Becke, by the grace of God, and by that same grace, etc., I greet you.*
>
> *I heartily regret that the book you so desired went to a more deserving party whom you will not wish to move against; someone protected by the crown as well as the pope. But be at ease that it is in safe and secluded hands. It shan't grace the world again to confuse and confound. Consider your mission done and my dealing with you equally at an end.*
>
> *With all God's grace and mercy,*
> *Crispin Guest, humble Tracker*

Dusting the ink with sand, he then folded the parchment until it became a neat pocket. He wrote the bishop's name on the outside and slid it carefully under the string that Jack had used to secure the bundle. 'That will do nicely.'

'Will you take it now to the bishop yourself? Should I accompany you?'

'No, Jack. I want you to bring your family back to the house. They have been too long away. But first, buy some food to celebrate.' He dug into his pouch and handed him some coins. 'Let's have something of a feast.'

Jack smiled as he stared at the coins. 'That it will be, sir.' But then he frowned. 'It'll be dangerous, master. The bishop will not be happy. His men might make his displeasure known upon you.'

'I shall be just fine, Jack. Don't fret over me.'

Crispin grabbed the bundle, took the scrip off the peg by the door, and slipped it over his shoulder.

He made his way to East Cheap, asked a few people, and found Walter Spillewood's humble lodgings up some outside stairs. As he climbed he was reminded of his old lodgings on the Shambles above the tinker shop, and then he gave a wayward thought to Martin Kemp the tinker and his harpy of a wife. He decided he did not miss them.

He made a fist and knocked hard on the door. When his double answered he gasped and took several steps back.

'I did as you said, Master Guest,' he insisted. 'I did! And I sent that missive to you to tell you so.'

'I see that.' Crispin pushed his way in, looked bluntly around before kicking a chair away from the small table and seating himself. He rocked it back on its legs and slammed his muddy boots up on to the man's table.

Spillewood's face soured. 'Make yourself at home.'

'I don't mind if I do. You know, I've been sweeping up after you, Spillewood.' Crispin unsheathed his dagger and used the sharp tip to clean his nails. Spillewood eyed the blade and took another step back.

'Whatever do you mean, Master Guest?'

'The people you've cheated. Does the name Edward Howard jog your memory?'

He feigned thinking about it, even tapping a finger to his chin.

'Oh, come now, Spillewood. Surely you remember the man. A fat merchant with a fat purse, who hired you to steal some money back from his nephew?'

'Oh. Oh, yes. Now that you mention it.'

'Where's that gold he paid you?'

'It wasn't gold and, well, you are sitting in it.'

Crispin made a show of looking around before he sheathed his dagger. 'I see. I hope you have striven to obtain honest work.'

'I am trying, Master Guest. But it isn't easy.'

'A man with your talents? You should find something quickly.' He made as if to think about it. 'Oh, *I* know. You can do a job for me.'

'How . . . how much does it pay?'

'Pay? *Pay?*' He swung his legs down from the table and rose, stalking toward him. 'You think I should pay you after you have used my name so carelessly?'

Backed against the small bed, he raised his hands defensively. 'No! No, of course not. What I meant to say is, what *day* would you like me to start?'

'That's what I thought you said. It starts today, Spillewood. In less than an hour.' He reached into his scrip and took out the wrapped bundle. 'You must take this package to Charing Cross and wait for a man in a plain carriage. And put on that red cote-hardie you used to wear to look like me. You'd better make haste. You haven't much time.'

Spillewood stared at the bundle and blinked. 'But . . . that's all? Am I not to receive something in return?'

'Oh, I imagine you will. Make haste, Spillewood. Noon will come before you know it.' Crispin turned his back and left the room, trundling down the stairs two at a time. He might have been whistling.

TWENTY-ONE

C rispin set out to the Horse and Dog Inn, but well before he reached Fenchurch, he saw the beggar Hugo Crouch slipping along the road, trotting close to the buildings under the shadows. Should he confront the man again? It was strange how he was always there, always just steps away from Crispin. The more he watched the man, the more unsettled he felt. He was obsessed with the dead. He followed Crispin. It was possible that *he* killed those men. And yet no one remarked seeing him.

Perhaps it was time for Crispin to do a little following of *him*.

He slowed and fell back behind the beggar, who seemed intent on his destination. Perhaps this time he wasn't following Crispin, for he did not seem to notice him as he hurried along in a strange, sideways gait. He kept swatting at his ears as if shooing away flies. It was probably those voices he heard, and swatting at them was the best he could do to chase them away . . . besides outrunning them as he seemed to do as he hurried ever faster.

He came to a church and passed through the lychgate, but instead of following the flagged stone path to the steps of the church, he veered away toward the churchyard.

Once the man was around the corner, Crispin followed. His back to the church wall, Crispin watched the man retreat further into the churchyard. He trotted here and there, looking at the headstones, until he stopped, staring curiously at one in particular. It seemed to have been recent, at least by the soil mounded over the burial place that had no grass grown yet over it. He positioned himself on the mound and sat, legs folded under him. He bent toward the stone, closed his eyes, and cocked his head as if listening.

Crispin realized that he probably was.

He crept forward until he was several yards from the man. But, without opening his eyes, Hugo nodded. 'I hear you there, Master Guest.'

'Very well. I am here.'

'So you *do* hear them.'

'I do not. But I worry, Master Crouch, that you do more than listen to the dead.'

Hugo still had not opened his eyes. 'I don't know your meaning.'

'I mean . . .' Crispin stepped closer. 'That you first *make* them dead.'

He opened his eyes at that. 'Murder?' He rocked back with a roaring laugh. 'You think I murder? So that I can hear even *more* voices? You are as mad as they say *I* am.'

'Are you?'

'Oh, aye.' He rubbed at his nose, a smile still crinkling his face.

'I don't know, Master Crouch. I think that you followed me all over London and even to Westminster, and murdered those men with whom I consulted.'

Hugo closed his eyes again and slowly shook his head. 'It's easy to blame a beggar, isn't it, Master Guest? But it isn't what's true. I am no murderer. I need no more voices in me head. But I can tell you this. Them murdered men. They cry out to me. They tell you to look. To look for a man what you know and what is there and there.'

'What the devil is that supposed to mean?'

'The dead, Master Guest. They don't make no sense sometimes. Especially the murdered ones because it came sudden on them like a surprise. They can't believe they're dead.' He snapped his dirty fingers. 'Like that.'

'But what you said makes no sense.'

'And I told you why. The murdered are all mixed up; all arse up, head down.'

'"For a man that I know and what is there and there"?'

'The dead. It's their way.'

'I will investigate, Crouch. And if someone remembers you even a street away from those murdered men, I will be back for you.'

'I have no fear, Master Guest. I am not lying. But the dead know who murdered them. They are telling you.'

He didn't mean to shiver, but the manner of his saying it and the place that they stood . . . gave him pause.

'Well then?'

'And I told you. You'd know the murderer . . . there . . . and there.' He pointed into the dark undergrowth.

'Nonsense,' said Crispin. He turned away without another word. And when he looked back, Crouch was still sitting on the grave, rocking gently back and forth.

Was the knave telling the truth? He was mad so there was no telling what he knew or didn't know, but his confession of what the murdered told him . . .

It was damnable. He had no leads. He had no other ideas. He stood in the road like a lackwit, staring up at the buildings. Where had he been going? Oh, yes. To the inn to talk to Hugh Ashdown. He got back on the way to the inn and saw it as he came to the crossroads.

An ordinary inn, with two floors and a red tiled roof, green in patches with moss. Hurrying to the inn yard, he stepped up to the sheltered portico and opened the door.

The usual crowd, the usual noise. He spotted the innkeeper and motioned him over. 'Good day to you, innkeeper. I am looking for Hugh Ashdown.'

'He the one with them nuns?'

'Yes, that would be him.'

'Aye. Well he's gone.'

'Gone? What do you mean "gone"?'

'He took his leave. Won't be returning.'

'But . . . the nuns. Are they still here?'

'Oh, aye. Said they'd leave in the morning.'

'Did they know about Ashdown's leaving?'

He shrugged. 'Not my concern, is it? I got me payment.'

Crispin grumbled. 'When did he leave?'

'Oh, must have been an hour ago by the bells.'

Crispin barely controlled his ire. 'Thank you, sir.' He left quickly, standing in the inn yard and looking hopelessly around him.

'When I get my hands on you, Ashdown . . .' So the coward fled. What was he to conclude from that? That he feared what Crispin would uncover? That Crispin would find that he was a murderer?

If he fled would he go to Norwich? Is he even from there? These were questions he might have asked had the knave not fled.

He turned back toward the inn. Should he ask Dame Julian? The thought soured even as it was poured out. No, he didn't want to trouble her. To do so seemed . . . sacrilegious.

But then again, perhaps she wasn't who she said she was. After all, an anchoress leaving her anchorhold on a whim? Were saints given to whims?

He took a step back toward the inn and stopped again. He'd read many a story of the saints, and they seemed to do a great deal on a whim; smiting their enemies with beasts and fire, bringing cows back to life, calling for storms. And she'd had visions of Crispin, so Ashdown had said. Still, what if she were mixed up in all this. What if she were not the real Julian of Norwich?

He took another step . . . and stopped once more.

Hadn't he felt the strange tingling in his hand when she touched him? That had only happened to him when he touched a true relic. No, he knew she was who she said she was. It was a solid truth in his heart. He looked down at his fingers, the fingers that had touched her. He rubbed them together. He remembered the feeling and it sent a shiver over his shoulders. He would not disturb her.

There was little left to do but hasten back toward the Shambles. This sense of unease in a case unsolved burned in him like a live coal. The only thing that could extinguish it was the catching of a murderer.

He got to the old poulterer's and opened the door. Jack and his family had not yet returned. No doubt the shopping had delayed him, or perhaps Helen or Little Crispin required their naps. He sighed, thinking of his own son. He wondered about his early life. If he took to naps. Crispin hadn't, so he'd been told. How he longed for them now!

A knock at the door interrupted his confused musings. He stared at it. The knocking was insistent and unceasing. He took the few steps and pulled it open.

'Master Guest, you did me a disservice,' said Spillewood, out of breath and spilling into the room.

'Me? A disservice to *you*?'

Spillewood lifted his bruised chin and straightened his dusty cote-hardie. 'Yes! You sent me on a mission that you *knew* would place me in harm's way.'

'I didn't *know* it . . . but one could hope.'

He jabbed a finger at Crispin. 'You are no gentleman!'

'No, indeed. That is the crux of it, Master Spillewood, and why I hold my name and reputation dear.'

Spillewood ran his hand over his mouth. 'I escaped with my very life.'

'Sit down, man.' Crispin pressed him into a chair and went to fetch him ale from the jug on the sill. 'There,' he said, handing him a cup. 'Drink up and tell me what transpired.'

Spillewood slurped up the ale and wiped his mouth with the back of his hand. 'You deliberately put me in harm's way, Master Guest. Very well. Maybe I deserved it. But I am not trained as you are in arms or in fighting my way out of a situation. It was very unfair.'

'All right, Master Spillewood.' Crispin tried hard to keep the laughter out of his voice. He sat across from him. 'Tell me.'

'Well . . .' He took another drink before setting the cup down and caging it with his fingers. 'I went to Charing Cross as you instructed. And anon came a carriage with a most disagreeable man as its driver. He said not a word, but the man in the carriage did. He asked if I had it – mistaking me for you, mind you – and I said I did. Well, my voice obviously didn't satisfy, as the man exited the carriage and looked me over. 'You are not Crispin Guest,' he said. I bowed and told him that you had sent me with this package, which I gave him. He tore it from my hands, ripped off the wrapping, and looked at the book and read your missive. And I must say, he was very angered by this. He signaled to the driver, who bounded off of his perch and headed straight for me with evil intent. I ran around the wagon, eluding him as best I could. That man in the carriage tried to trip me but I managed to kick him and he fell back into the thing. The driver pursued me and I barely got away in one piece. And so, if you don't mind, I don't think I shall be doing you any more favors, whether you threaten me or not. I am what I am, Master Guest, and I am no martyr.'

With his hand over his mouth, Crispin managed to stifle his mirth. 'Well . . . that is a tale. No, Master Spillewood, I consider your debt paid.'

'Thank Christ!' He got to his feet and headed for the door.

'Then consider that nothing on this earth will ever compel me to want to impersonate you again, Master Guest. The lesson is learned. I hope this is the last time we will ever see one another.'

'I hope so too, Master Spillewood. As long as you cleave to the straight and narrow path.'

'You can be certain of it.' He grabbed the door latch and flung wide the door . . . but a man was standing there, disheveled, dirty, with a torn houppelande.

Spillewood looked back at Crispin. 'Another one of your errand boys, no doubt.'

The man – Hugh Ashdown, as it turned out – looked from Spillewood to Crispin. 'God's wounds. I've been looking all over for Crispin Guest . . . and now there's two of you.'

Spillewood didn't wait. He shoved Ashdown aside and left as quickly as he could. But Ashdown looked ready to fall over. Against his better judgment, Crispin helped him to a chair, for it looked as if he sorely needed it.

'Well?' he said, looming over him.

'Well what? I have been injured and abducted and kept under lock and key. What has happened to the book?'

TWENTY-TWO

C rispin held himself in check. He wanted nothing better than to fall on Ashdown with his fists. He walked away and paced instead. 'I was going to ask you the same thing. As well as a host of other things. For instance, whether Dame Julian knew about your devilry or not.'

Ashdown cradled his head. There appeared to be dried blood in his sweaty and disarrayed hair. 'Master Guest, I beg you to talk more quietly. I feel as if my head has been cracked like an egg. It has been so for these last three days. Or has it been longer?'

Crispin turned to look at him. Really look at him. He leaned in and peered at his face. 'You . . . you are the man who gave me the book.'

'Yes. Days ago. I think. Where is it?'

'I . . . gave it to *you*.'

'Master Guest, you seem a bit confused. *I* gave *you* the book.'

'Yes, and then when Dame Julian came to call, I gave it back to you.'

'Dame Julian? Who by the mass is that? I never came to call until this very moment. I had a devil of a time finding you. First, I was directed to Bread Street and then finally here . . . where I found two of you. Or . . . did I imagine that? With my head aching so, I'm not sure.'

'Dame Julian, man. Of Norwich.'

'The anchoress? Oh no, I do not know her. And if she is an anchoress, why is she traipsing all over England? Master Guest, I am confused enough for the both of us.'

'I must confess, I am confused too.' Crispin looked him over. Yes, he was the man who had given him the book. But . . . was he the man who had come when Julian of Norwich paid him a visit? It was all so strange he began to wonder if it had ever happened. He mulled it for a few moments. 'Master Ashdown – you *are* Hugh Ashdown, are you not?'

'No. My name is John Pickett.'

'But you told me your name was Hugh Ashdown.'

'No, no! Don't you see? That was *his* name. *He* has been impersonating *me*!'

The pins in the lock fell into place. 'You too?' He got up and faced the man. 'Master Ashdown – I mean Pickett – perhaps you had better relate the whole tale.'

The man called John Pickett who looked remarkably like Hugh Ashdown sat back in the chair. He didn't look well. His face wore a gray pallor and his eyes had dark pouches under them. On closer examination, the two men looked similar, but not as alike as Crispin had first thought. Much could be hidden under a hood.

Crispin snatched the cup from the table that Spillewood had used and poured more ale in it. He handed it to Pickett, who drank thirstily. 'Ah,' he said when he took a breath. 'For this relief, much thanks. He starved me, left me alone. I think he meant to kill me.'

'The beginning, sir.'

'The beginning,' he parroted vaguely. 'The beginning was a year ago. I met a man in the Holy Land, a lord. His name was Henry but he gave no other name. I didn't recognize his arms, but his father is a duke . . .'

'Henry Bolingbroke. He is the Duke of Lancaster's son.'

His face wore shock. 'Bless me. I didn't know. He . . . he was a congenial man. I'm a merchant, you see, and I had done my pilgrimage. It was arduous. Many sea voyages and travel over land in strange caravans with men who spoke—'

'I am aware of travel in the Holy Land, sir, for I have been there myself.'

'Oh. Oh, yes. You were Lancaster's man, weren't you?'

'Yes. Go on.'

'Well, Lord Henry, as he would be called, spoke of this and that. I told him I was returning to London straight away and he got a strange look all of a sudden. He told me, "Master Pickett, if I give you a book, then I should like you to take it to a good friend of mine in London. His name is Crispin Guest and he has a most unusual occupation." He said it like that. And he further told me that once I had given it to you, you would know what to do with it. He gave me some coins for my trouble – which I tried to refuse but he was so insistent and kind about it – that I took

them and began my journey back to England. I arrived not too
long ago to Yarmouth and met a man there at an inn. Well, you
know what happens in an inn when one is drinking. You tell tales.
And I told him mine. He asked about the book – which I don't
remember mentioning but I did tell him about Lord Henry and so
. . .' He rubbed his temple and winced. 'Anyway, I had speculated
as to what the book could be. While waiting for a ship in Jaffa I
had a man look at it to get an idea . . . and he told me what it
said. Read out part of it for me. Well! Master Guest, I didn't know
what to make of it, but if this lord vouched for you, I knew you
would do it credit. I still wasn't certain about this book, but I had
made an oath and I was bound to carry it out. I'm afraid I told
the man at the inn more than I intended. He explained that he was
a Lollard and that such books should be destroyed. It was then
that I awakened to what I was doing and I worried that he might
become violent. So I told him that perhaps it was all a tale for I
was in my cups. I soon went off to bed and didn't see him in the
morning. And then I set out for London—'

'Not Norwich?' Crispin interrupted.

'No. I had no business in Norwich. I had to return to London
and, remembering my duty, I sought you out. But to my surprise,
you weren't anything like he said. You were entertaining crowds
with your feats of bravery. From Lord Henry's description I took
you to be a humble man.'

'And so I am, sir, or try to be. You met my double.'

'The man who was just here? Yes, I see that now. It was a
good thing I did not approach him immediately, for I had since
discovered from others that you could be found easily at the
Boar's Tusk, and you look very like him—'

'*He* looks like *me*, which was deliberate in order to deceive.'

'Yes, quite. So I found *you* in the Boar's Tusk . . . I did, did I
not?'

'You did. And have caused me no end of trouble since.'

'Forgive me for that, Master Guest, but Lord Henry never told
me to expect that. I delivered it to you, and shortly afterward, I
was coshed on the head. See?' He bent over to show Crispin the
bloody lump. 'He tied me up and left me for dead for days in
some mews somewhere in London, leaving me neither food nor
drink. I have only just escaped. I worried over what might have

happened to you. That's why I didn't go to the sheriffs . . . but now I suppose I should have done.'

'And this man to whom you told your story. Did he look like you?'

'I did not see the resemblance at first, but I did on seeing him again. He looked like me, a slightly younger version, perhaps.'

'And he has come to me with an equally strange tale, using just enough of your own story to confound and confuse me. He claims to be a follower of Julian of Norwich. And on some whim, she came to see me.'

The shocked expression again washed over his face. 'I can hardly believe it.'

'Neither can I. But he had befriended her.'

'Do you suppose he told her he was a Lollard?'

'I shouldn't think so. Was it because of his Lollard teachings he sought out the book to destroy . . . and to murder all those who knew about it?'

'Good Christ! He murdered?'

'Yes. I didn't know what else to do with the book but to find out what it meant. I went to three different men, two in London and one innocent in Westminster, and one by one in my wake they were murdered. I have no doubt now that I would have been next.'

'And you think he did the killing?'

'I am convinced of it. Where did he hail from, Master Pickett, and what was his real name?'

'Hugh Ashdown, for all I know. He said he was a Lollard and the way he spoke of his beliefs seemed a bit, well, tilted. He frightened me. And when he hit me and tied me up, he told me that I was getting what I deserved to help the filth of the world – that is what he called it. That the Bible in its pure state was the only Scripture, and any other was to be destroyed along with all who knew of it. Why he did not kill me straight away, I do not know. Divine intervention, no doubt.'

'I have come across difficulty with Lollards before, but none so deadly.'

'If you don't mind, Master Guest . . .' He rose, still holding his head. 'I have done my Christian duty by warning you. And now I think I shall return to my home for succor.'

'If I had a horse to give you, Master Pickett, I would.'

'You are as Lord Henry said you are, Master Guest. I am sorry for bringing these troubles to your door.'

'And I am sorry on your behalf, sir. Can I help you home?'

'No. My home is not far. God keep you, Master Guest.'

'And you, sir. Oh, one thing more. Did Ashdown say where he lived?'

'Come to think of it, I think he said Raundes . . . which I believe isn't far from Norwich, if that helps.'

'It does indeed. Thank you, Master Pickett.' He watched the man make his slow progress down the Shambles toward West Cheap. Ashdown would take the Aldgate road toward Norwich and Raundes, then. If he had a horse he'd be long gone. But what if he hadn't gone? What if he was working with other Lollards? Lollards had been like pests lately, at every corner crying out their preaching, and now, as he looked to the Shambles, suddenly he couldn't find even one. But, of course, he knew where they'd be at court.

I don't want to go back to court, he moaned. The king was still in mourning. But Crispin did have Lancaster's livery . . .

With a sigh from the center of his being, he trudged back home to fetch the tabard.

He made it back to Westminster Palace and kept his hood low over his face. When he passed St Stephen's open doors he saw the glow of the candles over the queen's bier, and the figure of the king still kneeling there.

He pressed on, asking servants where he could find Thomas Clanvowe, one of the king's courtiers. He was directed here and there, but it was never quite the right place. He turned the corner in the depths of the palace and unexpectedly encountered the king's chamberlain, Sir Thomas Percy. Crispin turned on his heel and headed in the other direction, when the man called out to him.

When will I ever learn? he admonished himself. He stopped, took a moment, then turned.

'You're Lancaster's man—' He stopped with widened eyes. 'God's legs, Crispin Guest.'

'Yes, my lord. I am Lancaster's man.'

'What the devil are you doing here?' he hissed out of the side of his mouth, searching up and down the corridor for spying eyes.

'In the service of the king, looking for a murderer.'

Percy's eyes remained wide and his mouth hung loose. 'What?'

'My lord.' Crispin sidled closer. 'You might be able to help me.'

'I will not!'

'Find a murderer, sir? Why would you hesitate?'

'I . . . I didn't mean that, Guest.'

'All I need do is find Sir Thomas Clanvowe.'

His shock changed to exasperation. 'Last I saw him he was in the great hall, arguing with some knave.'

'Ah, then I thank you.'

'Guest,' he hissed again as Crispin turned to leave. 'Make sure your exit is quick.'

He bowed. 'Always, my lord.' He hastened through the corridor back to the hall.

Clanvowe, looking dour and staring at the floor, was making his way back into the palace when Crispin stopped him.

He didn't look happy. 'Bless me, it's Crispin Guest. Again.'

'Yes, sir. And, begging your mercy, its best to keep your voice down when saying my name.'

He nodded, eyes darting to each courtier nearby.

'If you please, I am looking for a man who might try to contact you. His name is Hugh Ashdown—'

'That miscreant? I just now sent him packing. He talked nonsense of some scheme of his. Those who share my philosophy of faith need no zealots in the mix. It is a calm and quiet use of our minds that I prefer.'

'I agree. It is safer that way, though you might wish to tell the street-corner preachers the same, for the king's patience might wear thin.'

'Indeed. That is exactly what I expressed to the man.'

'And since you turned him out, did you catch which way he had gone?'

'Why should you want to pursue him? He's a fool.'

'And a murderer. I must apprehend him.'

'Not . . . not the queen?' he said confidentially.

'No, my lord. We have put that to rest. But three other innocents.'

'By the mass. In that case, only a few moments ago, he was following the river back toward London.'

'Thank you, sir. God keep you.' Crispin made a hasty bow and took off running over the tiles, past the door, down the steps, and through the courtyard and the gate beyond. He scanned the people along the road but there were only the usual citizens with their carts, horses, and other animals. But when he glanced lower toward the bank, he saw a man hurrying along wearing a houppelande that looked familiar.

Crispin dove down the angled bank and shouted. The man turned. It was Ashdown, and his look of surprise and then fear spurred Crispin on, especially when the wretch took off running.

'No, you don't.' Crispin ran faster, catching up. He was no more than a few yards behind when he leapt and tackled the man, both rolling further down the bank over the rough stones. They stopped with Crispin straddling the man on the ground. 'I have you. And I got the whole story from John Pickett.'

Now the man truly *was* surprised. 'He escaped?'

'And now you admit your guilt. I'll have you for murder and abduction.'

His face, so mild before, molded into an ugly mask of contempt. 'That vile book needed to be destroyed. And all who knew of it.'

'Two of those men knew nothing about that book, you fool. You killed innocent men. And for what? A foolish book that no one could read.'

'But *you* knew what it said. *You* translated it. Soon everyone could.'

'You were working for Becke all along.'

'Alas, no. But our purposes at least in this did cross paths.'

'He would eliminate you and your Lollard ways if he could. He is no friend of yours.'

Ashdown frowned. 'That makes no matter in the end, Guest. I have accomplished my deed. My reward will be great in Heaven.'

'I will see that you get to Hell sooner than that!'

Ashdown squirmed. Crispin punched him in the jaw. The man took on a bleary expression for only a moment. And when he seemed cognizant again, Crispin spit out, 'And what of Dame Julian? You deceived her. You, with your devil's tongue, lied to so saintly a woman.'

His face twisted again. 'She . . . she knows nothing of this. She will go back to where she belongs in her cell and no one will hear of any of it.'

'I will tell her. I must. She needs to know.'

Anger blazed in Ashdown's eyes. He turned his face toward the wrist that held him down and bit hard.

'Damn you!' Crispin slammed his fist into the man's face again. Blood spattered over Crispin's sleeve and Ashdown's face jerked to the side. His eyes grew hazy. 'What have you done with the book?' Crispin demanded.

Ashdown shook his head, licked the blood from the side of his mouth. 'Burned it,' he said distantly. 'In my room. It's done, Guest. There isn't a thing you can do now.'

Crispin grabbed his coat and shook him. 'You're done too. You'll hang for your treachery.'

Ashdown had seemed blurry, but he suddenly jerked hard, wresting himself from Crispin's fists and knocking him over. He scrambled up the bank, but Crispin heaved forward and clasped on to his gown, pulling him back. They both lost their balance. Crispin tumbled arse over heels. Ashdown windmilled his arms, but it did him no good. He arced downward, smashing his head against the rocky bank before he tumbled into the Thames. He floated face down for a moment until he sank below the churning water.

Crispin hurried down the stony bank and wetted his boots, standing in the water at the edge, but he could see nothing. Even looking down the river's swiftly moving current yielded no bobbing body. He stepped back up the bank, scanning the river a long time, long enough for a man to come to the surface to breathe. Long enough to make certain he'd never come up again.

A few men who had stopped to watch the altercation helped him up to the road and asked him what had happened.

'A murderer found his due, is all. Do you trust me to go to the sheriffs myself? I am Crispin Guest.'

'The Tracker?' said one man. 'The one on the Shambles?'

Crispin sighed his relief that at least a few still recognized him and where he lived. 'Yes. Do you trust me to go?'

'Aye, of course. God bless you, sir.'

Crispin asked the names and addresses of the witnesses, cradled his sore, bitten wrist, and trudged back toward London, satisfied that justice had been done.

TWENTY-THREE

Crispin, in his wet stockings and coat, waited in the sheriff's hall with Hamo Eckington, the sheriff's clerk. 'If you don't mind my saying,' said the old clerk, 'you look worn through, Guest.'

Crispin lifted a brow. 'Why ever would I mind your saying that, Master Eckington?'

'Send Guest in!' came the call from the chamber.

Crispin sauntered by Eckington, who seemed offended by Crispin's remark. *And well he should be.*

'What have you to tell me now, Guest?' asked Sheriff Whittington.

'The end to the three murders, my lord.'

'Oh? Well then. Proceed.'

'A man from Raundes called Hugh Ashdown. A zealot Lollard bent on getting the book from my possession. He abducted the man who had given me the book with the purpose of letting him die, alone and starving.'

'Good God.'

'He followed me throughout London and killed those men, any who knew of the book. He impersonated the poor man whom he abducted and allowed me to be lulled into thinking he was a friend of . . . an important personage. In the end, he burned the book, and I fought with him on the banks of the Thames in Westminster. He hit his head on the bank and fell into the water. I looked for him to jump in after, but I think the current took him to the bottom where he surely drowned.'

'Ah, Master Guest. What a tale.'

'Indeed.'

'Well. You shall, of course, appear at an inquest.'

'Of course, my lord. There are witnesses to my altercation who clearly saw what happened.'

'So our bishop friend didn't have a hand in it then?'

'It appears not, my lord.'

'That is a mercy. I dreaded dealing with him.'

'I can well imagine.'

'Tell your story to Hamo and then you are free to go.'

He bowed. 'Thank you, my lord.'

Crispin told his tale again – slowly – to the aged clerk, who kept having him repeat certain passages, and then left as soon as he could.

Crispin walked along Newgate Market, stripped the Lancaster livery off his cote-hardie, and balled it up under his arm. It had been a very long day and he wanted nothing more than to sit down to a supper of Isabel's cooking and play with his namesake again.

It wasn't long till he felt steps treading in the same rhythm behind him. When he stopped and turned, he was face to face with a smiling Hugo Crouch.

'Well?' he asked warily.

'The voices, Master Guest. They are calmer now. They thank you for giving them rest.'

A deep shiver assailed him and he wanted nothing more than to run from this man, from his words, from the image conjured in his mind. But he stood his ground and kept his face neutral and said nothing.

'It's a fine thing to give peace to the dead. Ah, you have a rare gift, Master Guest, no mistaking. It isn't just anyone who can do it. As rare a gift as mine. A gift and a curse, eh?'

Still, Crispin kept his lips shut tight, looking down his nose at the beggar.

'A curse because it never ends, does it?' Crouch went on. 'But every man must make his way in the world. You're better for it, I daresay. Better than you'll ever know.' Crouch smiled, winked knowingly, and gave a little salute. Humming to himself, he turned heel and wandered in his strange sideways gait off to God-knew-where.

Crispin watched him and wondered how many such men lived in London like Crouch. Was it a rare thing? He hoped so. Rather like madness itself.

He mulled his thoughts and continued his journey back home. Just as he was crossing into the Shambles, a man on the street approached Crispin and touched his sleeve. 'Are you Crispin Guest?'

God's blood, what now! He still hadn't sloughed off the strangeness of Hugo Crouch, but he looked the man over and warily replied, 'Yes.' Before he could ask, the man handed him a parchment and quickly walked away. Dreading what the missive might say, he unfolded it and read:

> *To the most honorable Tracker Crispin Guest, I bid you God's grace and my greetings,*
> *Sir, I hope that this afternoon is a felicitous time for myself to make a visit to you. I have sent a message as you have described and I shall presently take myself to your doorstep. I do hope you are at home and that we can visit.*
> *In all the mercy of the saints and of God Himself,*
> *Christopher Walcote*

Crispin read it through several times and smiled. That damned boy was persistent, he'd give him that. He looked up and realized he'd need to trot home to get there in time to intercept the boy. He got to within sight of his lodgings just as Christopher was arriving, walking by himself without an escort.

'And just what do you think you are doing, Master Walcote?' Crispin asked, strolling forward and trying to even his breathing. He stepped up the granite step and unlocked the door.

'Why are you all wet? Did you get my message, Master Crispin?'

'I received your message only mere moments ago.' He stood at the door and let the boy tromp through. 'Must I explain it in detail to you? You are to message me to see when I will be home and if I can accommodate you. It might well be that I have visitors or clients or must travel out of town. And here you are without a servant to escort you. What would your mother say?'

'She'd scold me,' he said, distracted. He was fingering the leather scabbard hanging by the door.

'And rightly so. As it happens, I am expecting the return of my apprentice's family.'

'Oh, I like Jack Tucker!'

'So do I.'

He seemed to run out of conversation, and there was no

time to give him his fighting instruction today. Crispin stuffed the livery into the coffer by the door, sat on it and pulled off his wet boots. 'Did you hear what I said, boy? Today is not a good day. You must give me more notice and then *wait* for my reply.'

Christopher heaved a great sigh and looked around, moving to the bottom of the stairway. He glanced up the stairs, trying to see beyond the gloom above. 'Is that your chamber up there? It's a small house, isn't it?'

'Yes.' Crispin stood back in his stocking feet, fitting his thumbs in his belt. 'It is a humble dwelling for a humble family.'

'I suppose. Do you truly have no time for me now, Master Crispin? It is hard for me to get away. My father has me spend more and more time on the business, and soon I will have no time at all to learn about swords and such.'

'I . . . I am sorry to hear that, Christopher, but after all, your father is only sharing with you his trade, a trade that will make you as wealthy as he is.'

'But *you're* not wealthy.'

He felt the sting but shrugged it off. 'No. I was once. And now my life is difficult. I must earn my wage to put food on the table. I have many mouths to feed now. Believe me, Christopher, though there are many responsibilities with having wealth, it is far better to be wealthy than to be poor.'

'But our Lord Jesus says that it is easier to fit a camel through the eye of a needle than for a rich man to get into Heaven. And He is always talking about the poor. Isn't it better to be humble and poor in the eyes of God?'

'Hmm.' Crispin rested his hand on the boy's shoulder and steered him toward the table. Crispin sat and he held the boy before him. 'You know your Scripture well. That is good. But, the truth is, God does love the rich as well as the poor, but perhaps He spares a little more love for the poor because they need Him the most. The poor hunger and are cold without a proper roof over their heads. Do not envy the poor, lad. But, on the other hand, when a man is wealthy he has responsibilities. He must make certain to help shelter and feed the poor. God wishes for him to do this. He must give charitably. He must never degrade the lowly.' And, in that instant, Crispin thought of Hugo

Crouch. '*For to each man to whom much is given, much shall be asked of him; and they shall ask more of him, to whom they betook much.* Do you understand that?'

'No, sir.'

'It means that the more you have – a wealthy man, for instance – the more is expected of you. When I was a wealthy man, I was obliged by my position to make certain that my tenants had enough to eat and were protected from outside forces. I gave generously, prayed for their welfare, and saw that the priests in the chapel prayed for their dead. Some wealthy men think that it means they may spend as much as they like, but we all must tithe to our parish churches and we must all be certain that our fellow man eats and is clothed.'

'I . . . think my father is generous.'

'I'm sure he is. And he does not brag of it. That is best. For God knows what we do in secret. It is only the braggart who must go about yelling about how great he is.'

He nodded slowly. 'I see. That is a good lesson, too, even if we can't use swords this time.'

Crispin smiled. 'Yes. Everything in your life will be a lesson. And it is up to you to pay careful attention.'

'I will, Master Crispin.'

Crispin rose and walked to the door with the boy. 'Next time you will wait for my letter?'

'Yes, sir. But . . . there is one thing that has been troubling me.' He slowed and turned at the door. He looked up and Crispin realized the sadness in his eyes. He crouched low and took the boy's shoulders.

'What is it, Christopher?'

'I don't have many friends. I mean . . . close. Like . . . like Martin used to be.'

His heart swooped. The boy's friend. He was dead now these two years.

'Why did Martin have to die?' His eyes were glossy, but the stubbornness of his set chin fought the tears.

Crispin gazed at him solemnly. 'You know why.'

Christopher lowered his face. 'I know,' he said softly. 'He was a murderer. But he was also my dearest friend. And John Horne deserved it. I should have killed him myself.'

'Then *you* would have died. And your mother would have been greatly aggrieved.'

'I know. Is it a sin to pray for Martin's soul even if he was a murderer?'

'Oh, no, child. It is a very great thing to pray for those we loved, even if they did wrong. Especially so.'

He nodded, put his finger to his mouth, and gnawed on a knuckle before he seemed to realize what he was doing and took it out, wiping his finger on his coat. He screwed up his mouth and raised his eyes to Crispin again. 'Master Crispin,' he said quietly, seeming to choose his words. His fidgeting hands stopped and fell to his sides. 'Are *you* my father?'

Crispin snapped up straight and blinked down at the boy. 'You . . . you must never ask such a question!'

'I don't look like my father – Clarence Walcote, that is. I look like you. Tell me.'

He shoved him by the shoulder toward the door. 'It's time for you to go home, Christopher.'

He dug in his heels. 'Please tell me. The servant I brought with me last time. I heard him talking to the other servants. That's why I came alone. Master Crispin, please tell me and I shall never bring it up again.'

Stricken, Crispin stood before him. He shook his head. 'I cannot.'

'I love Clarence Walcote. I do. But I would just like to know—'

'No, you don't!' Crispin turned away and paced across his hall. 'You don't want to be the son of a pauper.'

'But you were a knight!'

He halted and swung toward the boy, viciously. 'But not any more! Harken to me, boy. I . . .' But what he was about to say died on his lips. Instead, his shoulders slumped and he shook his head. Quietly he said instead, 'It hurts my heart that I cannot acknowledge you.'

Christopher's eyes lit and his face beamed.

'I would,' Crispin went on heedlessly. 'I would, believe me. But your life is far better off if you forget about me. Clarence Walcote *is* your father. He is wealthy. He is respected. That is something you cannot have as my son. You would be branded a bastard. Do you understand what that means? To those around you? To even your servants? Being a bastard is not any kind of honor. It will follow you all your days.'

The joy in the boy's face faded. 'My mother. Did she . . . did she commit adultery? It is a great sin.'

'No.' He sagged. He wanted to dash his head against the wall. Why hadn't he told the boy no? Why had he all but admitted it? Because he had selfishly *wanted* to tell the boy. It was too late to take it back now. 'No, Christopher. We . . . we were together before she married your father.'

He seemed to release all tension in his small frame. 'Good. That is a great relief to me. I love my mother dearly.' He gnawed on his finger again before tearing it from his mouth once more. 'Is it so much of a sin . . .' His voice was quiet, spoken to the door he was facing. 'Is it so much of a sin . . . to be glad that *you* are my true father?'

Crispin swallowed. His mouth was parched suddenly. 'Clarence Walcote is a good man. Not every man can or should be a knight, just as not every man can be a good mercer.'

The boy snorted but Crispin faced him again, giving him his sternest expression. 'Christopher, you must never speak of this again. Please. For your sake and that of your mother. And, under the circumstances, perhaps . . . perhaps we should not meet again.'

'No! I want to learn these things. I want to learn them from *you*. I might need it someday. We might go to war.'

'I doubt very much that *you* shall need to go to war.' Above all, he had to protect the boy. But he had a great need to teach him these skills, skills that he excelled at and had loved at Christopher's age. The boy might never be a knight as Crispin had been, but a man needed to know how to fight. 'Well . . . you must promise me that you shall never speak of this. To anyone. Even to me.'

'I will, Master Crispin! I swear!'

'Good. Now . . . it's time for you to go home. When Master Jack returns I will have him accompany you. You must not travel alone unless you are deemed old enough.'

'I wish . . . I wish *I* had been Master Jack.'

'He had a dreadful childhood. Alone, impoverished, begging for scraps. Why on earth would you want such a thing?'

'Because . . . then I would have been raised by you.'

It was every bit like a gut punch. Crispin staggered back slightly, holding his stomach that had seemed to steal his breath. If only it could have been. If only . . .

He shook it free and straightened. 'You were raised by a loving father. Never speak of it. You promised.'

'I know,' he said, head lowered. 'I'll go.' He even walked toward the door and Crispin thought he intended to go through it. But suddenly he turned, looked up at Crispin, and launched himself forward, wrapping his thin arms around Crispin's waist. Crispin's arms embraced him before he could think. He looked down on that dark head of hair and a wave of pride washed away the sadness . . . at least for a moment.

A knock on the door drew them apart.

'You see,' said Crispin. 'Your governor has come seeking you out. You must never try to elude him again.'

But when he opened the door expecting a servant, the person of the Duke of Lancaster filled the doorway.

TWENTY-FOUR

John of Gaunt first looked at Crispin, but then his gaze fell to the boy beside him. Then he looked at Crispin again, and then the boy.

'Your Grace.' He bowed, then elbowed Christopher to do the same. 'My lord, may I present Young Christopher Walcote, son of a mercer. Christopher, this is John of Gaunt, the Duke of Lancaster.'

Christopher gasped. 'Oh, my lord!' He bowed again. 'It is an honor.'

John leaned over, reached out his hand to shake the boy's, and smiled. 'It is a very great honor to meet such an accomplished mercer.'

'Oh, sir. I am only the son of a mercer. I am still learning my trade.'

'Ah, well then. It's a proud trade. I've no doubt you shall excel at it.'

Christopher looked up at Crispin. 'Yes. I am proud of my father.'

Crispin grabbed his shoulders and steered him toward the door. 'Christopher, you must wait outside for Master Jack to take you home.'

'I can have one of my men do it,' said the duke. 'Young Walcote, tell my man there that he will escort you home.'

'I will. Thank you, my lord. Farewell, Master Crispin. I will write *and* wait for your reply next time.'

'God be with you, Master Walcote. Fare you well.'

The boy waved to Crispin as he slowly shut the door. And when it was shut at last, Crispin crumpled into his chair and covered his face with his hand. 'God's blood, what have I done?'

'What *have* you done?'

'He asked me if I was his father? And I . . . I couldn't deny it.'

'All he needs is a looking glass. God's legs, Crispin. He is your very image. I remember that boy from years ago. I hoisted him on my own shoulders.'

He shook his head, still covering his face. 'I couldn't tell him it was a lie.'

'Well . . .' John pulled a chair from the table and sat next to him. 'You admonished him to silence, did you not?'

'Yes. But he's a boy.'

'And boys love to tell secrets. Though, if he is anything like you, he will keep it well.'

He raised his head. 'Will he?'

'I daresay there are still some secrets you have never told.'

'I daresay there are.'

'There you have it.'

He put his anxiety aside and stared at John. 'What are you doing here?'

'That's a fine thing. Your old mentor comes to visit and that's how you greet him?'

He smiled. 'I apologize. I merely wondered . . .'

'I wanted to see if all is well with that troublesome book you talked about.'

'It is well. We are . . . all well. And by the way, the book came to me because of Henry.'

'What's that you say? *My* Henry?'

'The very same. It seems he obtained it in the Holy Land and gave it to a man to give to me.'

John seemed embarrassed and then annoyed. 'Well. I shall have to have words with him when next I see him.'

'Yes. Please do so.'

They sat quietly for a moment, each in their own thoughts.

'Will you have wine, John?'

'No, thank you. It is only a brief visit. I wanted to see these new lodgings.'

'But you already saw them.'

They both glanced around, assessing together. When their eyes met, they laughed. 'It is better than the old one,' said Crispin.

'But where is this full house of yours?'

'Jack has gone to fetch them. I sent them away while this other business happened. It wasn't safe.'

'*Henry*,' muttered John. 'I'm glad it's concluded.'

Crispin surveyed the duke's line-etched face. 'Lady Katherine sent you, didn't she?'

John bristled. 'And what if she did?'

Crispin laughed. 'I'm glad she did.' He was satisfied when the duke smiled too. 'Will you marry her?'

It was an impudent question, but he felt that they were Crispin and John again and did not fear his mentor's wrath.

John's expression softened. 'It is my fondest desire to do so. Crispin, a little advice.' He leaned in toward him and Crispin edged forward as well. 'If you come across a woman whom you love, do not hesitate. Marry her. Time is fleeting.'

'How I wish you had given me that advice some eleven years ago.'

John glanced toward the closed door, no doubt thinking of the boy who had just passed through it.

'Do you regret your marriages, John? They made you wealthy. They gave you peerage.'

'I was young and ambitious. No, I don't regret them. At least, I did not at the time. But with the passing of years and at the twilight of my life—'

'Surely not.'

'And yet I feel it. We've traveled to many places, Crispin, you and I. We've fought many a battle. Hard battles.'

'I regret none of that time with you.'

He patted Crispin's leg. 'Nor I. But that time is catching up to me.'

'Me, too,' said Crispin. He remembered the stitch in his side running after Ashdown.

'It's been a good life for me, Crispin. I am grateful to God for putting Katherine in my path.'

'You mean putting that rogue Chaucer in your household, for she *is* his sister-in-law.'

'Geoffrey,' he chuckled. 'The two of you were thick as thieves. Have you seen anything of him at all?'

'Not for many years, to my great regret.'

'I am sorry. That is my fault, too.'

Crispin said nothing. They both knew the truth of it.

'But I digress,' said John. 'We were speaking of our lady loves.'

'I'm afraid I had – out of my own stubbornness and arrogance – let mine slip through my fingers.'

'The mother of that child?'

'The very same.'

'Ah, Crispin,' he said with a sigh. 'I am sorry for it. A woman who seems to know all one's faults and builds up all one's successes is more valuable than pearls. Katherine has been faithful to me for all these years. It is time to marry her. To marry for love. What a novel idea.'

'Will the king allow it?'

'He might.'

'And the Beaufort children?'

'I will plead that they be legitimized.'

Crispin nodded. He would never be able to acknowledge his own son. All the world would know instead that Christopher was the rightful son of Clarence Walcote. It might not be as it should be, but it was the best they both could hope for.

The door swung wide, and Jack Tucker blustered in, arms full of packages and baskets.

John and Crispin rose to greet him.

Jack stopped, gawking.

'What did you stop for?' cried the woman behind him. 'Jack, you're blocking the way.'

Not knowing whether to cater to the duke or to his wife, Jack did nothing.

'What's amiss? Are you mad?' Isabel Tucker pushed her way through, cradling the baby at her hip in one arm, and holding on to Little Crispin's hand with the other. 'Oh!' She, too, stopped when she beheld the duke.

'Madam,' said the duke with a bow.

Crispin took some of the packages from Jack's arms. 'Isabel, may I present the Duke of Lancaster?'

'God blind me,' she muttered as she dropped into a curtsey.

'The pleasure is mine, Madam Tucker. Jack, this is quite a brood.'

'Aye, sir. I mean, yes m'lord.'

John approached Isabel and smiled at the baby. 'May I?' He put out his hands to take her.

Stunned, she could do nothing but comply.

John held her properly – Crispin expected he had done it before – and cooed appropriately into little Helen's face. 'You're a pretty one. You'll have beautiful red hair like your father, won't you?' Thankfully, she gurgled a smile instead of howling as she was wont to do.

John turned toward the little boy at his feet, boldly staring up at him. 'And who is this young man?'

'His name is Little Crispin,' she said with a shy turn of her cheek.

John flicked an amused glance toward Crispin. 'Is he now? Well, young man. What have you to say?'

His ruddy cheeks plumped with a grin. 'God's blood!' cried the boy clearly and at the top of his voice.

Crispin knew he shouldn't but he couldn't help it. He burst out laughing.

AFTERWORD

The records show that Richard's queen, Anne of Bohemia, died of plague or some sort of illness. She came from Bohemia (the kingdom of Prague) and met and married Richard when they were only fourteen. (By the way, they were only the fifth royal couple to wed in Westminster Abbey, and there wasn't another one for 537 years!) She spoke no English but soon learned it. They were both young, and perhaps relied on each other – the two of them against the world – and soon grew very close. Richard was completely besotted with her. There is some disagreement among historians as to why they were childless. Either one or the other couldn't produce a child, or Richard – who had become obsessed with his ancestor Edward the Confessor – chose to live a celibate life with his wife as Edward had. However, Richard was also obsessed with dynasty and the divine right of kings. It seems unlikely given his overall ideals about kingship that he would willingly choose not to procreate to continue his line. We'll of course never know the truth of that.

Richard did burn down – or cause to have burned down – his palace at Sheen, which had stood on that spot along the Thames since Henry II's time in 1125. But the burning happened later than described. For the purposes of my drama I had him burn it down right away. For a long time, Richard refused to enter any room that Anne had lived in. Anne was a great intercessor, protecting the weak from the king's wrath. She, as many a medieval queen did, supported hospitals for the poor and other charities. She was also able to curb Richard's worse tendencies of revenge and unwise decisions. After she was gone, Richard made some very poor choices that soon proved disastrous for him.

When he married again, his second wife, Isabella of Valois, was only seven years old at the time in 1396, and they never lived as husband and wife. She, of course, was widowed three years later.

As for the Judas Gospel, it had, as many of the apocryphal gospels, a different voice from the four chosen gospels we know of today. There are other apocryphal gospels – the gospels of Thomas and Mary Magdalene, for instance. Its presence certainly made Crispin think about what it means to be a faithful Christian, when the most auspicious decision one could make in his day was whether to follow Lollard tenets or keep with the more orthodox teachings of the Catholic Church. Lollards did not believe that baptism and confession were necessary for salvation. They believed in the laity reading Scripture in their own language, and they considered asking intercession of saints and statues a form of idolatry – essentially, the beliefs that would eventually come to fruition in Henry VIII's Reformation.

The Judas Gospel or Codex does indeed exist. It is thought to have been created in the second century by Gnostic Christians, an early Christian sect that believed there is special knowledge that only few people possess of innate human divinity. The Judas Codex likely came from an earlier Greek version. Gnostic gospels were suppressed by early Christian fathers like the Greek cleric Irenaeus, who wrote his treatise *Adversus Haereses* (Against Heresies) in about CE 180. The only known copy of the Judas Codex (carbon-dated to CE 280) and written in Coptic, didn't turn up until the 1970s, but through a series of intrigues good enough for a Crispin mystery, it finally turned up again in 1983.

Julian of Norwich was a real person, though probably never left her anchorhold – her religious reclusive cell, into which she was likely literally bricked up – at St Julian's Church in Norwich, where she lived most of her life as an anchoress. So it is all my fiction that compelled her to leave it and seek out Crispin. No one knows her real name. She was known as 'Julian' because of the church she was attached to. She held a great many reforming ideas about the faith and, though it often was against the orthodoxy, she became an important Christian mystic and theologian honored by the Anglican Church, though not beatified or canonized yet in the Catholic Church. There is, however, a movement to name her a 'Doctor of the Church', that is, saintly persons who have contributed to the understanding or revealing of theology or doctrine ('doctor' is Latin for 'teacher'). Out of the thirty-six Catholic Doctors of the Church, only four are female:

St Teresa of Ávila, Catherine of Siena, St Thérèse of Lisieux and St Hildegard of Bingen. Julian's 1395 writings (written a year after she met Crispin, just saying) were collectively known as *Revelations of Divine Love*; this is the first published book in the English language to have been written by a woman.

And finally, some of you might have found the name Sir Richard Whittington familiar. Have you ever heard of Dick Whittington and his cat? It was seventeenth-century folklore that told of how Whittington started out as a poor man but raised himself to wealth after he sold his cat to a rat-infested area. But none of it is true. He certainly wasn't raised poor and no one knows if he ever owned a cat, but he did do great things for London, among them:

- He was Lord Sheriff, and served as Lord Mayor four times, and also as a member of Parliament
- He financed drainage systems in the poor areas of Billingsgate and Cripplegate
- He built a hospital for unwed mothers
- He created a public toilet with 128 seats!
- And added to the bulk of Greyfriars library

Nevertheless, the story about him and his cat has outlived his good works, and was a favorite pantomime from the pre-Victorian era to today, getting the most performance time during Christmas. Who doesn't like a good cat story?

If you liked this book, please review it. More can be found about the Crispin Guest series on my website, JeriWesterson. com. Crispin will return in another mystery that will take him and Jack far from home in search of the mythical Sword Excalibur in *Sword of Shadows*.